The Battle of the Void

Void

The Ember War Saga Book 6

Richard Fox

ISBN: 1533433984
ISBN-13: 978-1533433985

CHAPTER 1

Hale knocked his boxing gloves together and stepped out of his corner. He raised his guard, keeping his eyes locked on his opponent as he advanced toward him. Hale's shoulders burned from the past three rounds of exertions. His jaw ached from a solid cross that landed against his cheek and each new breath sent shivers of pain through bruised ribs.

He hadn't felt this alive in months.

Hale snapped out a jab that his opponent batted aside, then swayed back to dodge a hook that breezed past the tip of his nose. Hale dropped his right hand and swung it into his opponent's side; it hit home with a grunt of pain. Hale brought his arm back to repeat the blow, which left him open for a sudden uppercut.

The taste of leather and sweat filled his mouth as his head snapped back and he backpedaled until the ropes caught him. Hale got his hands up just before a flurry of blows rained down on him. He sidestepped and felt the turnbuckle against the small of his back.

A blow hit him in the temple, sending a flash of white across his vision. Another hammer blow thumped into his chest hard enough to send his mouthpiece flying as his lungs had the air slapped out of them. His opponent took a step back, then shimmied from side to side, showing off before he came in to finish the fight.

A flush of adrenaline went through Hale's body and he lowered a shoulder and charged. He collided with his opponent and got his hands wrapped around the man's knees, knocking the man off balance and slamming him into the mat. Hale landed on top of him with enough force to rattle the ring.

Hale rose up, intent on pounding his opponent into the floor. He got a few inches into the air when he found himself stopped by a hand hooked behind his neck. An elbow to the side of his head knocked him dizzy. He felt the world spin around and suddenly he couldn't get air through his throat.

His skull felt like a balloon about to pop as his opponent's choke hold cut off blood to his brain. Hale pawed at the arm wrapped around his neck, then tapped the mat. The hold relented and his opponent shoved him away.

The Marine lieutenant got a good look at the mat, stained with sweat and dirty from countless bouts before his. Hale breathed hard, then tried to push himself up on shaking arms.

"What the hell, Ken? We're supposed to be boxing. *Boxing*. Not grappling," his brother Jared said.

"Since when are elbows and rear chokes part

of boxing?" Hale spat a wad of bloody spit onto the mat.

"Since you decided to tackle me, jackass. You all right?" Jared touched his brother's shoulder and Hale pushed his hand away.

"Fine. My pride hurts more than anything since you hit like scrawny five-year-old." Hale sat up and leaned against the ropes. "Sorry...sorry. I haven't had a fight that was anything but life or death in a long time. Trying to box is frustrating. Everything inside me just wants to go all out and win."

Jared backed into the ropes and slid down to sit next to Hale.

"This isn't combat, Ken. I'm not the Toth or the Xaros. You having trouble getting them out of your head?" Jared asked.

"I've had nothing but the fight since this war started. After we retook Earth, it was training for Anthalas. Gunney Cortaro and I used the months we spent waiting to get back to Earth with the Dotok to do more training. Then we finally get back and I've got to deal with the Toth, and then more Toth on Nibiru. This has been my first week off since…"

"We went to Lake Mead with Mom and Dad? Couple months before we went up for the Saturn colony." Jared wiped an arm across his forehead and huffed. "Lake Mead's gone. Xaros erased the Hoover Dam. Place is a normal river valley again."

Hale spent a moment remembering that boating trip, campfires and war stories from his father after a few too many beers. He'd brought Durand out for a few days, back when they'd just started dating. Both parents had liked her, but his Japanese mother had trouble understanding Durand's thick French accent.

"You get the Terra Nova application?" Jared asked.

"What?" Hale snapped out of his reverie.

"Terra Nova. The colony world that's supposed to be out of reach of the Xaros. I thought you'd be a shoo-in for an application, you being a war hero and all. Application deadline is in two days."

"I have several thousand unread e-mails on my Ubi and no time to waste on something like…wait, why two days?"

"Some techno babble about 'gravity tides' and the Crucible's ability to get the colony ship to the system. Next jump window isn't for another fifteen years…then not again for basically ever. The colonists will be all on their own for a long time," Jared said.

"You got an application? This open to just anyone?" Hale asked, doing some quick math in his head. Whoever was on that colony mission would miss out on the next wave of Xaros coming from Barnard's Star. Assuming what Jared said about Terra Nova being out of reach from the Xaros was true…that world was an insurance policy against humanity's extinction if Earth fell to the Xaros again.

"I did. They screened the whole population looking for people with more than one skill set." Jared shrugged. "Guess my civil engineering degree and passing the fundamentals exam gave me some bonus points above and beyond being a Marine. What did you get your degree in? Underwater basket weaving?"

"History, you ass. And the only reason you took that exam was because Mom threatened to lock you out of the house if you didn't. So you going to apply?" Hale pushed his gloved hand against his jaw and felt a slight click.

"I wanted to talk to you and Uncle Isaac about it first. See what you think," Jared said.

"Why do you need our approval? You're a grown man. Sack up and make your own decision." Hale stuck his other hand under his arm and pulled it free of the glove. He stuck a fingertip into his mouth; it came away smeared with blood.

"It's not like I'm going to Mars to work the fortification parties. Terra Nova…no one but Ibarra and that probe friend of his knows where it is. I go and there ain't no coming back for fifteen years," Jared said.

"Why do you even want to go?"

"Do you know what it's like being your brother? Couple times a day some dingbat will see 'Hale' stenciled on my armor and think I'm you. 'What was it like on Anthalas? What's Ibarra's ghost like in person? Can you sign this for me?' I get to tell them I'm the *other* Hale. The one that hasn't done anything."

Hale jabbed his brother with his elbow.

"You were on the Crucible. You held the beachhead against the Toth. Not too shabby," Hale said.

"That fight with the Toth was not going my way. Only reason I'm still alive is because you and that armor showed up. Nothing I've done is as relevant as saving the human race or hobnobbing with alien dignitaries," Jared said.

"Tell you the truth…I've just been lucky. Or unlucky. I've got good Marines following my lead, even when I don't exactly know what the hell is going on," Hale said.

"Now you're all modest about it. If I go, Ken, it's because I want to make a new home for us all. All the time I've spent dirtside reminds me of what we've lost. Even when we went to Mom and Dad's house…it didn't feel like home," Jared said.

"I took my Marines up to Oahu for a training drop, getting familiar with the Karigole cloaks." Hale turned his face away from his brother. "We were standing on Waikiki and I could see Diamond Head. I'd been in the same place before the Xaros, but without the people, the city…it wasn't the same."

"Like when Grandpa talked about Manhattan. How it wasn't the same after the Twin Towers came down and that new Freedom Tower went up."

"Yeah," Hale nodded. "You go to Terra Nova. I'll follow up the next time the door's open. Want me to pull some strings? Ibarra owes me a couple favors."

"Don't you dare! What part of me wanting to get ahead on my own merits didn't you understand?"

A trill came from a pair of gym bags lying in

a corner.

"That you?" Jared asked.

"Yeah." Hale got to his feet and opened his bag. He took out an Ubi slate and frowned. "Admiral Garret moved up our briefing time. Got to run."

"Fine. You go back to being super important." Jared got up and threw a half punch at Hale's stomach. "I'll go make sure my platoon of doughboys aren't drinking out of the toilet or lighting themselves on fire for fun. Just like regular Marine privates."

****

Stacey Ibarra walked through the arched corridors of the Crucible. She looked up to the tall ceilings at the strip lighting that had been installed since she and Hale's Marines had wrested control of the wormhole gate away from the Xaros. Her toes caught on a lump in the sand-like floor and almost sent her falling.

"We fix the lighting but not the damn floor," she mumbled. The line of light running around the edge of a doorway twice her height blinked on and off. "I know which one it is, thank you, Jerry," she said to the Qa'Resh probe that controlled the station.

"You seem to have some difficulty controlling your locomotion," came from the walls. "Perhaps the alcohol in your system is affecting your cognitive abilities."

"The problem is that these floors are still made out of this solid sand crap, not that I had two beers with dinner before I took the shuttle up here." Stacey ran her hands over her jumpsuit and her fingers through her hair.

"The chemical composition of your breath is more consistent with three whiskey sours than two beers," the probe said.

"Shut up and open this door." Stacey glared at the tiny camera attached to a touch screen bolted onto the wall. "And don't mention any of this to my grandfather."

"He already knows." The doors opened as a line appeared down its center. The basalt-colored material crumbled to the sides as tiny flecks seemed to fall away and were reabsorbed by the walls as the gap in the door grew.

Bastion, where she and the rest of the Alliance's ambassadors worked to defeat the Xaros invasion, had its quirks, but the way the Crucible functioned sent shivers down her spine.

The doors opened quickly and she stepped into a dimly lit room. A man dressed in a simple gray tunic and pants sat on a bench behind a force field, the energy wall glittering as a breeze from the hallway wafted in from behind Stacey and caressed the barrier. The man had his hands on his knees, his chin resting on his chest.

"Malal?" Stacey took a cautious step into the room.

"I don't like this," he whispered through the air.

"You know the routine. Show it to me." Stacey held up her hand and glanced at a tiny screen embedded into a skintight bracelet.

Malal's chest shimmered like humid air over a fire, morphing into a field that looked like dancing Damascus steel and then shifted aside. A spherical device made up of connected hoops was embedded in Malal's chest. Green lights flashed on the screen.

"Good." She lowered her hand.

"I made my agreement with you and the Qa'Resh." Malal lifted his head, his face nothing but a featureless mask. "Which I will honor. I find this object offensive."

"Why? Because I can annihilate you with a command or because the governor keeps you bound to the capabilities of a mere mortal?" Stacey asked with a half grin.

"Again. We have a bargain. This governor of yours presumes I will seek to break the agreement."

"Sorry if we don't trust you. Your previous history of luring races to Anthalas with the promise of immortality then consuming their life force leaves us a bit skeptical. Let's not forget when you possessed a Marine and tried to convince Captain Valdar to bring you back to Earth so you could rinse and repeat with the consuming. We just went through this with the Toth. Our patience is short," Stacey said.

Malal waved a dismissive hand in the air, one of many human gestures he'd picked up.

"We'll be leaving for your vault soon, but there's been a change to the plan. You will identify the codex we need to complete the Crucible and tap into the Xaros travel network, as planned. But I will be the one to return the artifact to the Qa'Resh, not you," she said.

Malal's chest closed around the governor. He stood up and walked to the force field, dark pools forming where his eyes should have been.

"Impossible." He bent slightly at the waist to bring himself eye to eye with Stacey. She felt her heart skip a beat as the ancient entity looked her over. "You cannot understand what the codex is or how to transport it. It would be like expecting one of your planet's canines to teach calculus."

"My body is a little different than the other humans who've had the misfortune of meeting you. The Qa'Resh sent me the tools I need. You'll guide us to the codex we need and I will handle the rest," she said.

"And my key? What of that?" Malal's fingertips touched the force field, which swayed as he ran his touch from side to side.

"I will bring that back as well."

Malal rammed a fist into the energy wall with enough force to send ripples across the entire surface.

"That is not the deal!" Malal thundered.

"You named your price, Malal!" Stacey jabbed a finger at him. "You'll get exactly what you want, but under our terms. If that's not acceptable, I can turn you into a hot puddle of goo or drop you into one of the four gas giants orbiting the sun. I'll even let you pick which one. I hear the center of Jupiter is nice this time of year."

Malal took a step back. "Once…I was a god. Worshipped on countless seed worlds. My effigy cut into the side of mountains. Entire mythologies based on the forms I inhabited on a whim. Now I'm bargaining with hairless apes, trusting them with my future."

"And what will you get in return for our deal?" Stacey cocked her head to the side.

"Revenge," Malal said. "Revenge that has been waiting for millions of years."

"That's right. So you can put up with me a bit longer," she said. "Now put your face on. Time to get to work."

****

Corpsman Yarrow sat on a bench and took a small notebook from a thigh pocket. The *Breitenfeld* had been under a MALCODE condition red, no electronic devices of any kind allowed on the ship since he and the rest of the team had returned from their R&R trip to Hawaii. He clicked a pen and wrote in the date on the top of a blank page.

"Then I said to the guy, 'Hey, how do you

know the Dotok aren't into that?'" Standish said to Orozco as the two Marines sat down on Yarrow's bench.

"And the military police found the guy bound and gagged outside the gate to the Dotok sanctuary the next morning?" Orozco asked.

"That's the one! I haven't laughed so hard since we had new guy looking for the cloaked Mule." Standish reached over and gave a red-faced Yarrow a quick pat on the shoulder. "Don't worry, kid. We haven't forgotten about that."

"You're lucky the internet is still out," Orozco said. "That video would have gone viral."

"You said you deleted it," Yarrow deadpanned.

"Oh, sure we did," Standish nodded. "Didn't we?"

"I might have a copy somewhere on my Ubi," Orozco shrugged.

"Guys, come on, you promised—"

"Don't sweat it, new guy," Standish said. "We'll keep it between us and maybe…" Standish's fingers darted to Yarrow's notebook and plucked a photo from between the pages, "your girlfriend."

Standish raised the photo beyond Yarrow's reach as the corpsman snatched at it. The small photo showed Yarrow and a bikini-clad woman with lavender-colored hair snuggling on a beach chair.

"How is Lilith doing these days? She have a sister? I keep asking but you never answer." Standish handed the photo back to Yarrow, whose face had gone several shades redder.

"She's fine." Yarrow tucked the photo into a Velcro pocket on his uniform. "Ibarra's got her and the rest of the ones we rescued from Nibiru working on Toth technology, helping salvage what they can from the *Naga* and all the other wrecks in system. And no, she doesn't have a sister. If she did, there's no way in hell I'd take the hit for introducing you." Yarrow looked at Orozco, the well-built, blond-haired, blue-eyed Spaniard. "But some of her friends were asking about you, Oro."

"What have I got to do?" Standish asked as

Orozco's laughter filled the briefing room.

"You tried being a little less creepy?" asked Bailey, the team's sniper, as she and Egan sat on the bench behind the three Marines.

"I was the first human to meet the Karigole," Standish said. "The first human to set foot on an alien planet. Then there's the Dotok and Nibiru. I should have a-a set of commemorative stamps, at least! Maybe an action figure. What do I get? I catch every crap detail Gunney comes up with and get to go toe to toe with every face-eating alien we come across. You're still welcome for that save, Bailey."

"Haven't you been busted down to private three different times?" Egan asked. "What was it for? Larceny? Destruction of property...disrespect to a commissioned officer?"

"That last one was alleged and I'm not allowed to talk about it," Standish said. "Sergeant Torni was there for that and she...she's not here anymore." The Marine's face darkened and he took a seat next to Yarrow.

More of the *Breitenfeld's* crew filed into the briefing room. Yarrow recognized some of the bridge crew, Durand, and one of the Ma sisters from the fighter squadron. A man with a half-dead face pushed a wheelchair-bound woman into the room.

"Who're they?" Egan asked.

"Two of the Iron Hearts, Kallen and Bodel," Yarrow said. "We don't see them out of their armor that often."

Yarrow watched as Bodel pushed his right hand off the wheelchair's handle. The soldier's left arm hung slack at his side as he tucked a blanket around Kallen's legs and adjusted a shawl over her frail shoulders.

"What happened to them?" Egan asked.

"Bodel got hit on Takeni," Standish said, his voice low. "I think Kallen's been in that chair her whole life."

"Jesus, why are we putting them on the front lines?" Egan asked.

"You've never seen armor fight, have you? They might not be much outside their armor…but they're terrifying on the battlefield," Standish said.

Bailey frowned. "Standish, there was some story about you and them floating around when I first joined the squad. What did you do?"

"I can neither confirm nor deny any such wild tales." Standish crossed his arms.

"Where's Steuben? Lafayette? Aren't they always early to these kinds of things?" Yarrow asked.

"Gunney said something about Steuben dealing with that new Karigole village out in Kenya," Egan said. "The Karigole matriarchs aren't entirely convinced that we humans really don't want to eat them like the Toth. Steuben's been trying to talk them down, get them to stop setting traps for the resupply ships. Lafayette's been on the Crucible since we got back from Nibiru, special projects."

"So they're not coming with us?" Standish asked.

"Guess not. I wonder if we're getting some other mission experts coming with us. Where ever we're going," Egan said.

A side door near the front of the room opened and everyone rose to their feet as Captain Valdar strode into the room. Stacey Ibarra and a civilian man in a plain jumpsuit followed behind him.

"Shit," Standish said. "Not her again."

Yarrow focused on the civilian man. His face was eerily stoic, eyes dead as a mannequin's. The man stared straight ahead, uninterested, as the room settled down on Valdar's order. The longer Yarrow watched, the more certain he became that the man wasn't even breathing.

The man's head snapped to stare straight at Yarrow. One side of the man's mouth pulled up into a smile, like there was a line connected to the corner of his lips. Yarrow felt a stab of fear in his chest, then calm. He felt something trickle out of his nose and wiped the side of his hand across his face. A small smear of blood stained his fingers.

A hand touched his shoulder. Yarrow looked over and found Cortaro and Hale behind him.

"You alright, Yarrow?" Cortaro asked.

"Sure, Gunney. Just the damn dry air on board," Yarrow said.

His lieutenant and head non-commissioned officer traded a glance.

"Let's get to it," Captain Valdar said. "Given the MALCODE order, we're doing this the old-fashioned way. Slides."

A crewman brought out an easel. Large sheathes of attached paper rustled as he set it next to the captain, the words OPERATION INDIANA in simple black and white on the top sheet.

"You've all seen the preparations in orbit with Eighth Fleet. Our mission stands apart from theirs. Slide." The crewman flipped a sheet of paper over. A map of the galaxy was on the next sheet, a red dot in between two of the arms. "This is where we're going." Valdar pulled a pointer open and tapped the red dot. "It is, on a galactic scale, in the middle of nowhere. The target is dozens of light-years from the nearest star, nebula or anything else of interest. The only other place we'd find a more perfect void is intergalactic space. Slide."

The paper flipped over, revealing a picture of a giant object in space. The structure brought back Yarrow's memories of a jade puzzle ball, layers of intricately carved spheres within each other. His grandfather had one, a memento of a trip to Okinawa before the Chinese conquered the island.

Not a real memory, Yarrow reminded himself. He was a procedurally generated human being, grown in a tube and implanted with a lifetime's worth of skills and memories. He did his best to discount everything that he remembered prior to joining Hale's team aboard the *Breitenfeld*, the first moment he knew that something truly happened and wasn't a construct from Ibarra's computers. Yet he couldn't deny that everything he remembered from before he learned the truth of his existence had no bearing on the kind of person he'd become.

"This is a laboratory of a long vanished, advanced alien race." Valdar's eyes flicked toward the still man sitting beside Stacey. "Lieutenant Hale encountered a remnant of this race on Anthalas. Their technology powers the omnium reactor that will make a difference in our next fight with the Xaros."

"We've got the reactor, sir," said Commander Utrecht, the ship's gunnery officer, from the front row. "What more do we need? Wouldn't it be more useful with Eighth Fleet than going on another snipe hunt?"

"What's he complaining about? Not like he's the one that has to go boots on the ground to find this stuff," Bailey muttered.

"Captain, may I?" Stacey stood up. Valdar motioned to the podium and stepped aside.

"After the encounter with Xaros leadership on Takeni," Stacey nodded to the two Iron Hearts, "and some…additional research, we determined that the Xaros are more than just the drones. There is a leadership caste, one we can either negotiate with to end the war or eliminate." Murmurs spread through those assembled. "I'm for the latter, if anyone cares.

Reaching that leadership is difficult, unless we can complete the Crucible we have orbiting Ceres. Once our gate is fully operational and tied into the Xaros network, we can strike a fatal blow to the Xaros.

"We lack the technical know-how to complete our Crucible, and that's where this star vault comes into play. The technology we need is here, and since the *Breitenfeld* is our only other ship with a jump engine…off we go." Stacey stepped away from the podium.

"You called it a vault," Kallen said. "How're we going to get into this thing if it was built by someone more advanced than the Xaros?"

"We have a…technical expert," Valdar turned his head to the still man, "on loan to us from the Qa'Resh."

Anxiety squeezed Yarrow's chest as the puzzle pieces fell into place. He reached for an absent sidearm and started to get up. A heavy hand pressed against his shoulder and Hale leaned over.

"It's alright, Yarrow. We're safe from it," Hale whispered.

Yarrow's memories of Anthalas were hazy, but he still had nightmares of the moment the sphere of omnium hidden deep beneath an ancient pyramid invaded his body and took it over.

"No! Sir, we can't trust—" Yarrow struggled against Hale's grasp until Cortaro grabbed Yarrow's arm with a vice grip.

"Stand down," Cortaro said, using the command tone all Marine leaders could call on when the time to follow orders without hesitation was required. Yarrow's hands balled into fists, his breathing quick and shallow as the still man got to his feet.

"You may call me Malal." The words came without his mouth moving. "This is *my* vault. I will be your guide. Some of you know me…" He looked to Hale and his Marines.

"I take back what I said about Stacey. Now we're really good and fucked," Bailey said.

"You have nothing to fear from me," Malal said. "This one," he pointed at Stacey, "has me on a short leash, as you say. Just follow my lead. Things will be fine." His face pulled into a too wide smile, revealing pointed teeth.

"If you'll excuse us," Valdar said to Stacey. She and Malal left the room. Angry questions rose from the audience and Valdar raised his hands to ask for calm.

"I know," Valdar said. "I've had to ask a lot of you since this war started. Transporting an ancient entity is not what I thought the next phase of the war would be, but here we are. Stacey and Marc Ibarra assure me that the entity calling itself Malal is contained and harmless. Don't ask me to explain the tech, but it can't manifest any of the abilities we observed on Anthalas. If it steps out of line, Ensign Ibarra has the means to destroy it."

"That make you feel any better?" Standish asked Yarrow.

"No," Yarrow said.

"Stow it, both of you," Cortaro growled.

"This vault is far behind Xaros lines," Durand said. "Wouldn't the Xaros have found it and destroyed it by now?"

"The Xaros typically preserve any technology from extinct civilizations, but Malal and the Qa'Resh believe the Xaros haven't discovered the vault. Malal claims it is well hidden and the chances that the Xaros stumbled upon it in deep space are very low," Valdar said.

"Hey, we're in for a cakewalk," Egan whispered.

Orozco reached over and punched Egan in the thigh.

CHAPTER 2

Admiral Makarov stood on the open ramp of a Mule transport, her boots clamped to the deck and one hand mag-locked to a strut. Readouts flashed against her helm's visor as she looked through the void of space to the cruiser passing a few dozen yards beneath her feet. As commander of the Eighth Fleet, there was never enough time. Not enough time to address every maintenance issue, correct mistakes to operation orders, lead simulation exercises and a whole litany of problems that came up as the head of a military organization of tens of thousands of sailors and dozens of ships.

Her solution to the time crunch was to combine events whenever possible, which was why her senior staff officers were crammed into the Mule while she inspected the refit on the *Macta*.

Calum, her harried and overworked executive officer, stood just behind her, an Ubi slate in one hand.

"The next batch of shipboard security augmentees will arrive in…eight hours, ma'am," Calum said. "The adjutant has them prioritized for the *Gallipoli* and *Tarawa*, which will bring the *Tarawa* back to full strength after the accident."

"The investigation was supposed to be complete last night. What of it?" Makarov asked. She leaned forward slightly and focused on a work party on the cruiser's hull. Bright motes of light flared from plasma torches as the workers attached a black slab of armor to the ship.

"The inspector general determined that a doughboy mishandled a breach charge. Most of the casualties resulted in the doughboys' inability to react in time to vacuum exposure. They were fresh constructs, ma'am. None had been through the shipboard training programs we've put into place since the incident," Calum said.

A sailor with petty officer rank adorned with two stars pushed his way through the mass of staff officers and stopped next to Makarov. Command Master Chief Holck, the top enlisted sailor for the entire fleet, grabbed the strut opposite his commander, the magnetic plates in his glove holding him firmly in place as the Mule banked around.

"The doughboys aren't that bright, Admiral," Holck said. "My chief's mess is complaining that getting them up to speed is taking time away from their other duties."

"And are they telling you that the doughboys aren't worth the effort? That they're mass-produced and are expendable?" Makarov asked.

"Some say that," Holck said.

"No life goes to waste in my fleet." Makarov twisted around to address her staff. "Doughboy, proccie, true born, doesn't matter. We're all in the same fight." She pointed at her adjutant. "Get copies of our training programs to Ibarra and tell him to make the next batch of doughboys smarter. Save us some time."

"We'll get pushback from the effect on the production schedule," the adjutant said. Makarov turned around very slowly and stared at the man. "And I'll tell him we don't care," he said quickly. "I'll get it done soon as we're back on the *Midway*."

Makarov reached toward the cruiser and touched her thumb and middle finger together. She flicked the fingers apart and her visor zoomed in on the half-dozen sailors working along a seam of an armor plate that covered most of the ship's prow.

"Where are we on the armor retrofit?" she asked.

Lafayette, the cyborg Karigole, stepped between two staff officers. He wore no space suit, merely a helmet and attached air tanks, his artificial body proof against the void.

"Across all hulls...total ablative armor installation is at sixty-five percent, ma'am," Lafayette said.

"We were supposed to be at eighty percent yesterday," Makarov said.

"The omnium reactor is the only thing in system that can produce the armor resistant to Xaros disintegration beams." Lafayette put his hands behind his back. He walked to the edge of the ramp, his feet clapping against the deck with each magnetized step. "The reactor is producing nothing else and consuming a good deal of our pure omnium reserves in the process."

"Is that a compliment, Mr. Karigole?" Makarov asked.

"A dispassionate observation. To fully equip your fleet in time for the launch window," Lafayette touched his fingertips together to make a circle, "the reactor would need to produce this amount of omnium, but it can manage only this." His hands closed into a circle half the size.

"I'm not even convinced the armor will work," Makarov said. "If the omnium reactor had been repurposed to hull construction, I would have twice as many ships."

"Your fleet's new armor plating is based on materials we recovered from the banshee troops on Takeni. The armor can withstand a blast from a Xaros disintegration beam. I witnessed it firsthand," Lafayette said.

"The encounter with the Xaros leader?" Makarov asked.

"The same. The armor is thick enough to withstand a single direct hit from a drone construct up to destroyer size, similar to what Admiral Garret encountered during the Battle of the Crucible. I encourage you to avoid getting hit by anything larger," Lafayette said.

"'Don't get shot,' good advice," Makarov said. "Of course, the purpose of this mission isn't to get in a fight. XO, where are we on the minelayers and the new *Manticore*-class frigates?"

"*Abdiel* squadron will take on the last of the graviton mines with the next delivery from Luna," said Calum, the XO. "The breakers on the *Naga* found another intact heat sink that should bring the *Griffin*—"

A flash of light came from the cruiser. Makarov reflexively brought her free hand over her eyes, blinking hard to clear the afterimage.

"What the hell?" Makarov found the work party on the hull and counted five sailors. One was missing.

"A plasma arc," Lafayette said. "The armor is made up of Xaros material. It can react unpredictably when exposed to high temperatures."

Makarov saw a shadow pass over the star field. She thrust her hand into a boxy propellant gun from a bulkhead, ripped it out of its holster and leapt into the void.

"Pilot, bring the Mule about and prep the atmo chamber!" Makarov pointed the gun toward the shadow and fired. Streams of particles spat out of tiny nozzles, pulling her away from the Mule.

She caught sight of a sailor tumbling end over end through space, the arms of his vac suit singed black. The IR broadcasters in her suit tried to link with the stricken man, but an amber fail icon came up on Makarov's visor.

"Sailor? Can you hear me?" Makarov slowed down as she got closer. The burns to the vac suit looked worse up close, the outer layers blackened and cracked, but she didn't see any blood or air venting into space.

She reached out and tried to grab his foot as it swung toward her. Her hand clamped down on his ankle for just a moment until his momentum pulled him away.

Makarov cursed and let off another spray to close in on him again. She got an arm around his waist and pulled him close. Her inner ear protested as she took on his spin. She grabbed the sailor by the shoulder and spun him around. The young man inside the helmet had his mouth open, screaming.

Makarov pressed her visor plate against his, and the anguished sound came through.

"Sailor! Look at me!" Makarov ordered.

The sailor's eyes opened wide. He looked at Makarov and then let out another pained cry.

"What's your suit integrity?" When he didn't answer, Makarov slapped her free hand against the sailor's head. "Suit. Integrity."

"S-stable. Oh God, my hands. Are they still there? Please tell me they're still there," the sailor said.

"Your hands are right where they're

supposed to be. The pain is a good sign. It means the nerves are still intact. What's your name?" Makarov asked.

"Yeoman Warren." He grit his teeth and tried to pull away from her.

"No, you don't, Warren. Stay right here. You know who I am?" Makarov opened the control panel on Warren's chest. The fried screen explained why his suit hadn't flooded Warren with painkillers.

"You're…oh, I'm really in deep shit now, aren't I?" Warren asked.

"You're going to be fine. I see my Mule coming for us now. They'll get you back to a sick bay and you'll be back on duty in no time, understand?" Makarov watched as Warren nodded.

The Mule swooped in a few moments later. Makarov pushed Warren into the open cargo bay and waited until he was secure in the emergency atmosphere compartment.

"Button up and get him to the *Midway*," Makarov said. She swung her body toward the cruiser and accelerated, the propellant box pulling hard against her shoulder.

"Ma'am? Where are you going?" Calum called after her.

She landed on the *Warsaw* a minute later next to a charred hunk of armor and five surprised sailors.

"Everyone alright?" Makarov asked.

"No injuries, ma'am," said a petty officer with the name "Tibbins" stenciled to her suit.

Makarov looked over the damaged armor and found a melted lump of metal that had once been a plasma torch.

"You were running the torches at their highest setting, weren't you?" Makarov asked.

Tibbins locked her heels together as best she could and stood up straight. "Yes, ma'am. I ordered Warren and Liu to violate the safety regs. We were behind schedule and the faster we could—" Tibbins stopped as Makarov raised a hand.

"Where are your safety lines? Three points of fixed contact are required for all EVA work details," Makarov said. "And where is the alert team on Dutchman duty?"

"We weren't...issued any, ma'am," Tibbins said. "We haven't had a Dutchman team on deck since last night. Personnel shortage, I heard."

Makarov felt bile rise in her throat.

"Tibbins, get your crew to sick bay and have them looked over." Makarov touched the screen on her forearm and opened a channel to the soon-to-be former captain of the *Warsaw*. "Captain LaRoche. This is Admiral Makarov. I will see you, your chief of the ship and your XO in the ship's wardroom in ten minutes."

****

Corporal Brannock kept his back to a bulkhead as more Mules and Destrier transports landed on the *Midway's* cavernous flight deck. The shuttles leapfrogged over each other with the coordination of a ballet, and Brannock kept his fingers crossed that the automated landing systems kept up the good work.

He'd helped clean up the wreckage from an ALS malfunction on the *Warsaw* after the Battle of the Crucible. A shiver went down his spine as the memory came back to him.

"They say who we're picking up?" said Lance Corporal Derringer, the other Marine who'd been shanghaied into this task with Brannock.

Brannock shrugged. "'Personnel augmentees' is all I got from First Sergeant. Pick up, get them to berthing and report back for the next 'hey you' detail."

"I thought this was some babysitting mission. Why the hell do we need so many warm bodies on the ship? Showers are a hassle. Can't even eat in the mess hall because we can't find a seat. Now we need *more* bubbas? I thought the company was already at full strength," Derringer said.

"You think too much for a lance corporal, you know that?" Brannock checked the time on his forearm screen and sighed. "Hurry up and wait. Hurry up and wait."

Derringer scooted closer to Brannock and did his best to whisper over the constant roar of engines.

"I heard from my buddy on the *Dallas* that we're going through the Crucible. That could take us…anywhere. You hear about all the crazy stuff the *Breitenfeld* does when they go through?" Derringer asked.

"No, and neither have you," Brannock said. "The *Breitenfeld's* always on black ops missions. I heard the crew is nothing but proccie cyborgs, like that one Karigole that Admiral Garret is always walking around with."

"I heard they were all true born, handpicked by Ibarra before the war to be some kind of elite crew," Derringer said.

Brannock's forearm screen beeped.

"Here we go…pad ninety-four." Brannock pointed to their left and made his way down the line of shuttles, dodging around cargo sleds and packs of loaded-down Marines coming off the flight line.

Brannock saluted a tired-looking Marine

lieutenant as he descended from the Mule parked on pad ninety-four. Brannock glanced at the name stenciled on the lieutenant's void suit: Hale.

"You're with Alpha Company, 19th Regiment?" Jared Hale asked.

"Roger, sir. You're assigned to us?" Brannock asked. His company had plenty of new second lieutenants and more than its usual allotment of first lieutenants. He dreaded the answer, sure that his company was about to have more chefs in the kitchen than it really needed. But this lieutenant…he had that faraway stare of someone who'd been in more than one battle. Having him around might help the less experienced officers.

"Not me, my boys," Jared said, turning his head to the open cargo bay. "Indigo! Fall out."

A dozen massive soldiers rose from their seats and stomped down the ramp. Each was almost six and a half feet tall with mottled skin in shades of green and brown. They carried simple-looking rifles with oversized triggers and handgrips to match their bodies. Each had a sledgehammer slung over their shoulder. None spoke a word as they stepped off the ramp and formed a row with parade-ground precision.

"These are...are..." Brannock's mouth kept working, but no words came out.

"Doughboys, that's right," Jared said. "Bio-constructs. They'll respond to simple commands and will protect you against any nonhuman threat. Just think of them as military working dogs, just with guns and a bit smarter than your average German shepherd. Don't piss them off." He cocked a thumb at the nearest doughboy, one with scars covering his face. "I saw Indigo here crush a Toth warrior's skull with his bare hands."

"Toth...enemy," Indigo said, his voice a rumble of boulders.

Jared turned to Indigo.

"You and your squad have done very good, Indigo," Jared said, speaking a bit slower. "I am very proud of you."

"Good," the doughboys repeated the word and nodded vigorously.

"You're going to go with Corporal Brannock and you'll do what he tells you to. Understand?" Jared asked.

There was a pause before Indigo said, "Sir…leave?"

"Yes, that's right. Corporal Brannock, he's your sir now."

"Sir no leave," Indigo said forcefully.

"Orders." Jared held up a finger and Indigo pouted. "You are all good soldiers. You have a new mission. Fight enemies!"

The doughboys nodded and repeated Jared's last two words.

"I have to go. I'm sorry, boys. I really am." Jared slapped Indigo on the shoulder.

Indigo shot an arm around Jared and pulled him into a bear hug.

"Too tight! Too tight!" Jared wheezed and Indigo let him go. Jared straightened out his vac suit and gave Brannock a look.

"I'll take good care of them, sir," the corporal said.

Jared nodded and went back into the Mule.

"Squad," Brannock said and the doughboys snapped to attention. "Follow me."

CHAPTER 3

Valdar gripped the armrests of his captain's chair and fought to keep his bearings as a cascade of white light assaulted his eyes. Every time the *Breitenfeld* went through a wormhole, the experience varied. Jumps into the Crucible were brief, almost pleasant, but jumps from the Xaros gate into the far reaches of space were almost torture.

The oppressive light vanished suddenly. Valdar looked up and saw a wall of distant stars beyond his ship.

"Damage report. Is the cloak active?" Valdar asked.

"All decks reporting in…" said Ericcson, the ship's XO. "Nothing significant to report."

"Cloak is active," Commander Levin said. "Battery power holding steady, for once. Looks like the Akkadian engineers really did fix the energy leak."

"Maintain silent running. Have the deck and

turret spotters searching for the vault. We'll weigh anchor once we have a bearing," Valdar said. He unbuckled his safety harness and took to the walkway running behind each of the bridge's workstations. He stopped at the front of the bridge and passed his gaze over the thin band of stars before him. Below the ship lay a vast abyss, punctuated by a few pinpricks of light, lost stars cast into the darkness.

"Geller," Valdar said to the ship's navigator. "How far to the nearest star?"

"There's a shallow gravity well eight light-years away," the young ensign said. "The margin of error is pretty high with passive sensors. Must be a rogue star. After that…nothing for hundreds of light-years."

"Which was the point," Malal said. He and Stacey Ibarra stood next to the holo table at the rear of the bridge. Unlike the rest of the crew in their combat-rated vac suits, Malal wore nothing but simple coveralls. "Deep space is uneventful. Safe. I leave my vault next to a star and I've got to worry about supernovas, stellar drift, and all manner of mundane concerns. And that rogue star is six light-years away. I accounted for its passing. My vault is secure, I assure you."

Valdar wasn't entirely sure how Malal managed to access the IR network to speak. The *Breitenfeld* was under combat conditions, the atmosphere drained to mitigate the risk of fire and decompression damage.

"Where is it, Malal?" Valdar asked.

"We had to jump in beyond the detection capabilities of the Xaros, if they're here," Stacey said. "We should have come in far enough away that they'd think the wormhole was nothing but a random fluctuation in the fabric of space-time."

"She's right, sir," Geller said. "The dimensional shift would be little more than—" Valdar banged a fist against the railing. "I'll stop talking. I should know better than to…spotters have something!"

"Send it to the holo table." Valdar strode across the bridge and got to the edge of the high-walled table as an image materialized.

It wasn't the sphere-within-spheres of Malal's vault. It was a crown of thorns nearly a mile in diameter. A Xaros Crucible.

"What were you saying about your vault being secure?" Valdar asked.

"Impossible," Malal hissed.

"I have a tendency to believe my own eyes, and I don't see your vault," Valdar said.

"You spoke of other security measures," Stacey said to Malal.

Malal reached into the holo tank and rotated the image around.

"If I could access but a fraction of my true capabilities…" Malal gave Stacey a sideways glance.

"Never," she said.

"Then you filter out all electromagnetic radiation coming from the area around the Crucible but from this frequency." Malal rattled off a series of numbers as Stacey tapped the touch screen on her forearm.

Color sapped away from the holo, leaving the Crucible the color of ash. The vault appeared for a split second, several times the size of the Crucible, the internal spheres spinning in different directions from the other layers. The vault vanished with a blink.

"Another protective measure," Malal said. "If the vault detects anything on an intercept course, it cloaks. Undetectable but for a few moments at a shifting frequency only I know."

"And yet…" Valdar pointed to the Crucible. "How do we know the Xaros haven't cleaned the place out?"

"Because I spent thousands of years undisturbed by the drones when they came to Anthalas. The Xaros preserve; they do not explore. The presence of the Crucible is of little consequence. You have a cloaked transport ship. That will get us to my vault without alerting the Xaros," Malal said.

"We're not seeing any drones," Stacey said. "So the Crucible should be on standby. The Xaros are nothing if not resource conscious. It shouldn't detect us while cloaked, but if they start an active scan, they'll see us in a heartbeat…This Crucible is a lot smaller than the others we've encountered. Odd."

"So we can get in and out without a fight?" Valdar asked.

"So long as we're sneaky about it," Stacey said. "The guard dog is asleep. Stay quiet and you can get past. Make noise and we've got a problem."

****

Hale grabbed his gauss rifle from a rack and swung it over his shoulder. Magnets snapped the rifle into place. He filled a bandolier with anti-armor grenades and snapped magazines full of cobalt-coated tungsten bullets onto his utility belt.

"Sir," Yarrow said from behind him, "Gunney Cortaro sent me up to ask you if we should bring a spare set of suit breakers for the Iron Hearts." The corpsman's matte-black armor seemed to mute the colors of the arms room around the young Marine. The new and improved (and supposedly disintegration-beam-resistant) armor was less bulky, while boasting longer battery life and improved augmented strength for the wearer. Hale had decided to curb his enthusiasm until the armor proved itself in the field.

"Yes, grab another set," Hale said. "Better to have it and not need it than need it and not have it. Why'd he send you?" Hale glanced at his forearm screen and found Cortaro, and the rest of his squad, were off-line.

"Gunney's got the team doing some…corrective training."

Hale suppressed a smile. The snide comments and lack of focus from some of the Marines during the mission briefing had Cortaro red-faced with repressed anger. Cortaro was a believer in alternate disciplinary measures: an extra hour of intense physical training in lieu of written counseling statements had a much more profound effect on a Marine's behavior. Hale understood that he led the team. Cortaro ran it.

"Yarrow," Hale said, "is this mission with Malal going to be an issue for you?"

Yarrow pressed his lips into a thin line. "Thing is, sir, I barely remember any of it. I remember us on that floating pedestal where Malal's orb was…then just a few flashes of memory until we were on the *Breitenfeld* in the middle of all that gray. I see Malal and part of me…" Yarrow tapped his knuckles to his chest.

"Fear?"

"Some. But fear is just a physiological reaction to stress. My body getting ready for fight or flight. I don't let it control me. I've tried putting the whole thing behind me. Dealing with being a fake person that's only a few months old has been more of an issue than something I barely remember."

"You're not fake, Yarrow. Not to me, not to the team." Hale slapped the corpsman on the shoulder and motioned to the exit. "Let's get to the flight deck before Gunney beats the others into paste."

CHAPTER 4

The *Midway's* command bridge was a near riot of activity as sailors and officers went through the ship's final prep before it weighed anchor from orbit around Ceres. The ship's captain and XO called out terse commands to the sailors manning each work pod while the admiral commanding the entirety of Eighth Fleet had her attention on the holo table to the rear of the bridge.

Admiral Makarov, clad in her armored vac suit and with her helmet under the crook of her arm, conferred with Admiral Garret next to the table as wire diagrams and stats for each of her fleet's ships floated up through the holo table.

"Are you ready, Makarov?" Garret asked.

"My fleet is back to full strength, we're loaded to bear with quadrium munitions and my ships have the new aegis armor. I'm ready to charge the gates of hell. Escorting a mine-laying task force doesn't exactly scratch the same itch," Makarov said.

"I'm not sending you into deep space to pick a fight. Drop your mines, gather what intelligence you can on what's coming out of Barnard's Star and get back here. I want your ships on the line when the Xaros arrive," Garret said. "The longer we have to get ready, the better."

Makarov's cheek twitched as she tried and failed to smile. Makarov didn't care for Garret's veiled statements. Eighth Fleet's mission was to slow down the Xaros, nothing more. The return of her fleet was a secondary concern.

She'd seen the projections. If the Xaros held to form, they would arrive in five years. Every month she could delay their foe would mean more ships, orbital emplacements, fighters and troops ready to defend the solar system. If she lost her fleet to hold off the Xaros for more than a month, the battlefield math favored the loss.

To Makarov, every fight was winnable and she and her fleet were anything but sacrificial lambs. They were Dragon Slayers.

Her hand tapped a control screen and twelve nearly identical ships appeared in the tank. Long, unarmed objects that looked like giant round shields ran along the hull inside giant racks.

"Task Force Scorpion will carry the day," she said. "Their graviton mines will slow the Xaros and my guns will make sure fewer ever reach Earth."

"I'm sending a good portion of the entire fleet with you, Makarov," Garret said. "Come back quick just in case the Toth feel like coming back for more punishment."

"I thought they were in chaos after the *Breitenfeld* killed the leader, Mentiq," she said.

"From what we've gleaned through other Bastion races that have contact with the Toth, their whole species is as fucked up as a football bat, but

59

one overlord is consolidating power. We didn't plan on them coming for us the first time. I'd rather have you back just in case."

"We could use another *Naga* for parts." Makarov nodded her head quickly.

"Don't go picking a fight…but if you find out how well the *Manticore*-class frigates do in the field, I won't complain." The supreme commander of Earth's forces stepped away from the table and extended a hand to Makarov.

"Good luck," Garret said.

"God helps those who help themselves, but we will pray to keep the powder dry." She shook his hand. A team of heavily armed Rangers and a pair of Doughboys escorted Garret off the bridge.

Makarov sighed in relief once the other admiral was gone. She hated sharing the command deck with anyone. She wasn't sure if the foible was meshed into her personality by whatever process Ibarra used to grow her mind in the proccie tube, or if Garret was just an overwhelming bore.

"Calum," she rapped her knuckles against

the holo tank, "are we ready to weigh anchor?"

"Aye, aye, Admiral. All ships report green across the board. Ready for your word," Calum said.

Makarov sat in her command chair and strapped herself in. The rest of her staff followed suit.

"Signal the Crucible to prepare the wormhole. All ships set for zero atmo conditions and   burn on my mark." She slipped her helmet on and readied the fleet-wide channel. With the press of a button, the microphone in her helmet connected to every single IR speaker in the fleet. Every sailor, embarked Marine and doughboy could hear her.

"Dragon Slayers," Makarov said, not fighting a smile as the bridge crew pounded fists against their workstations. "We stand on the precipice of a great task. The Xaros are coming to finish what they started. We, the Eighth Fleet, Earth's mightiest defenders, will travel to deep space and seed the void with mines. Task Force Scorpion's graviton mines will slow those metal bastards to a snail's pace and when the Xaros do finally reach Earth, we will be waiting for them. We will be waiting for them with a star fleet the likes of which humanity have never dreamed of. Then, we will teach them the same lesson we rammed down the Toth's throat: Earth is ours.

"Now, we weigh anchor to carry out this great task. We're not looking for a fight, but if we find the Xaros, not one of them will get past us while we still live. Makarov, out."

She closed the channel and pointed two fingers at the conn officer. The *Midway* shuddered as her engines roared to life. The carrier was the first through the Crucible as the rest of the fleet followed close behind.

****

Makarov pressed the back of her hand against her helmet, but the white light invading her eyes didn't relent. A whine roared in her ears like a thousand mosquitoes.

"Conn! What is going on!?" Makarov shouted.

"This is supposed to be completely normal, ma'am," Lieutenant Santiago said. "The space-time fissure hasn't resolved because we've got so many ships coming through—"

"How much longer?"

The whine and blinding light faded away together. Makarov's command crew touched their helmets, eager to rub eyes and ears after the assault.

"That was damn miserable," she grumbled. "I feel bad for Valdar."

Makarov pulled up a screen from her armrest. A list of her ships with unlit red and green lights popped up. Green lights filled the board as her fleet came through the wormhole.

"I want status reports from every ship. Keep to the IR. The fleet is on silent running until I say otherwise," Makarov said. The vid screens surrounding the bridge showed the void beyond the hull, stars stretched to infinity. "Conn, are we where we're supposed to be?"

"Looks that way…pulsar triangulation puts us just outside Barnard's Star. You can see it on screen two, deep red star to the bottom left of the screen," Calum pointed.

Barnard's Star, a mere six light-years from Earth, was invisible to the naked eye from the Earth's surface. This close, the star looked like a ruddy dot with a fuzzy halo of light around it.

"What's wrong with it? The halo?" Makarov asked.

"Wait one…" Santiago turned his attention to the screens around his workstation. "The team in astrometrics thinks the distortion's from a comet swarm passing the star or an ice giant broke up somewhere in the solar system."

"Barnard's Star wasn't like this before we left…the time dilation." Makarov felt a ribbon of fear unfold in her chest. The light from the star was several years old by the time it reached Earth. Jumping close to it closed the delay from what they saw and what was actually happening to it. She tapped her fingers against her armrest in frustration.

"Roger, Admiral. On Earth, the Barnard's Star we saw was years old. We're a hundred light-hours from the star now, almost real time by astrophysics standards," Santiago said.

"Let's not pretend this is some sort of coincidence," Calum said. "The Xaros own that star. They must have done something."

"I want a full scan on all mathematically possible routes from that star to ours," Makarov said. "Pull the fleet into a lens formation, front to Barnard's Star. We stay on combat alert until we've got the lay of the land." She unbuckled her restraints and went to the engineering pod.

"Status on the jump engines?" she asked.

"Fully charged, but we can't jump back to Earth for another twenty-eight hours, ma'am. Our arrival sent a wave of quantum flux through local space-time and the engines can't—"

"Twenty-eight hours, thank you," Makarov said.

"Ma'am." Captain Randall, standing next to the conn station, tapped two fingers against his thigh once Makarov turned and looked at him, a signal that something needed her attention immediately.

"We've got a mass shadow on the scope," he said. Information had a way of leaking off a command bridge and morphing into a rumor. Her staff knew better than to make offhand comments that could metastasize into something that would worry or otherwise distract the crew.

Makarov tapped a button on her gauntlet and put up a cone of silence around her, just large enough for her, Randall and Santiago. With the bridge at zero-atmo, the three could speak through IR without eavesdroppers.

"What?" she asked.

Santiago, his face pale, motioned to a screen with trembling hands. A smooth sphere punctuated by dark circles the size of cities filled the screen, great brass-colored rings around the equator. The pale white surface looked like a black net of thin filaments covered it. The perimeter wall of a great crater surrounded silver doors marred by swirling patterns.

"That…is not what we're expecting," Makarov said. "Ibarra's probe said the Xaros travel from star to star in a maniple, like a school of fish made up of individual drones. This is…"

"It's on course for Earth," Santiago said. "Mass and circumference are about equal to Luna, accelerating at almost one gravity. Should reach the outer solar system in…four years, maybe add a month for deceleration."

"That's too soon. Way too soon," Calum said.

"That's why we're out here," Makarov said. "To slow them down. We could launch every last round of ordnance into that moon and it would make absolutely no difference. But these…" Makarov zoomed in on the brass rings around the moon. "Are they active?"

"There's an Alcubierre field around the planetoid, same as we saw on Ceres before the battle," Santiago said.

"The graviton mines should rip it away,"

Calum said, "in theory. They weren't designed to counteract something of this magnitude."

Communications requests from captains across her fleet popped up on her visor. They saw the same thing she did.

"Tactical," Makarov went to her holo table, "any reaction from the Xaros?"

"Negative, ma'am," said a commander at the gunner's station. "At best-known speed, we're eight hours from contact with the Xaros."

"Set fleet to atmo condition amber," Makarov said. The fleet would re-pressurize, but the crews would remain in their vac suits, ready for an immediate return to combat conditions at a moment's notice.

"I want all ship captains on holo conference in ten minutes. We'll figure this out."

Makarov gave a series of commands to the warrant officer manning the holo table. The fleet and the distant Xaros moon floated before her a few seconds later. Her brow knit as a bad thought came to mind. She reached into the tank and zoomed in on the moon until the dark filaments of the net came up, heavily pixelated.

"Get me a better picture of this," she said over her shoulder, "now."

It took another minute before one of the *Midway*'s spotters sent up an image from their high-powered telescopes. The pixels smoothed out, revealing the oblong body of a drone, stalks joined to another drone. The net encompassing the moon was nothing but drones. Millions and millions of drones.

****

Holograms of Makarov's captains joined her around the operations table. All bore serious, stoic expressions, exactly the same mask of command Makarov wore. She didn't care if each of them were full of doubt and fear, so long as they didn't show or act like they were influenced by those emotions.

"Eighth." Makarov ran a hand through her short hair. "This isn't what we planned on. This isn't what we trained for. The Xaros moon, hereby designated Abaddon, is on course for our solar system. We can't destroy it, but we're going to figure out how to slow it down or knock it off course so it spends the rest of time plowing through empty space."

"Ma'am." The holo of the captain directly across from Makarov changed into a rail-thin man with a weak chin. Captain Delacroix, the commander of the minelayer task force. "My engineers ran the numbers. It will take almost a full complement of mines from just one of my ships to have any effect on Abaddon's Alcubierre field."

"And will that do any good?" Randall asked from Makarov's side. "I can cycle the *Midway*'s Alcubierre drive on and off in hours. I'd bet money the Xaros can do it faster."

"The graviton mines are designed to disrupt the warp fields…" Delacroix rolled his eyes. "We don't have time for the PhD version. Watch." His holo tapped a screen invisible to Makarov.

The holo above Makarov's table distorted

into Abaddon, surrounded by a grid shell, a single *Abdiel*-class vessel in front of it.

"That grid is the moon's Alcubierre field. Now watch." Delacroix hit a button and a mine shot off the rails and exploded. Motes of light hit the shell, to no effect. "One mine is about as good as pissing on a forest fire, excuse my language. But if we…" All the mines exploded and showered the grid. It wavered and fell away.

"Now," Delacroix lifted a finger like a college professor, "knocking it down is one thing. Keeping it down is another. A certain graviton density can retard the formation of a new field." A line of minelayers stretched out from the Xaros moon. Mines shot away from the *Abdiel*-class ships and filled the space along the moon's route with graviton particles. "We do this and it will slow their advance by up to fifteen years, even send them off course if we can maintain the effects long enough. I make the assumption that the Xaros can't make a sharp turn when steering a moon."

"What's the catch?" Makarov asked.

Delacroix cleared his throat. "I need to set off no fewer than twenty graviton mines within three thousand kilometers of Abaddon's surface." The assembled captains shook their heads and mumbled curses under their breath.

"That's practically knife-fighting range with the drones wrapped around the surface. You understand that?" Makarov asked.

"I do, ma'am." Delacroix raised his chin slightly. "You asked me how to slow it down. This is the only way the math works."

"Thank you, Captain. I only ever want the unvarnished truth from any of you." Makarov swiped a screen and the tactical overlay with the entire fleet returned. "Our next course of action is to destroy the rings—which will take down the field, correct?" she asked Delacroix, who gave her a thumbs-up.

"The rings around Ceres are of a composite metal that's a good deal stronger than even our new aegis armor," Kidson, her chief gunnery officer said. "Ibarra and his probe weren't real forthcoming about how to wreck the rings—or even the Crucible—should the need arise. Now we've got to figure this out on our own."

"I don't know how much damage we have to inflict on the rings," Delacroix said. "Maybe a single solid hit, maybe we have to break it into a thousand pieces."

"So we're in for some discovery learning," Makarov said.

"Ma'am." Delacroix's holo shifted to that of a woman with a long braid of red hair, Commander Brantley from the destroyer *Halifax*. "I'll take the hit and play devil's advocate. If we're in a bad tactical situation, why don't we return to Earth? Come back with a better solution."

"The short answer is 'we can't,'" Delacroix said. "That moon creates enough of a dip in space-time that our single jump engine doesn't have the power to get us all back to Earth. We could all jump away, but then we'd sit in deep space for years waiting for the engines to recharge with dark energy."

"I can get the *Midway* back," Makarov said, "but I will be goddamned before I leave anyone behind. We knock this thing on its ass and it'll take us a few months at full burn to get clear of the mass shadow. We're sending everything we learn back to Earth at light speed. That'll give them months of warning about what's coming their way. Succeed or fail."

Makarov swiped her touch screen and a new tactical overlay appeared. Her captains leaned in to study. Some crossed their arms in frustration; others nodded slowly.

"We need information," Makarov said. "And for that, we're going to give the hive a good kick."

CHAPTER 5

Hale buckled himself into the turret ball and grabbed the control sticks. He swung the turret through its full range of motion, spinning the *Breitenfeld's* flight deck around him.

"Standish, how's the dorsal turret?" he said into the IR.

"Little sticky going past the aft, nothing to worry about, sir," Standish said. "Can barely move my arms after my hundredth squat thrust into a pull-up but who's complaining? Certainly not me. Learned my lesson, I tell you."

"We've got the armor bolted down," Cortaro said through Hale's comms. "Bit tight in here. Let's hope whatever we're bringing back isn't too big."

"I've got clearance to lift off," Egan said. "I thought I'd have more time to break in my new co-pilot, but beggars and choosers, right?"

"Lafayette assured me that my piloting skills are thoroughly adequate," Orozco said.

"You hear that everybody?" Standish asked. "He's adequate."

Standish and Cortaro's icons blinked and entered a private channel.

"Get us off the deck and engage the cloak, Egan," Hale said.

"Roger, sir."

The Mule shuddered and rose higher. Hale felt the shuttle jiggle as the landing gear retracted. The hull wavered and faded into nothing as its cloak activated. Hale glanced from side to side. The seemingly absent Mule made him feel like he was almost floating in midair inside the turret ball.

"Cloak looks good," Hale said.

"—Never wear a corporal's stripes if you don't—"

"Cloak good!" Standish said over Cortaro before he switched back to the other channel.

"Here we go," Egan said as the Mule accelerated forward. The shuttle passed through the *Breitenfeld's* open bay doors moments later. Hale scanned the sky until he found the Crucible; tiny gold flecks imbedded in the thorns twinkled against the wall of stars of the distant galactic arm. He looked back to the ship, but it was gone. Hidden behind its own cloak.

There, seemingly floating in the vast depths of the void, Hale got a sense of his own importance in the grand scheme of the galaxy, and it felt utterly irrelevant.

"Cut your forward velocity to zero in eighty-seven seconds," Malal said.

"What happens at eighty-eight?" Egan asked.

"You will smash into the outer hull and not survive the experience. That would complicate my task," Malal said.

"Reducing speed," Egan said.

Hale felt a slight tug against his restraints as the Mule slowed.

"Stacey. I don't see a damned thing out here other than the Crucible," Hale said. "Are you sure—"

The vault appeared right in front of the Mule. The outer sphere was enormous, easily a dozen miles wide and far larger than any spaceborne object humanity had ever constructed. Titan Station could have fit in the gaps on the outermost sphere with room to spare. Geometric shapes and swirls played out across the surface.

"See it?" Stacey asked.

"Yeah, it's here all right. How do we get in?" Hale asked.

"Stop close to the surface, but do not land on it," Malal said.

"Roger," Egan said and the Mule closed on the vault slowly. "I can see it…but it's not anywhere on my screens. There's not even a hint of gravity from that thing. I did a flyby on Deimos. Even something that small played hell with navigation."

The Mule came to a stop almost fifty yards above the surface. The outer sphere raced past with enough velocity that it reminded Hale of the time he and his brother played too close to the train tracks as children. Jared had come precariously close to getting hit by a speeding locomotive and both had received a licking from their mother's wooden spoon when their parents learned of the incident.

"How are we going to get inside?" Hale asked. He caught a few glimpses of the fourth layer of spheres, but the gaps never stayed open for more than a few seconds.

"Open the hatch," Malal said. A few seconds later, the unsuited Malal floated past Hale and stopped feet from the vault's surface.

"I'm *not* getting used to him," Standish said. "Just so everyone knows."

Malal reached for the surface and tendrils of coherent light stretched from his fingertips to the spinning metal. A plane of blue-white light stretched across the surface, and the spheres continued moving without any apparent effects. The plane grew until it was wider and taller than the Mule, and then stopped.

Malal lowered his hands. The plane faded away, revealing a long tunnel with a bright light in the far distance. The tunnel looked like it went on for miles and should have cut through the moving spheres. Yet the tunnel and spheres didn't interact, even though everything from Hale's point of view told him the tunnel should have been ripped apart or jammed the spheres into motionlessness.

"I think I'm going to be sick," Egan said.

Malal floated to the side of the tunnel, bent at the waist slightly, and motioned for the Mule to go inside like he was a doorman welcoming them to a hotel.

"Get us inside, Egan. I don't like it out here anymore than you do," Hale said.

****

Hale grabbed a lever on the side of the turret

and pulled. His seat came loose and he dropped down onto the Mule's deck. Two of the Iron Hearts were still bolted to the deck in their compact travel forms; four of his Marines dragged the third down the ramp and onto the tunnel floor. Hale ran down the ramp and found Stacey and Malal near the Mule's nose.

"Malal, what is with this place?" Hale asked. "How far does this thing go?" The end of the tunnel seemed to fade away into the distant light. Malal stood still, eyes closed.

"He's…thinking," Stacey said. "Trying to communicate with the vault."

"Is this in line with what he told you we'd find here?" Hale asked.

"We certainly didn't expect a Xaros Crucible. Or slightly less than Earth standard gravity and a breathable atmosphere waiting for us," she said.

Hale tapped his forearm screen. The air was thin, equivalent to almost eight thousand feet above sea level on Earth, with a higher percentage of oxygen.

"Yarrow?" Hale asked.

"Should be good to breathe, sir. Might take us a bit to acclimatize, but it'll take the strain off our life support for sure," Yarrow said.

Elias rose to his full height behind the Mule. His new armor had a more ascetic character than the old blocky armor he'd worn at the beginning of the war. The cut of optics into the helm, shoulder pauldrons and molded breastplate almost made it look like Elias had come from a medieval battlefield, if the knights of old carried twin-barreled gauss cannons and a rail gun that could destroy a starship with a single hit.

How far we've come since the day I got Ibarra out of Euskal Tower, he thought.

"Stay on internal air until we've got a better read on the rest of this vault," Hale said. "Stacey..." The lieutenant turned around and found Stacey with her helmet off and tucked into the crook of her arm.

"Was I supposed to wait?" she asked. "Yes, I see that vein on your forehead twitching. Should have waited."

Malal's head jerked up. "I have found what we seek. Follow me."

"Why did you have to look?" Hale asked. "Isn't everything just where you left it?"

Malal walked down the hallway, his bare feet slapping against the lit squares.

"Echelon formation," Hale said. "Two armor lead, one rear."

Elias and Bodel stomped ahead of Malal, the hum of their gauss cannons heavy in the air as they passed. Cortaro, Bailey and Standish fell in a few steps behind the armor, weapons ready.

"This is foolish," Malal said. "You think we're at risk in here? In my vault?"

"Why don't you worry about getting us to the codex and I'll handle security," Hale said. He glanced over his shoulder and saw the hallway meld together beyond the Mule. The twisting bulkheads snapped apart, and the opening they'd come from was gone, replaced by a hallway that extended to a distant point of light.

"Ugh, sir?" Egan asked.

"I saw. Malal…how're we supposed to—"

"You don't understand, human. Your mind cannot even grasp how this vault functions. Tell your walking machines to stop. They passed the door," Malal said.

"What door?" Nothing but an endless hallway stretched ahead of them.

Malal stopped and turned to his right. He snapped his fingers, and a sealed doorway twice the height of the armor appeared without a sound, embedded against the bulkhead.

"You use pocket dimensions," Stacey said. "The Qa'Resh have the same technology."

"They have a feeble imitation of my technology. Cribbed from the decayed remnants of my civilization. Did they ever tell you where they came across the ruins? One of my brethren must have been sloppy before the ascension." Malal touched the door and it slid aside, revealing a pitch-black wall.

"Who wants to go first?" Malal asked.

"Into what? There's nothing there," Hale said.

"What do you mean?" Stacey asked. "You don't see the garden?"

Malal tilted his head to Stacey. The flush of a dark-colored rash spread over his face then faded away.

"Your mind can't grasp a multidimensional space, perhaps like explaining color to the blind. One of my labs is beyond this door. Go on," Malal said.

"Then why can she see something?" Hale asked.

"Perhaps she is not entirely human," Malal said.

Stacey shrugged her shoulders slightly. "It's complicated."

"To hell with this." Hale stepped toward the doorway. His reflection appeared, like he was staring into polished obsidian. He stopped a foot away from the doorway…and his reflection did the same with a slight delay.

Hale stepped into the doorway, his limbs tingling as he passed through. His lead foot found nothing but air and he stumbled forward, splashing into water up to his knees, and found himself surrounded by wide-leafed plants that came up to his shoulders. The plants' thick stalks ran from lumps of mossy soil that just barely broke the surface of ice blue water and stretched out for dozens of yards in a haze-filled enclosure. The water lapped at a patch of ground covered in silver grass. Hale made for the solid ground, sloshing water around him as he moved.

Elias came through the doorway, his cannons up and ready.

"What is this?" Elias asked. His helm swung from side to side. "My thermal lenses must be malfunctioning. Everything in here is the same temperature."

Hale got onto the patch of ground. The haze thickened until he couldn't see more than a dozen yards away from him. The sound of more Marines and armor splashing in the water carried through the air.

"Up here." Hale waved a hand in the air. Cortaro directed the team into a hasty perimeter on the silver knoll.

Malal and Stacey stayed in the water. The ancient entity touched one of the plants and motes of light ran up and down the stalk and filled the leaf with streaks of light. Hale jumped into the water and stopped next to the pair.

"This is your lab?" Hale asked.

"No." Malal cracked the stalk with his hand and ripped the leaf away. The plant withered instantly, leaving him holding a blackened mass.

"I don't know what this is."

****

Malal's feet shifted through the silver grass. He bent over and plucked a blade free, then tossed it into his mouth.

"Did he leave the water running, or something?" Standish asked Stacey from the edge of the security perimeter. She'd kept her eye on Malal, waiting for him to "reorient himself."

"Maybe these plants are some sort of ancient alien mold that just got out of hand."

"Your guess is as good as mine," she said.

"I would hope yours would be better," Standish said. "On account of you being his chaperone and hobnobbing with all that crazy stuff on Bastion."

Malal walked off into the haze.

"Follow him," Hale said.

Stacey ran over to Malal and matched his pace. The grass grew longer, covering their ankles as they progressed through the haze.

"Care to explain what all this is?" she asked. "Some experiment of yours gone out of control?"

"I've located my lab. Some…thing managed to break into my vault and alter the landscape," Malal said. "Not Xaros. Not anything I recognize."

The haze faded away. Neat rows of white trees with tall, arched branches reached twenty feet into the air. The trees glowed from within, the light diffusing into darkness not much farther into the air. There was something very familiar about those trees…

"They altered the landscape? Can you even find your way around anymore?" she asked.

"The intruders locked everything into place beyond the first dimensional door. The compartments are now linked together, whereas I'd had them all within their own domains. Whatever did this violated my vision, my plan," Malal said.

"How can you tell?" she asked.

"I feel the energy from the power grid." Malal put his hand on a glowing tree and the bark darkened and cracked beneath his touch. "Feel the growth polluting every corner of my sanctum. Feel it linked to each and every project that I spent millennia perfecting."

"What about the codex? Is it still here?"

"There are voids." The tree dimmed. Leaves fell from branches and shriveled before they hit the ground. "Voids in the pollution where my more sensitive projects were kept. My wards and ciphers hold true."

The trunk cracked in half, one side falling to the ground, crumbling into dust.

"If you two are done wasting time…" Hale motioned into the bands of trees with the muzzle of his rifle.

"Movement," Bodel said, "on foot, two o'clock from our direction of travel. I can't make out the distance in this fog…but it's coming in fast."

"Shield the principal. Take cover behind the trees," Hale said.

Elias and Kallen stepped over to Malal, protecting him with their armored bulk.

A clipped staccato noise came from the distance, dozens of high, oscillating yelps.

"That sound like barking to anyone else?" Egan asked.

Stacey took her gauss carbine off her back and got closer to Malal behind the armors' legs. The entity was her responsibility, and she wasn't entirely sure how vulnerable he was while he had the Qa'Resh governor inside him. She keyed off the safety and felt it hum in her hands.

Kallen glanced down at her. "You shoot me and I will be upset," she said.

"What? Why do you think I'd do that?"

Elias turned his helm to her, and then looked back into the fog.

"Oh, right, I did shoot him in the face…that one time," she said as the panicked memory of Elias ripping open her stricken elevator and bouncing a bullet off the soldier's helm came back to her. "You're still mad about that?"

"Incoming!" The snap of gauss rifles erupted around her.

The ground shook as the double clap of Elias's twin cannons spat bullets that blew a tree into splinters.

Stacey struggled to even see what the Marines were shooting at. She glanced at Malal, a serene expression on his face.

A streak of orange and white shot into the air over the forest. It reached an apex then dove onto Kallen. A clang of metal on metal broke in the air and the armor stumbled backwards. Stacey watched in shock as Kallen tipped over and came down on her like a felled tree.

Malal yanked Stacey out of the way. She bounced off Elias' leg and nearly dropped her carbine.

A leonine form with gleaming tusks savaged Kallen's armor, teeth and claws drawing sparks as they ripped across her helm and shoulders.

Stacey swung her carbine up and fired from the hip. Bullets hit the ground next to Kallen then stitched a line up her flank and into the attacker. The beast yelped in pain as it curled up, its fanged snout biting at a smoking crater on its rear haunches.

Kallen's massive hand grabbed the beast and swung it into a tree, shattering it like a dropped wine glass. Smoke poured out of the half still in the armor's grasp, the stench of ozone invading Stacey's helmet.

She gagged and doubled over. Malal

touched a button on the side of her helmet, and a blast of fresh air blew across her face as her armor sealed itself off from her surroundings. She went to her knees, fighting her body's desire to vomit.

"You OK?" Yarrow patted her on the shoulder.

"Hate…that smell…" she said. Kallen's shadow loomed over her. The armor had the rear half of the beast held by a whip-thin tail. Two divots of cobalt blue marred Kallen's side armor.

"No hard feelings," Kallen said, dropping the remains at Stacey's feet. Clear liquid seeped out of a mess of shorn wires and sparking power lines.

A high-pitched screech filled the air, a sound she remembered from her childhood when a dog had been hit by a car, breaking the poor animal's spine and legs.

"Come," Malal said.

Stacey followed him to the source of the noise. Hale and Cortaro stood near a tree, hunks of bark blown free by the Marines' gauss weapons. Their weapons trained on one of the injured beasts.

It looked like a saber-toothed tiger made out of white and orange glass. Streams of light raced over its surface, swirling around the ends of its missing front legs. It tried to crawl through hunks of broken glass, the remains of the rest of the beasts that attacked.

"What the hell is it?" Cortaro asked. "Is it…alive?"

"I can tell you," Malal said. "May I?" he asked Hale.

"Be my guest," Hale said.

Malal grabbed the beast at the base of its skull. Screams of fear filled the air as he lifted it into the air. His other hand wrapped around the neck. Stacey's stomach went into knots as the thing seemed to beg for mercy as it shivered in Malal's grip.

Malal tore the head free from the rest of the body, and silence returned to the grove. Malal dug a finger into the exposed skull and removed a glowing cube. He wrapped his hand around the cube, fingers morphing into a solid mass.

"This is unexpected," he said.

"Care to share the details?" Hale asked.

Malal tossed the cube over his shoulder.

"They are an echo. Android approximations from a dead world," Malal said. "These things mimic the tusk-cats from the eastern hemisphere, not the planet's sapient species that called itself the Jinn."

"What about the Jinn?" Stacey asked. "Are they here too?"

"No," Malal said. "The Jinn are gone. Extinct by my hand."

****

Hale and Cortaro walked close to each other, their eyes watching opposite flanks for the small column of Marines and armor as they made their way through the neatly spaced rows of the glowing trees. There hadn't been another sign of the tusk-cats, or any other wildlife, since the last encounter.

"I cross-leveled ammo," Cortaro said.

"We're still green on battery life and supplies, but we have a couple more fights like that and we're in trouble."

"We didn't come here for a scrap, but we're going to win every one we get into," Hale said. "Malal says we're not far from the lab with the codex. Let's hope that's the last stop we have to make in this damn fun house."

"Hope isn't a method, sir."

"Yeah, yeah." Hale walked faster and opened a private channel to Stacey. "Ibarra, fall back and talk to me."

Malal didn't seem to notice as Stacey fell back to join Hale.

"Help you?" she asked, still on their suit-to-suit channel.

"Why is that thing helping us?"

Stacey looked away. "The Qa'Resh made a bargain with him. I don't know all the details, but he'll help us complete the Crucible, give us a shot at winning the war."

"A 'bargain'? In return for what? I saw what

Malal did to the Shanishol on Anthalas. There were rivers of dead in that city, Stacey. He set himself up as some sort of prophet and lured thousands to their death. What kind of deal did they cut with him?" Hale asked.

"Again, I don't know all the details." Her words were clipped, guarded.

"He wanted *us*. When we had him on the *Breitenfeld*, he wanted to know how many humans were left so he could catch up with whoever left him behind…it's the proccies, isn't it? Did the Qa'Resh promise him a planet full of them once the war's over?"

"No!"

"Thought you didn't know the details," Hale said.

"The Qa'Resh aren't like that. They helped us against the Toth, gave us the location of Terra Nova to help us survive when the council voted to abandon Earth to the Toth." Her face fell as she realized what she'd just said.

"What? The alliance voted to do what,

exactly?"

"This is between you and me. Bastion wanted to let the Toth take some of the proccie technology—and every other human being left on Earth—then repopulate our home with a more compliant human population, the kind that doesn't violate resolutions to save the Dotok…or assassinate enemy leaders," she said. "The Qa'Resh are hard for me to fully understand, but they're on the side of the light, like us."

"Malal doesn't want a nice summer home on the beach and a pension. What did the Qa'Resh promise to get his help?"

"I don't know," she said through grit teeth.

"Your grandfather tricked the whole planet for decades. Engineered a scenario where there was enough of a fleet to retake the Earth after it sidestepped the Xaros invasion. I have a hard time trusting him, and something tells me your apple doesn't fall too far from his tree," Hale said. He cut the line to Stacey and moved back to Cortaro.

"I see a wall," Elias said. "Twenty rows of

trees ahead."

"My lab," Malal said.

CHAPTER 6

Makarov double-checked the seals on her helmet and lowered her head in prayer.

God, don't let me screw this up. Amen.

She touched a strike cruiser in the holo before her and opened a channel to the captain.

"*Gallipoli*," the captain said, a feed of his helmeted face appearing next to his ship.

"Parris, you ready for this?" Makarov said.

"We've been ready for the last half hour. I've got my squadrons in the void and three Warthogs tethered to my hull. Waiting for the word," Captain Parris said.

"The word is given, good hunting,"

Makarov said.

Parris cut the transmission. The *Gallipoli,* a frigate, and two destroyers accelerated away from the rest of the fleet, their course plot taking them wide around Abaddon's rings. A diamond popped up on the course plot, the maximum engagement distance for the *Gallipoli* and her escorts' rail cannons. Their mission was simple: attack the rings so Makarov and the fleet's scientists and engineers could gather data for the next step.

The minutes ticked by as the *Gallipoli* closed on the firing point without action from the Xaros. Sweat dribbled down the back of her vac suit and fell onto her visor. It reacted to the moisture, vibrating until the drop dissipated.

"We've got movement," Kidson said. A single point on the drone net lifted off the surface, aimed directly for the *Gallipoli.* The net broke apart, the needlepoint of drones keeping toward the approaching human ships, the rest of the net reknitting itself over the surface.

"Abaddon's acceleration is slowing,

ma'am," Santiago called out. "Down almost twenty percent to two gravities."

"Is the net part of the propulsion system?" Calum asked.

Makarov opened a channel. "Scorpion, what's your read on this?"

Delacroix's face popped up next to the *Abdiel*. "The data is fascinating…a bit preliminary for a definitive answer."

"The separated drone mass comes to nearly a hundred thousand individual drones," Kidson said. He glanced at a flashing screen. "Video from the *Gallipoli.*"

A window opened in the holo. The needle of drones broke into thousands of individual drones, all swarming toward the *Gallipoli*.

Makarov saw the projections for her ships to reach the firing point and the intercept times for the drones. She opened a channel to Parris.

****

Captain Parris reached into his holo table and traced routes with his fingertips. He looked at his XO and shook his head.

"Parris?" Makarov's full-body holo came up next to him. "We're looking at the plot and—"

"It's pointless, ma'am," he said. "If we turn tail and run, the drones will be all over us before we could expect support from the rest of the fleet. I stay the course and I've got a fight on my hands before we hit range on the rings. Damn things are a lot faster than we'd seen before. My guess is they're combining their Alcubierre fields to get at us that much sooner."

Makarov's face betrayed nothing as her holo wavered.

"We'll take the shot. You have my word, Admiral."

"Good hunting." Makarov's holo vanished.

"Helm," Parris strapped himself into his command chair, "all ahead full. Guns, I want a full spread of q-shells and flechette rounds on that mass from every ship. Beat them back as long as you can.

Save a broadside for the rings as soon as we're in range."

"Aye-aye, Skipper," his tactical officer said from her pod. "The big guns never tire."

Parris opened a channel to his wing commander. "Raven, you've got to pick up the strays that get through the bombardment. Keep them off us as long as you can."

"Awful lot of drones heading right for us. Sure hope this ain't a one-way trip," Raven said.

"Stop hoping and get ready to start shooting." Parris pressed a button and prepared to address every ship under his command.

"This is *Gallipoli* actual. We've got a fight on our hands. Our mission is to knock a chunk off those rings and get back to the fleet. Make 'em pay, *Gallipoli* out."

The rail gun batteries fired, the first ventral battery a split second after the other two, rocking the ship from side to side. Flashes from the other ships' rail batteries burst like lightning deep within a thundercloud.

The first quadrium shells erupted against the line of approaching drones. Pale blue jagged tendrils of electricity arced through the leading drones, burning some out of existence and knocking thousands more off-line. Flechette rounds followed a split second behind the q-shells. They broke into spikes two meters long and ripped through the disabled drones, impaling several drones before being robbed of their killing momentum.

The bombardment hit the attacking drones like a series of shotgun blasts, blowing hunks out of the giant mass.

The needle broke apart, forming into a giant cloud of drones.

"Guns, adjust cannon fire, wide dispersion across the entire front," Parris said. "Conn, how long until we're in range of the rings?"

"Five minutes at current velocity and heading, Skipper," the ensign at the conn said.

"Combination!" Commander Hudson called out. "Xaros are forming into…looks like one hundred drone constructs, disintegration cannons visible."

Parris called up the spotter's feed on his screen. The frigate-sized constructs gathered into a dozen tendrils and accelerated toward the *Gallipoli* like grasping fingers, single drones darting ahead of the larger ships.

"Flechettes won't have much of an effect on these larger ships," the gunnery officer said.

"Load lance shells. Take out the leading constructs." Parris glanced at the time plot to the firing point. The Xaros would reach him before that—he was certain of it.

His ship's rail cannons kept firing, launching another salvo every forty seconds. The capacitors blinked with warning. The rate of fire pushed the ship's systems to the limits and rested on the knife's edge of permanently damaging the battery core.

Just the way they'd trained.

"Targets engaged!" Raven said. *"Got almost fifty drones coming from—"* the transmission filled with static and the sound of a gauss cannon

rattling the wing commander's cockpit *"—way too many. I'm down three Eagles and—"* It cut off in a hiss of static.

The icon for Raven's Eagle flashed amber. Damaged.

"Constructs entering range, enemy cannons readying to fire," Hudson said.

"Conn! Evasive maneuvers!"

The ensign flipped a plastic cover off a series of four yellow buttons and pressed one. Thrusters bolted to the dorsal frame, all with their own independent power systems, flared to life and pressed the *Gallipoli* down.

The recoil from the sudden acceleration slammed Parris against his restraints. Scarlet lances of energy snapped over the ship's bow. The thrusters cut out and Parris settled back into his seat.

"Conn?" he asked.

"We can still make the firing point, and I think I lost a filling," the ensign said.

"Sir, the *Cabo* took several direct hits. I'm not getting anything from her or the crew," Hudson

said.

A coherent beam of energy struck the ship's starboard side. It cut across the aegis plating like a surgeon's laser, gyrating the ship beneath Parris. The beam cut out, leaving a smoking furrow in its wake.

"Damage report," the captain said.

"Minor damage to decks seven through twelve…primary lift to the flight deck off-line," Hudson said.

A smile came to Parris's face. The aegis armor worked as advertised. Ships hit by Xaros beams of that magnitude had been gutted like a fish during the Battle for the Crucible.

At least we have a ghost of a chance now, he thought.

A drone cut across his bridge, an Eagle blazing gauss rounds hot on its tail.

Drones landed on the ship's hull. Ruby beams stabbed into the aegis plating, slowly cutting through the armor.

"Get the gunships on those boarders, now!"

Parris ordered.

"The Xaros constructs are reforming," Hudson said. "They're...fusing into a single mass, sir."

"Tell the *Ancona* to continue their mission. Get fire on those rings. Helm, adjust course for the new construct. Ramming speed," Parris said.

The bridge went silent. An out-of-control Eagle slammed into the ship and broke into an expanding cloud of debris.

"Ramming speed, aye, Captain," the ensign said.

The ship veered to the side. Parris got a glimpse of the rest of his task force, their point defense turrets raging against dozens of drones swarming over them. The new construct came into view: the hundred drone ships fit like bricks on a wall as they merged into a vessel several times the size of the *Midway*.

The *Gallipoli's* rail batteries flashed, scoring solid hits on the merging Xaros. Red light burned against the seams of the construct. Blisters of disintegrating drones broke out across the surface.

"Get video of this back to Makarov," Parris said. "Hitting them while they're merging might be a vulnerability."

The construct ripped apart like a desiccated ear of corn. The *Gallipoli* hit the fragments as they broke off, shattering them into burning embers.

"Conn, break off ramming speed and return us to our original course," the captain said.

A fragment twice as long as his ship twisted into a spiral...one end pointing toward the *Gallipoli*. Another hunk smoothed into a long dart and slid into the spiral. The dart shot through and crossed the void to the human ship in the blink of an eye.

It speared through the strike carrier and shattered her keel. The ship ripped into two halves that slammed into each other. Wrecked batteries dumped their stored energy and scorched the ship black. The remains of the *Gallipoli* spun through the void.

****

Makarov kept her head up, watching as the *Gallipoli* died. Data from the rest of Parris's task force kept coming in. They were holding their own against the drones swarming their hulls, but it wouldn't last much longer.

The icon for the *Cabo* blinked red. The captain reported boarders in his engine room and the ship exploded a few seconds later.

"Admiral, the fragments…" Calum zoomed in on what remained of the giant construct. The jagged remains broke apart and reformed into drones. The new drones made straight for the besieged ships.

Makarov slammed a fist against the side of the holo table. She'd sent them on this mission, and now she was helpless while they were torn apart.

The frigate *Ancona* broke from the pack, engines burning well beyond their safety tolerances.

"What's she doing?" Kidson asked.

"Taking a shot," Makarov said. Tiny icons

broke from the *Ancona*, lance shells closing on Abaddon's rings.

"Come on…" She opened and closed her hands into fists as the shells crossed the last few hundred meters…and missed. Xaros destroyer analogues closed on the *Ancona*. Damage icons popped up next to the *Ancona* as disintegration beams hit home.

New rail cannon tracks appeared, and the *Ancona* vanished from the plot, replaced by a yellow and black emblem. The *Ancona* was gone, but she got off one final salvo. The shells streaked toward the rings, and hit.

A cheer went up through the bridge. Makarov stayed silent and zoomed in on the point of impact. The shells knocked a hunk off the rings, exposing glowing pyrite within. The open wound grew bright, then pulsated from abyss black to burning bright.

"Lost the *Reno*…and the *Utica*," her XO said.

"I want every scrap of data we can get from

Abaddon and what happened to that merging construct when the *Gallipoli* hit it. Send everything to Earth as it comes in. Maintain ready alert. Tell the captains I will have them on holo conference in forty-five minutes," Makarov said.

"Search and rescue, Admiral?" Calum asked.

Drones swarmed around the dead ships.

"No, there's nothing to recover. I'll be in my ready room."

CHAPTER 7

Dotok women hurried their children into idling Mules, their engines kicking up a dirty haze on the mesa. Wind whipped through the air. Loose bits of cloth on the Dotok snapped like pennants.

Torni and Minder watched the evacuation play out. Torni remembered the tug of wind at her hair, the pungent smell of body odor and fear from the Dotok. She couldn't feel those sensations viewing the simulation, but her mind tried to fill in the blanks of what she *should* have felt.

"Why are we here?" she asked Minder. "I've been through this before. I know how it ends." She turned to the other side of the mesa just as Yarrow dragged the badly wounded Hale and Bailey into view.

"An amendment for my report to the Masters. Your actions here are difficult for the Xaros to comprehend. I hope to explain it better," Minder said.

The dirty and armor-clad Torni that had less than a half hour to live lifted a Dotok boy into the air and placed him in the waiting arms of his mother.

"Ask," Torni said.

"You are warrior caste. Your government spent significant amounts of time and resources training you in combat and communications. Replacing you, particularly after the reduction in Earth's population, would be difficult," Minder said.

"There wasn't a deep bench of other Marines to take my place after your drones killed everyone, you mean."

Torni watched as she dragged Hale into a Mule.

"Why did you sacrifice yourself for children?" Minder waved his hand through the air and stopped the simulation. He walked up a ramp and leaned over to examine a Dotok baby, swaddled against its mother's breast. "Look at it. It is useless in its current state. Completely dependent on others for survival. An obvious liability."

"The child is defenseless. I joined the Marines to defend the weak, those in need," Torni said. "You see a liability. I see the future. That child may grow up to be a great leader. A scientist who discovers a breakthrough that changes the lives of everyone."

"You gave up your spot and handed over your air tanks. Perhaps a half-dozen Dotok were saved. Tell me, would you have stayed behind for one child?" Minder walked over to a group of Dotok men herding wives and children up a different Mule.

"Yes," Torni said.

"What about this one?" Minder pointed to Nil'jo, the elderly First and leader of the refugees.

Torni hesitated.

"Interesting." Minder walked around Nil'jo, looking him up and down. "This one had obvious value. A leader. Presumably educated. Capable. You jump at the chance to die for a mewling lump of flesh that might not even survive to adulthood, but have to consider whether or not to die for this one."

"You sound like the Dotok. Their society classified each person by their worth, not their potential," Torni said.

"And when confronted with choosing to adhere to their culture or give in to these…nurturing instincts, the Dotok followed your lead." Minder rubbed his chin. "This behavior is counterintuitive to survival of the species. Curious."

"How is it with the Xaros?" Torni asked.

"Our castes are absolute. The Masters lead. I obey. We left the lower tiers to annihilation after the event. There was no discussion or debate." Minder went to Torni's frozen form. "I do not know how I can even communicate this concept of yours to the

Masters."

"Women and children first," Torni said.

"I might as well try to tell them that humans believe the color blue tastes like the number nine."

"That makes no sense."

"Exactly. Tell me, how many Marines would your officer have traded for a single baby?"

Torni looked into a Mule. Lieutenant Hale lay on a bench in a puddle of his own blood, his skin pale. Yarrow pressed a heat suture against a long gash on Hale's arm with one hand and attached a bag of IV fluid to Hale's armor with the other.

"That's…"

"Would he have landed all of these Mules, packed with civilians, next to a lone child and put everyone at risk to rescue it?"

"No, not if the Mules were at capacity."

"He could abandon his own spot." Minder shook his head. "You hesitate. The answer is unsure. At some point in the human decision-making cycle, there is a limit to what you will sacrifice. This lieutenant would not sacrifice a hundred human warriors for one life, would he? No. But he would fight to the last man to save a city, correct?"

"Correct. We manned the walls of New Abhaile against the banshees and your drones."

Minder snapped his fingers and the simulation ended. Takeni, the Dotok, and her frozen self all fell apart like they were made of grains of sand—sand that splashed against the ground and faded away, leaving Torni and Minder on a white plane with no shadows or end in sight.

"My task is impossible," Minder said. "If there was a single value to place on a life, some quantifiable variable, I might explain this to the Masters."

"I could speak to them," Torni said.

"No!" Minder snapped at her. "You will never pollute their existence with your presence—" Minder clamped his mouth shut.

"'Pollution'? Then why are you wasting so much time trying to understand us?"

"I am sorry, Torni. I still harbor old

prejudices. We suppressed the evolution of other intelligent species in our home galaxy. The Masters believed any interaction with the impure would distract from our great purpose," Minder said.

"What about the red one? The General. We've met." Torni crossed her arms.

"He is a manifestation of the drones' programming, not a Master. I have work to do, excuse me." Minder flicked his fingers and put Torni's consciousness in stasis, his laboratory replacing the blank simulation in a smear of light.

Photonic copies of Torni's mind floated atop pedestals, radiating away from his workstation in concentric circles. Lying to Torni about the General and the Xaros was necessary; previous iterations of her mind refused to cooperate once she deduced the truth—that the Xaros would annihilate all intelligent life in the galaxy without remorse or hesitation.

Dangling the hope that she could sway the Xaros Masters away from total xenocide proved to be effective in eliciting her cooperation.

Hope. The concept was alien to Minder.

That the humans were so dependent on it made his work even more difficult. Minder stepped back from his workstation as the urge to add to his already lengthy report faded away.

Keeper had no interest in learning more about the humans. Minder would be erased as soon as Torni outlived her usefulness. The General had already launched an assault on Earth; humanity's extinction was all but assured. Completing the report was his duty, his purpose…and it would be the last thing he ever did.

CHAPTER 8

Malal stepped up to a three-story-high door embedded in a wall so tall the top was lost in the haze. He pressed fingertips to the door and ripples spread from his touch.

"Why are the doors so...big?" Bailey asked.

"You think my true form is like yours?" Malal asked.

"What do you really look like? The big-ass orb we found on Anthalas?"

Malal's head twisted completely around to stare at Bailey. "You truly wish to know?"

Bailey shook her head and stepped back.

The doors slid open to reveal a short tunnel

with pitch-black sides leading to a circular room, the walls covered with glass cylinders full of gray fog. Some glinted with specks of light; others had raging storms of multicolored lightning. A raised circular platform took up the center of the room.

"Here we are." Malal strode into the room.

Hale followed, his weapon ready against his shoulder. He cut around the corner into the lab, sweeping his muzzle around…and behind the door. The entrance was nothing more than a paper-thin slice of reality. He circled the door, and it vanished completely. He ducked his head round the side and found he could look into the doorway back to the orchard they'd come from.

"Iron Hearts," Hale said, "keep an eye out on your side of the doorway. We get separated, you head back to the shuttle."

"And who's going to fly it?" Elias asked.

"Or open up the bay doors?" Bodel asked.

"We all go home or nobody's going home, crunchy," Kallen said.

"Fine. Keep an eye out for anything that

moves," Hale said.

The rest of the Marines had entered the room and taken cover behind the platform. Stacey walked a step behind Malal as he walked around the room, scanning the cylinders.

Almost every inch of the laboratory walls was covered by the cylinders, but there was a blank patch the size of a normal doorway on the opposite side of the platform. Hale jogged around the cylinder. On the blank patch was a frozen shadow of an alien with a segmented body like an ant, its spindly limbs held up over its head like it was trying to defend itself.

"My first experiment," Malal said. "Complete failure, the essence was lost. Shame really, I rather enjoyed its company."

"What did you do to it?" Hale felt anger stir in his heart, a flicker of hatred that spread until his hands gripped his rifle so tightly that it trembled in his grasp.

Malal wagged a finger at him.

"We're not here for a history lesson," Stacey

said. "Where is the codex?"

"Yes, the codex…" Malal turned to the empty platform. "I will need control of my faculties."

"No. Not the deal." Stacey touched her forearm computer and the governor's metal hoops glowed bright enough that Hale could see them in Malal's chest.

"The interface doesn't use something so pedestrian as fingers and buttons. Loosen your hold. The Qa'Resh gave you the option," Malal said.

Stacey bit her lip.

"Hale, if he tries anything, shoot the governor. Something tells me he doesn't want to be a sludge of subatomic particles," she said.

"That works for me." Hale thumbed the safety off his rifle and pointed it at Malal's chest.

One of the hoops in the governor faded away, and Malal rose off the ground.

"Whoa! What is this?" Yarrow scrambled away from Malal as he floated toward the platform.

"Easy. All part of the plan. Kind of," Hale

said. "Shoot him if he acts out of line."

"Sure," Standish muttered, "I'll know just when the floating star god is about to turn from benevolent companion to face-eating demon. Did that in basic training."

When Malal's toe tips touched the pedestal, it came to life with a white glow. Three of the cylinders floated from the walls and formed an orbit around Malal.

"This is what you seek," Malal said. "Peerless knowledge of omnium manipulation. Discrete dimension communications…and…no."

"What? What's wrong?" Stacey asked.

"Corruption." Malal closed a hand into a fist and one of the cylinders shattered. The light inside the broken cylinder held its form for a moment and then dissipated into nothing. Hale heard the sound of a distant scream.

The two remaining cylinders floated down to hover in front of Stacey.

"The echoes. They tried to access my work and ruined it," Malal said.

"Do we have what we need?" Stacey removed a small pyramid-shaped object from a belt pouch and tapped one of the corners. It leapt from her fingers and spun like an out-of-control gyroscope.

"The schematics are parsed through several different vessels. We must have the complete record to open it…a security measure that is proving irksome," Malal said. "This data would have survived until the energy death of the universe. Leave it to lesser beings to ruin perfection."

The spinning pyramid spun around the two cylinders in a figure-eight motion, rays of light dancing between the objects.

"He serious about all this?" Hale asked Stacey over a private channel. "What if he's just playing us?"

"The best encryption methods we had before the war involved steganography based on cosmic background radiation with quantum keys," she said, "which are about as complex to Malal as pig Latin is to us."

"Which…means?"

"He could be playing us. I have no way of knowing. This recorder the Qa'Resh gave me will take in all the data. They're the only ones that can put it together," she said. The pyramid slowed to a stop, then floated to Stacey. She snatched it out of the air and returned it to a pouch.

"Malal," Hale put his fingertip on the trigger, "you went through an awful lot of trouble to protect all this knowledge. Without redundancy, you're risking everything on a single point of failure and something tells me you wouldn't make that mistake. Where are the backups?"

"Perceptive." Malal stepped down from the pedestal, moving through thin air like he was taking a set of stairs. "This is one of the ancillary laboratories. The forge will have the original documents."

"How do you know the Jinn didn't get into there too?" Hale asked.

"Because the vault is still here. If anyone but me had broken into the sanctum, a singularity

128

would have opened up and annihilated everything," Malal said.

"Hold on. There's a black hole in the middle of this place just waiting to go off?" Stacey asked.

"Correct. I will guide us," Malal said. "Bring your abominations into this room. I must reopen the door."

Hale sent a quick message to the Iron Hearts. The cylinders around the lab clinked against each other like wind chimes as the armors' heavy footsteps reverberated through the room.

"Malal," Stacey said, "is there anything else in here we could use in the fight against the Xaros? I don't want to waste this opportunity."

"You'll get what you bargained for, bright one. The rest of the records here all pertain to the grand question." Malal looked around the room. "The totality of my existence went to the answer, and here we are surrounded by a fraction of that work. Experiments that failed, experiments that brought me one small step closer to a solution. Once I'd solved the equation, I should have destroyed all of this. But…vanity."

"What was the question?" Elias asked.

"Must we die? Must our consciousness embrace oblivion when reality can no longer support even the concept of thought?" Malal's face pulled into a sneer. "That was our destiny, *is* your destiny. The cold abyss at the end of the universe, when all matter and energy decay into nothing. *I* found a way out. *I* opened the door to immortality…and my peers left me behind."

"Your people never had faith in God? Never thought you could achieve eternal life through belief in a higher power?" Elias asked.

"Spare me," Malal said. "We were that 'higher power' for countless civilizations until I found a more noble pursuit for our efforts. Humans are lucky they were nothing better than primates when our gaze passed over Earth. I will not waste any more time. Stand aside."

****

Malal opened a door into a sparse forest. Trees made up of intertwined vines as thick as Hale's leg joined the luminescent white trees. Tufts of tall grass formed bushes between the two types of trees, which alternated as the forest stretched into the distance.

The Iron Hearts took the lead out the door, the tops of their helms well short of the treetops.

"This is weird," Standish said as he and Orozco squared opposite corners around the door. Standish swung around and found the door had disappeared, same as the entrance to the lab. He knelt next to a tree trunk and kept his eyes peeled.

"What part?" Orozco asked. "Us in some crazy *hombre*'s secret stash or that we're babysitting the guy, helping him look for…I don't know, Excalibur or something." Orozco thumbed the control to his Gustav heavy cannon, spinning the three barrels to life.

"I know, right? How am I going to tell this story to all the impressionable and hero-worshipping ladies when we get home? 'Then he snapped his fingers and a dimensional gate opened up.' No one wants a one-night stand with a nut job. Well...I'm OK with crazy because I never use my real name and leave before they wake up." Standish shook his head. "But what I'm talking about is this forest. Why are all the trees evenly spaced? Even those bushes are smack between the trees. There should be bugs, critters all over the place."

"Maybe you're missing the forest for the trees." Orozco shrugged his shoulders, then scratched his back against a trunk. "Those tusk-cats weren't biological. Maybe the trees aren't either. Nature doesn't have a lot of obvious patterns to it. A setup like this can't be an accident."

"Maybe there's a planet where trees grow in an orderly fashion," Standish said. "Gunney Cortaro would love it there."

"So...there's a gardener? Someone that wants the forest just like this?" Orozco asked.

"That's my guess. You think he-she-it knows we're here?"

Orozco gave the long barrels on his cannon

a pat. "I haven't been subtle."

"Move out," Cortaro said from the middle of the formation as Malal closed the door. "We're half an hour from the next doorway. Stay alert. Stay alive."

Standish kept watch behind the formation as it moved into the forest. The eerie symmetry and layout of the place didn't bother him as much as the total stillness of the trees, like he was walking through a photograph and not a living, breathing place.

****

Hale touched a beaded cord hanging from his armor and shifted a black bead to the bottom. Keeping a pace count was a fundamental skill for Strike Marines; learning to keep track of his position without the aid of GPS was a novelty for someone raised in the always-on, always-connected environment of twenty-first century America like him. The American military hadn't relied on maps, terrain association and compasses for dismounted movement since the end of the Vietnam War. The skills came back to the fore once the Chinese disabled or destroyed the world's satellites at the beginning of World War III.

Having to trust Malal with the navigation irked Hale. He was the team leader; he was supposed to know where they were and where they were going. With no distant point of reference, the only thing Hale knew for sure was how far they'd gone since they left the lab: nine hundred yards.

Not for the first time, he wished Steuben was there. The Karigole warrior never tried to interfere with Hale's authority, but he would give a few private words of advice from time to time.

A whistling sound came through the air.

Hale stopped and raised a fist next to his head, signaling a halt. The tree branches remained as still as ever. No breeze caused the whistling, which grew louder.

"Anyone else hear that?" he asked.

"It's coming from up high," Elias said. His

helm titled up toward the dark sky.

Thumps sounded in the distance ahead of them, each new sound evenly spaced from the last. Hale couldn't keep count as the rhythm pounded the ground with the steady ferocity of an old belt-fed machine gun.

"Action front," Hale said, "hold your fire until we know they're hostile."

Elias put his palm against one of the glowing trees and shoved it over. Clear glass roots snapped and shattered as it tore free from the forest floor. Bodel and Kallen did the same and then rolled the trees toward Hale with a kick. The three trunks formed a field expedient, if somewhat sloppy, palisade.

"Take cover," Elias said.

The Marines crouched against the trunks as their internal light slowly faded away.

The sound of marching feet filled the air.

"Care to shed some light on what's coming at us?" Hale asked Malal.

Malal, standing tall and not taking

advantage of the felled trees to shield him, gave a slight shrug.

"Get down. Now."

"My form is proof against anything the physical universe could—"

"You're not invisible and standing out in the open will draw fire on those of us who aren't 'proof.'"

Malal's eye twitched, and then he sank down onto his haunches.

"Contact," Elias said, "dismounted infantry, hundreds."

Hale glanced over the trunk. Soldiers, made from the same orange and white glass as the tusk-cats, advanced toward them in a wide column, their pace in lockstep. The front rank carried tear-shaped shields and tall pole-arms that crackled with electricity. Bullet-shaped helmets stuck up from behind the shields, all without slits for eyes or breathing. There was no obvious leader, no banners and no sound other than the mass of feet hitting the ground in unison.

"Sir?" Cortaro asked.

The front rank lowered their halberds over their shields, pointed right at the Marines.

"Open fire!" Hale set his rifle to high power and pulled the trigger. His rifle kicked like a mule. The shot hit a Jinn's shield and blew it, and the soldier, into fragments.

The thunder of the Iron Hearts' cannons and Orozco's Gustav drowned out everything else as Hale tried to aim again. The torrent of shots from the bigger guns annihilated the first dozen ranks as Jinn soldiers exploded into dust. Despite the onslaught of fire, the advance continued.

Hale's rifle buzzed when he pulled the trigger and a battery icon popped onto his visor. He switched his weapon to low power and got off one last shot that blew the head off a soldier. The rest of the body took another step forward then fell to the ground.

"Low-power head shots!" Hale tossed away the dead battery and slapped in a fresh one.

Red spheres of energy the size of golf balls

snapped overhead and the smell of burning ozone hit Hale a moment later. The fire from the Iron Hearts came to a sudden halt.

The three soldiers were frozen in place. Willowy bands of electricity leapt from armor to armor.

"Elias? Can you hear me?" Hale asked.

He heard nothing but static in return.

The tree Hale leaned against bucked as a Jinn energy round hit, knocking Hale to the ground. The trunk blew into splinters as another round tore through, spraying Hale with tiny bits of shrapnel.

Malal stood over Hale, bits of tree embedded in his skin, and reached down to Hale.

"Get down!"

"How many times must I—" a Jinn round hit Malal in the back. Malal's smug face melted like a candle under a blowtorch. His entire body lost coherence and splashed to the ground, the glowing governor in the center of a quivering puddle.

"Malal?" Stacey crawled over and reached for the gooey mass, stopping short of actually touching it.

The roar of Orozco's Gustav firing at full cyclic tore Hale away from what had become of their guide. Hale grabbed his rifle and turned it back toward the Jinn.

The soldiers' advance stopped a few trees away, their halberds pointed skyward. They were still as statues. Orozco methodically swept his cannon across the soldiers, destroying several with each shot.

"Cease fire!" Hale shouted. Orozco's cannon died down a second later.

"Why'd they stop?" Cortaro asked.

"Don't know, don't care," Hale said. "Anyone hurt?" His Marines answered in sequence, no casualties.

The helms of Jinn soldiers toppled over and broke apart on a carpet of broken glass. Shields fell to the ground. Arms detached from bodies and the remaining Jinn disintegrated in seconds.

"Hale…" Elias' transmission came in riddled with static. The Iron Heart lurched forward, breaking away from a band of energy that clung between him and Kallen like a spider web. The web between the other two Iron Hearts vanished with a pop.

"That was miserable," Bodel said.

"What happened?"

"Our suits went into lockdown, everything off-line," Elias said. He touched a hand to his helm, as if dizzy. "Feel like I'm going to puke."

Kallen fell to her hands and knees and the armor rocked back and forth. Bodel and Elias went to her instantly.

"Yarrow," Hale said to the corpsman, "see what you can do for her. Stacey, is Malal…dead?"

Stacey ran the small triangle over the Malal-puddle and shook her head as she read off her forearm screen.

"The governor says he's still…around. Sort of." She put her hands on her hips.

"Can we take him with us?" Cortaro asked.

"In theory." Stacey poked the muzzle of her carbine between the governor bands and lifted it up.

The goo clung to the bottom of the governor and lifted up with it. "He's still one big mass. I think we can carry him, somehow."

"My drill sergeant always said it only takes one battlefield mistake to go home in a bucket," Standish said, "and we seem to be fresh out of buckets."

"Standish, empty out your pack and get Malal in there," Cortaro said.

Standish went pale beneath his visor. "But, Gunney, I already carried that probe in my head back on Nibiru. Who knows what this thing will do to me. What about Yarrow? He's still the new guy!"

Yarrow brandished his middle finger.

"That's right, there's some history between them," Standish said.

"I'll get it." Egan opened the pouch on the small of his back and handed off spare batteries, ammo magazines and tubes of ration paste to Standish. He picked up the governor with his fingertips and lifted it up, Malal clinging to the governor like a soaked towel on a hook.

"OK, here we go." Egan opened the pouch and tried to guide the lower edge of Malal into the opening. Malal flapped from side to side. Egan let out an un-Marine-like screech and stuffed the governor into the pouch, Malal's mass draping over the side. Egan scooped it up and tried to stuff it inside.

"Oh God, why is it warm? Why is it warm, Stacey?" Egan got the last of Malal into the pouch and zipped it shut.

Bailey crept over to Standish.

"Did you get that on your armor cameras?" she asked.

"All of it," Standish whispered.

****

Kallen's gauntlets trembled, digging into the bed of silver grass beneath her. The HUD integrated into the visor over her eyes flashed warning after warning as the synch rate between her and her armor dropped into the red zone that barely kept the armor functional.

"Desi, can you hear me?" Bodel asked her on a private channel.

"Mm-hmm," she managed as phantom pain stitched up her armor's back. If she had any sensation below the neck, she knew the pain would have been unbearable. She'd been diagnosed with Batten's Disease weeks ago, an illness that would rob what little faculties she had left…and kill her within the year. Her control over the armor had been slipping the past few days; whatever the Jinn hit them with had sent everything into a tailspin.

"Key my serum…I can't do it on my own," she said. A patch of warmth spread from the plugs in the base of her skull and the tremors stopped.

"Dr. Eeks said the serum would lose potency with every use. We need to get you out of here," Bodel said.

"I will leave with everyone else." She got to her feet and watched as her synch rate with the armor rose to marginal effectiveness. With a high synch rate, she could move with an air of grace and take on both Elias and Bodel in armor-to-armor unarmed combat and stand a good chance of winning. Now, she could shuffle forward with the finesse of an early-model Ibarra construction robot.

Yarrow, Hale and Elias spoke to each other a few yards away.

"Does he know? About the Batten's?" Kallen asked.

"The corpsman? No. Nothing he can do. Not his business," Bodel said.

"What about Elias?"

Bodel didn't answer.

"Damn it, Hans, you promised me."

"He was about to figure it out on his own. You've been degrading for too long for him not to notice."

"Why…why hasn't he said anything?"

"He's waiting for you to tell him. Assuming we get out of here, don't wait anymore. Some things need to be said." Bodel broke off the private channel.

Elias' legs locked straight. Armor plates

retracted and treads extended from their housings with a whirr of servos. His upper body slid down to the knees and the tracks hit the ground.

"Crunchies want a ride?" Elias said. "You two good?"

"No problem," Kallen said. It took three attempts before her armor transformed.

****

Hale ducked beneath a branch as Bodel rumbled beneath a vine tree. Keeping one hand, foot and a knee mag-locked to the armor and trying to keep his rifle ready for any sudden contact *and* ducking branches (which Hale suspected the soldier was deliberately aiming for) was an exercise in coordination and concentration.

"I've been thinking," Stacey said from the other side of Bodel.

"Bad habit," Hale said.

"What? No, listen. Those Jinn weapons blew the tree to smithereens. Why didn't they do the same to the armor?" she asked.

"I'm not complaining," Bodel said.

"Why'd they give up after they hit Malal?" she asked.

"Ibarra," Hale said, swaying back to dodge another dangling vine, "you're worried about a very distant target. I'm trying to figure out how we get into the next part of this vault without Malal. Then, I'm trying to figure out how we get off this rock without Malal to open up the outside. How long until we know if he'll be all right or we need to find out if any of these trees are edible?"

"We've got a structure at our twelve o'clock," Bodel said. The image of a wide and squat brown building popped up on Hale's visor.

"All stop. We'll go in on foot from here," Hale said. He jumped off Bodel's track before it came to a complete stop and rushed over to a glow tree. He zoomed in on the structure with the optics on his rifle. The building was two-stories high and looked like it had been cut from a single giant rock. There were no seams or doorways anywhere he could see.

"This is the place," Hale said. "Gunney, take your fire team and scout around the other side. Let me know if there's a way in."

Cortaro, Bailey and Standish took off at a jog.

Egan skipped to the side like he'd been hit with an electric shock.

"Gah! Damn thing moved." The commo Marine slapped a hand against the pouch containing Malal.

"Check on him," Stacy said.

Egan unzipped the pouch slowly. Dark swirls moved across the surface.

Malal's face formed and said, "Let me out."

"Jesus H. Christ!" Egan tore the pouch off and threw it against a glow tree.

A blobby arm slurped out of the pouch and the rest of Malal pulled free. Malal morphed back into his human shape, no worse for wear. He turned his head to Egan.

"You will never speak of this," Malal said.

147

"Fine by me." Egan went to his empty pouch and hesitated before picking it up.

"What happened? Are you…whole?" Stacey asked.

"The interaction between the energy field of the governor and the Jinn weapon proved…unpleasant," Malal said. "Had the weapon been a bit stronger, I would have been destroyed. To have my existence ended so close to my goal, and by the combined efforts of humans and Jinn. A tragedy."

"Nothing on the other side, sir," Cortaro said.

"I take it you have a way inside," Hale said to Malal.

"Yes. Give me a moment. Some things are still in flux." Malal's chin sunk to his chest.

"Form a perimeter," Hale said to the Marines. "Soon as he's done putting his face on, we'll move out."

"Hey, Ibarra." Standish waved to Stacey. She jumped off Bodel and went to him. Standish opened a pouch and removed one of the bullet-shaped heads from a Jinn soldier and handed it to her. "I figure you're the only one smart enough to figure anything out from this. Well, except for Malal, but he freaks me out."

"Thanks." Stacey rolled the object in her hands, her reflection wavering like she was looking into a pond disturbed by a strong breeze. It was half the diameter of her head, a tangle of ripped glass wires at the base.

"You know, there's no artificial life on Bastion," she said. "The Qa'Resh probes might make that definition, but they're so constrained by programming most shut down when forced to choose anything."

"Why's that?" Standish asked.

"The Xaros. Any computer system they can access they destroy. Bastion never bothered to recruit or even contact species that were AI and computer dependent. They'd never stand a chance once a single Xaros drone showed up in system and ripped every network to pieces," she said.

"Guess we were lucky we had the Second Pacific War, forced our military to learn to function without computers," Standish said.

"You think that was an accident?" Stacey asked.

Malal's face snapped up.

"I am ready," he said.

****

The largest cavern Hale had ever seen was the Tycho Dome on Luna. Jared's senior thesis on asteroid mining had caught the attention of an Ibarra Corporation headhunter, who arranged for Jared and Hale to visit the incomplete dome. Jared's trip included corporate briefings on the wonders of working for the wealthiest company in human history and a conditional offer of employment. Hale got space sick during the shuttle from the spaceport in Belize to Tycho and spent most of the trip clutching a bag ready for the contents of his stomach.

Luna's light gravity hadn't agreed with him then, and it hadn't gotten any better with time.

The Tycho Dome was three miles high at the apex, and with enough surface area to house almost a million people once complete. Hale didn't think one could suffer from agoraphobia beneath the Moon's surface, but he'd come close to a panic attack while his brother chatted up the project's engineering staff.

Tycho Dome was a child's sand castle compared to where Malal led them.

A great cylinder spun around a freeway-wide bridge. Lakes, green forests and concentric circles of structures filled the inner surface. All of it stretched so far behind them that the end was lost in a haze. Ahead, a solid pillar of light pulsated.

Hale used his forearm screen to send a dose of anti-motion-sickness drugs into his system. That the folded landscape rotated around the bridge did nothing to settle his stomach.

Malal opened his arms wide.

"Behold! My great work, my soul forge," he

said.

"Malal, is there anyone in those cities?" Hale asked.

"No one. Holding areas for the kindling, if you will. Come, you won't be the first to see this, but you will be the first to speak of it afterwards." Malal moved toward the pillar at a brisk pace.

"How does it work?" Hale asked.

Malal looked at Hale like a dog that had just messed the rug.

"I don't think your language has enough small words for me to explain it properly."

"Try me," Hale said.

Malal remained quiet for a minute then held up the palm of his hand. A box morphed out of his palm.

"What is in the box?" Malal asked.

"How am I supposed to know?"

"You aren't. You are to guess. Please, do so."

"I don't...a model of the *Breitenfeld*, how's that?" Hale asked.

152

The sides of the box sank back into Malal's palm, revealing a sparrow that flapped its wings and jerked its head from side to side.

"Incorrect, but inconsequential." Malal closed his fingers around the bird and dropped his hand to the side. "You are capable of creativity; you can imagine multiple possibilities. Tell me, where did that answer come from?"

"Just a guess," Hale said.

"And that guess is what makes you so wondrous. Animals do not imagine. Computers do not create. They follow a pattern set by those capable of independent thought. I will share something your physicists suspected but would never be able to prove. No matter what you guessed was in the box, you were right."

"You changed what was inside?"

"No. But in making a decision, making your guess, you created a reality where there was a model in the box," Malal said. "The universe reacts to your will. That is the ultimate power of sentience, and that power is quantifiable. Measurable.

Useable."

"You lost me," Hale said.

"You held on longer than I thought possible." Malal turned his attention back to the great pillar.

"Where's the 'so what,' Malal? What does all this have to do with those empty cities? What you did to the Shanishol on Anthalas?"

"Hale," Stacey tried to step between the two, "none of this is relevant to the task at hand."

"The power exists in sufficiently developed minds, but it is faint," Malal said. "When harvested in sufficient amounts, it can be bent to a purpose." He waved a hand up and down his omnium body. "To stave off the decay of time. Or, if at the right place at the right time, to open a doorway to another universe where the laws of physics are more...accommodating."

"And how many souls did you feed into this forge?" Hale asked.

"Lieutenant! Stop this line of questioning right now," Stacey said.

"What's done is done, bright one," Malal said, "and I have no time for regrets." He turned his face to Hale. "All of them. We harvested every advanced intelligent species in the galaxy. Every planet we nurtured to maturity fed the forge engines. We left a few primitive species behind, those not worth the effort to collect. Ironically enough, there was no suitably advanced civilization to counter the Xaros when they arrived."

Hale stopped. His stomach felt like a rock as the implications of what Malal just told him raced through his mind. He knew Malal was a monster, but the sheer scope of his crimes was almost impossible for him to comprehend...and this monster was their ally.

Stacey took a few halting steps after Malal, then came back to Hale.

"Hale, look, I know this is a lot to take in, but the Qa'Resh—"

Hale grabbed her by the shoulder, glared at her and opened a private channel.

"We are not doing this, Stacey. We can't

help that thing anymore. Not when the price of its cooperation is going to be paid in blood. Our blood!"

Stacey slapped his grip away. "Not your decision. Not mine either. In case you haven't noticed, we are up shit creek without a paddle in this vault, and in this war, without Malal. Play along until we're back on the ship. Can you do that, at least?"

Even when angry, Hale could see the reason behind her request.

"We're not done. Not by a long shot," he said.

Stacey opened her mouth to speak, then turned away.

"Problem, sir?" Cortaro asked as he came up from behind.

"Let's keep moving."

CHAPTER 9

Miles beneath Abaddon's surface, a control room came to life, a circular room with a flattened dome ceiling, identical to Crucible's command center. Workstations lit up with data on the human fleet, holo recordings of the *Gallipoli*'s final moments, replays of Xaros disintegration beams ripping across the aegis armor with less effect than expected against the humans' ships.

The presence of humans in deep space was an anomaly, one that must be reported.

A plinth in the center of the room glowed as pale light shone through the base, up through floating red plates of armor. The control room connected to the greater Xaros network and transmitted every scrap of data collected on the human fleet.

The light grew brighter. A burning sphere of light grew in the armor's chest. The spheres burst like a supernova, filling the armor with coherent light.

The General had arrived.

A swipe of his ethereal fingers brought up a real-time image of Eighth Fleet. The ship that carried his prisoner and had proven difficult to destroy on Anthalas and Takeni, the *Breitenfeld*, was absent. He studied the ships, noting their markings and significant improvements made to their weapons and armor.

They are using the omnium reactor they took from Anthalas. The General compared the ships arrayed against him with Torni's memories. His prisoner was of the human's warrior caste, but segmented to the human's ground combat arm. Her memories of the humans' fleet were fragmented, ancillary.

The largest human vessel, *Midway*,

corresponded with memories of a wrecked ship broken across a mountain range. *Is this the same ship?* the General asked himself.

The General compared Torni's memories of ships in battle over the Crucible to the humans' fleet and came to a conclusion he had some confidence in.

The humans had sent their entire fleet to stop his invasion. The fleet before him was a few ships less than what Torni remembered seeing in dry dock and in space. Human breeding patterns and maturation meant that the crews of these ships were the vast majority of the fighting force that survived the Battle of the Crucible.

If they risked their entire fleet to slow my advance…they're relying on the Qa'Resh alliance to protect their home world.

The theory fit the facts…but something galled at him. The humans had proved too resourceful, too clever, to make such a strategic misstep as sending everything they had to interdict the next invasion.

The eye slits in his mask burned as frustration mounted.

I will brush this irritant away and finish off what remains on Earth. The final outcome is the same. The General stretched his perception through the entire planetoid and felt the drone crèches. Proto-drones, little more than omnium sacks clutching the sides of hollowed-out caverns through the rocky interior, reacted to the General's command to mature into full-sized drones.

His arsenal was far from the dark matter halo around Barnard's Star, forcing the drones to transmute far more of the planetoid's mass to mature so quickly. Drawing on so much of the arsenal's potential would make for fewer drones once it arrived in the human's system.

There was a single tenet of warfare that the General held to with every operation against the intelligent species polluting this galaxy: overwhelming force. Even with the losses he'd sustain swatting this human fleet aside, he'd invade Earth with a force several orders of magnitude greater than anything the humans could hope to have standing against him. Their extinction was a near mathematical certainty.

Still…

The General ordered his drones to redouble their production. He would take no chances.

He watched the human fleet for hours and then he entered the conduit leading to the rest of the Xaros network and left his arsenal to the droids' programming. He would return, but first he needed more answers.

CHAPTER 10

The admiral turned an ornate handle on her bulbous samovar and piping hot water poured into a china cup, already half-full with deep brown tea. Her hand trembled and the cup rattled against the saucer in sympathy.

She set the saucer on her desk, spilling some of the tea onto an open notebook.

"Chyort voz'mi, guvno!" She wiped the spill away and picked up a pen. Every observation from the recent battle went onto the paper—every conjecture, every crazy idea that came to mind. She picked up a printed photo of the damaged construct and scribbled a note on the back.

"Ma'am?" came from the doorway. Calum leaned into the room. "Five minutes until the captains."

"Yes, I will be right…Calum, that ribbon. It fired off the lance that destroyed the *Gallipoli*. Why haven't we seen that tactic before?" she asked.

Calum frowned.

"Well," his head rocked from side to side, a sure sign he was thinking hard, "they were under duress. *Gallipoli* was going to pound them to dust if they didn't do something fast. The whole thing—the ribbon, the lance, all made out of drones. They lost a lot of combat power when they killed the *Gal*."

"We haven't seen kamikaze tactics from them," Makarov said. She chewed on the end of her pen then wrote furiously.

"Should I have them wait?" Calum cocked his head over his shoulder.

"No." Makarov jabbed a period and closed her notebook. "Time is valuable. I don't waste my time. I will not waste others'." She slammed back the hot tea. If it caused her any pain, Calum didn't notice.

When she arrived at the operations table, Delacroix's holo was ready and waiting across from her normal spot. The rest of her captains' holograms shifted from side to side, looking uneasy.

"Scorpion, what did we learn?"

Graphs formed in the holo, full of science jargon that Makarov didn't understand.

"We recorded fascinating readings at the moment the rings took damage. The space-time grade fluctuation perfectly followed the Kapur Theorem which will—"

"Skip to the end," Makarov said through grit teeth.

Delacroix rolled his eyes and Makarov resisted the urge to rip his face off.

"The damage to the ring disrupted the planetoid's Alcubierre field and cut its acceleration, but only briefly—not because the ring came back online, but because the drone net around the surface formed a new field." Delacroix nodded slowly. "The new field is just as strong, but the Kapur signature matches readings from recorded drone interstellar travel."

"And?" Makarov asked.

"And look at this." Delacroix swiped a screen and a graph with a slight decline came up. "This is the planetoid's gravity. As soon as the drone field came online, the pull of gravity from Abaddon decreased, and it is only getting weaker. Granted, it would take years to have any measurable effect…Yes, Admiral, I see that look and I'll cut right to the chase. The drones are consuming themselves to keep the Alcubierre field up and running."

A video of Abaddon's surface came up. Drones spewed from open portholes and melded into the net surrounding the planetoid. Burning embers traced up and down the net's filaments, like a lit cigarette wasting away.

"The power needed to keep this planetoid moving is enormous, and the drones were not designed for this. Hence, the Xaros use the rings to relocate large objects, not a drone net like we see now."

"We take the rings off-line permanently…what effect will that have on Abaddon?" Makarov asked.

"Assuming they keep the same acceleration, it would decrease the mass of drones arriving in our solar system by thirty percent," Delacroix said.

"Seventy percent of a giant shitload is still a giant shitload," Calum said.

"Correct," Delacroix said. "The ability of the drones to create their own field also puts my task force in a precarious position. The drones can power through the effect of the graviton mines. There's no way to stop Abaddon from reaching Earth." Murmurs filled the air as the rest of the captains reacted to the news.

"The strain…" Makarov tapped a finger against the side of the table, "you set off the mines and the drones will have to burn their candle at both ends to keep up the speed, yes?"

Delacroix's eye slid from side to side as wheels turned in his head.

"Yes, we have to monitor the consumption rate a bit longer." Delacroix's eyebrows shot up. His holo turned away from the table.

"I'm sure he will return in a moment with a brilliant deduction," Makarov said. "Now, if we can't stop this thing, then we must weaken it. Give Earth a better chance when it arrives."

Delacroix returned to the table, a smile across his face.

"Good news, everyone! I ran some simulations based on my idea—"

"My idea," Makarov said.

"Her idea, and we can force the Xaros to expend between forty and seventy percent of their total strength. How? Take out the rings, then Task Force Scorpion makes for Earth at best speed, seeding graviton mines every few light-hours for maximum effect. It'll be like forcing the Xaros to run uphill. Given the details, the forty percent solution is preferred, naturally."

"How do we get to seventy percent?" Makarov asked.

Delacroix went pale. "That's the worst-case scenario, given what we know about the Xaros' ability to highjack computer systems, and that the minelayers will only be a few steps ahead of Abaddon to maximize the effects. The ships can't run on automation. They have to continue to the limits of their life-support systems."

"The minelayers run ahead of Abaddon until air, food and water run out," Makarov said.

"And then the crews die," Delacroix said, swallowing hard. "My ships have to run at full speed. No other ship in our fleet can keep up with the minelayers."

"It may come to that," Makarov said. "It may come to that for all of us." She looked around the table. Captains straightened up as they found her gaze. "We are here, in the depths of the unforgiving void, to fight for Earth. Give her a future. We have a chance to win, and we are going to fight for it. There is no price we will not pay, no burden we will not bear. Am I clear?"

Calum tapped her on the elbow and

whispered to her.

She hit a flashing icon and the holo switched to a close-up of the damaged ring. Drones pressed into the exposed pyrite, melting, then morphing into the brass outer casing and the pyrite.

"Easy to conquer the galaxy when you have no supply chain to worry about," Calum said. "The drones convert mass to omnium, then to more drones, to whatever they need."

Makarov zoomed out. A circle of light opened on Abaddon's equator, then darkened as a swarm of drones poured forth.

Makarov felt her stomach knot. "Battle stations."

                              ****

Corporal Brannock wondered, not for the first time, just who he pissed off to get hull guard duty. The *Midway* had small bunkers across her hull where security teams would protect against drones attempting to cut into the hull. The idea had proven marginally successful during the Battle for the Crucible, even though casualty rates had been exceedingly high for those tapped to stand on the wrong side of the ship's armor and fend off Xaros drones with little more than a gauss rifle.

He shared bunker D-28 with Derringer, a Marine heavy weapons team and three doughboys. The heavy weapons team nursed a Gustav cannon mounted on a turret ring. The two Marines had spent the last half hour practicing detaching and reattaching the weapon, all the while cursing whatever naval engineer expected them to swing the weapon in a circle to engage targets coming from the other direction.

All wore the new combat power armor, the armor plates coated with the same material that made up the aegis plating. Brannock didn't care for the glossy sheen, but noise and light discipline had little effect when fighting in the void. The armor would, according to the quartermaster who'd issued it to him, protect them from a Xaros disintegration beam. The engineer went on to say that *not* getting shot was still the preferred method to survive on the battlefield, but anyone hit and not killed should write up the experience to benefit the next design iteration.

Indigo shook Brannock's shoulder.

"Sir. Sir!" Indigo pointed to the bunker's bolted door.

"How many times do I have to tell you not to call me 'sir'? I work for a living." Brannock pushed Indigo's hand away.

"Time to go see, corporal sir," Indigo said, his eyes wide with anticipation.

"Has it been thirty minutes? Fine. Derringer." He kicked the sleeping Marine's feet. "Taking the big boys on a little walk."

"This mean I have to wake up?"

"Yes, exactly that." Brannock detached the air supply lines running from the side of the bunker to his helmet. The doughboys did the same, wrapping the lines around their hooks just like he'd taught them when they first started their shift.

The doughboys didn't come across as

terribly bright, but they learned simple skills surprisingly fast. Brannock wished he could say the same for Derringer.

The corporal opened the door and stepped out onto the *Midway's* hull, his mag locks gripping the matte-gray armor with each footfall.

A squat void craft with wide wings sat on the hull ahead of him. It had ball turrets on the top and bottom of each wing, mounted to the fuselage, twin gauss Gatling cannons, rocket pods and a spine-mounted rail cannon. The new Osprey gunships had arrived only a few days ago, and he'd been keen to get a closer look.

The doughboys were even more eager to know more about the Osprey. They'd nearly gotten into a fistfight over who got to look through the bunker's view slits to see it. Promising to take them out to see the new weapon if they behaved for a half hour had calmed them down instantly.

There were two of the new gunships not far from the bunker, a flight of Eagles just beyond them. All were mag-locked to the *Midway's* hull.

Putting pilots and crews on the ship's surface took stress off the flight deck when it came time to get more fighters and bombers into the void.

Brannock glanced at Abaddon, glowing like a bale eye. There'd been no official word on the *Gallipoli* and the ships that left with her, but they sure weren't with the rest of the fleet in the void above his head.

"'Join the Marines! Fight a planet!' Let's see the recruiters use that line," Brannock said.

Indigo grunted, his default response to anything remotely complicated.

Brannock stopped a few yards from the Osprey and shrugged. "Here you go. Remember, no touching."

"No touching," the three doughboys said as one. They bustled past Brannock and pointed at the larger gun emplacements, grunting in approval.

"What the hell are those?" came from behind him. A pilot in a lighter, less armored vac suit walked up to him, his steps tenuous on the hull. The call sign "Zorro" was stenciled on his chest.

"You're asking me, sir? Thought you flyboys would be all over the new toys."

"Not the Ospreys…those." Zorro pointed at the doughboys.

"Yeah, them. Bio constructs made to look like us, minus the freaky skin and Cro- Magnon features. Guess Ibarra can't make proccies fast enough so now they're mass-producing these guys," Brannock said.

"What do they do?"

"Whatever we tell them, so long as you can say it with very small words. They fight like demons. I saw some footage of them in Hawaii ripping Toth warriors apart. I spent that whole fight on ship security detail, thumb way up my own ass." Brannock shook his head.

"I was in the upper atmo, knocking down their transports," Zorro said. "You think I can talk to one?"

Brannock called Indigo over. The doughboy went to the position of attention when he saw Zorro's lieutenant rank.

"At ease, soldier. Bend down a bit," Zorro said. He leaned close to Indigo's face and took a long look at him. "Amazing, isn't he? Ibarra creates life now. Same way he created us."

"What do you mean, sir? The proccies?" Brannock asked.

"Aren't you one too? The whole fleet are proccies." Zorro held up a palm to Indigo, who returned the gesture with a hand nearly twice as big.

"Suppose so. That rumor was going round the ship after the fight with the Toth. Then Admiral Makarov told everybody it didn't matter one way or another far as the military was concerned. I got better things to worry about than if my mom and dad were tubes. The parents I remember are dead, killed on Earth with everyone else."

"What's your name?" Zorro asked the doughboy.

"Sir, unit designation Indigo-347."

"How do you feel about being out here?" the pilot asked.

Indigo grunted.

"Don't bother, sir. They're as dense as armor. The only time I've ever heard them even laugh is when one of them passes gas," Brannock said.

"Sir." A massive hand shook the corporal's shoulder. He turned around and found another of his charges, Cobalt, pointing at an Osprey turret. The crewman inside banged on the shell and pointed to a piece of paper with an IR frequency on it.

Brannock manually set his receiver and said, "Yeah?"

"Shit's going down," the crewman said. "Xaros coming in hot and heavy. You better get back in your hole, Marine."

"Why am I always the last to know things like this?" Brannock grabbed the doughboys and pointed them to the bunker. Zorro had already left.

"Bottom of the totem pole, buddy. Good luck." The crewman closed the channel.

Rail cannons flashed to life across the fleet. Fighters lifted off from the *Midway's* hull and zoomed out of the flight deck. He glanced at

Abaddon and saw a dark mass made up of thousands and thousands of drones advancing on the fleet.

The rail gun battery behind the bunker crackled with energy then shot out a round with a white flash of light so bright it burned an afterimage into Brannock's eye.

"Shit!" Brannock repeated the word over and over again until he got back to the bunker and hustled the doughboys back inside.

"What's going on out there?" Derringer asked.

"Drones, coming right for us." Brannock slid aside a view port on the roof, letting him and the rest of the bunker see Abaddon and the battle unfolding around them.

"All hull security elements, prepare for contact," came through the ship's defense network.

"Now they tell us." Brannock checked the charge on his gauss rifle and chambered a round. "Lock and load."

The doughboys slapped magazines into their

oversized gauss rifles. The two Marines manning the Gustav said a quick prayer over the weapon.

"They tell you what's happening?" Derringer asked.

"Nope. We stick to our assignment, shoot any drones that make it to the hull."

"Fight!" Indigo slammed a fist against his chest then drew the pneumatic hammer off his back.

****

Holos shivered as the rail batteries did their work. Makarov watched as hundreds of projectiles traced from her fleet to the encroaching Xaros. The swarm was nearly ten times what the *Gallipoli* had faced, all single drones packed together.

Makarov closed her eyes for a moment, feeling the hum of the deck plates beneath her feet, the tremors of firing rail guns. Calm came over her. A warship was one of the few places she ever felt truly at home.

The leading shells detonated just short of the

drones, shredding hundreds into oblivion with razor-sharp flechettes. The swarm contracted as fire from Eighth Fleet peppered the mass of drones. The drones took more casualties as their close order left little room to maneuver away from the shotgun blasts from the shells.

"What're they doing?" Makarov asked.

"They must have thought we'd lead with the q-shells," Kidson said, "to try to mitigate that by spreading the effects through many separate drones."

"Commander Laskaris requesting permission to open fire with the energy cannons," Calum said.

"Not yet," Makarov said. The swarm tightened then flew apart to reveal a spiral construct ship. Four gleaming darts floated near the back end, each the size of a destroyer.

"Guns, concentrate lance fire on that launcher. All ships, engage maneuver pattern delta. Stay out of each other's line of fire," Makarov said. She slammed her palms against the table and mag-locked her feet and hands. The *Midway* lurched as the carrier activated its auxiliary thrusters to carry out the sudden maneuver.

In the holo, her fleet broke to a side. The weight of fire slowed to nothing as ship realigned.

The Xaros launcher shot out a lance, moving fast enough to reach her lines within a few tens of seconds. The lance's projected course jumped all over the place, then settled. It was heading for the cruiser *Warsaw*.

"*Warsaw*, all ahead full, now!" Makarov shouted.

The *Warsaw* surged forward and the lance's plot fell behind the ship.

"Guns, plot a—" Makarov stopped as the lance veered to the side. The weapon changed its course, heading straight into the *Warsaw*'s flank. Point defense batteries on the *Warsaw* battered the lance, to no effect. The lance slowed, but still hit the *Warsaw* with enough force to break through the aegis plates like they were paper and impaled the ship through the engines. The lance caught in the wreckage, its silver tip jutting between the number four and six thrusters.

The *Warsaw* listed to the side like a speared fish.

"Another launch!" Calum called out. The plot on the next lance resolved…it was coming for the *Midway*.

"Randall, emergency thrusters. Guns, hit that thing with q-shells and lance shells before it can maneuv—" A sudden downward acceleration sent blood rushing into her skull. Her hands snapped off the holo table and flew over her head. She felt the grip of her boots slipping off the hull.

Blood pounded against her temples and her vision darkened. She pressed her toes against the sole of her boots and the gravity linings in her boots tightened their grip on the floor. The acceleration quit and Makarov stumbled against the holo table and fell to the deck.

She pulled herself back to her feet. The incoming lance flew through clouds of q-shell electricity from exploded munitions as the rest of the fleet fought to save the flagship. The lance's projected path would take it into deep space. The disabled lance didn't correct its course and missed the *Midway* by an uncomfortable few hundred yards.

"Captain Randall," Makarov said to him on a private channel, "install another acceleration chair for me next to the holo table once the battle is over. I do not want my career to end with a smear on the ceiling."

"Aye-aye, Admiral," Randall said.

"New contacts…coming from the *Warsaw*," Calum said.

Drones poured out of the dead ship. Lumps of glistening metal sloughed off the lance embedded in the ship and formed into new drones.

"Launch! Another lance…on an intercept course with the *Tarawa*," XO said.

Whoever's leading the Xaros…he's damn good, Makarov thought.

****

Brannock scanned through his firing port, adrenaline coursing through his veins as he waited for the Xaros to arrive.

"Drone touchdown in sector thirty-seven! At least twenty all coming from the—" The IR transmission broke into static.

"Should we go help?" Derringer asked.

"Thirty-seven is on the exact opposite side of the ship," Brannock snapped. "This is our sector. Our job is to keep drones off that rail battery until someone tells us we have a new job."

"I just don't want to spend this whole fight on my ass," Derringer said.

"Careful what you wish for, boot," one of the Gustav gunners said. "I was on the Crucible, saw a drone tear five Marines to pieces."

"Enemies…soon?" Cobalt asked.

"Maybe soon. Watch your sector, big guy," Brannock said. He tapped a fingertip against his rifle. The anticipation was proving worse than the thought of facing the Xaros.

A point defense battery down the hull opened up and rapid flashes issued forth from gauss cannons.

He caught sight of a drone off the port bow and his heart skipped a beat as it veered straight toward the ship. A flurry of bullets smashed the drone to bits. An Osprey zoomed over the bunker and banked away.

"Why are we out here, again?" Derringer asked.

"Drones! Drones coming in twelve o'clock high!" The transmission was from bunker four, on the opposite side of the rail cannon.

"Up! Up!" Brannock grabbed the handle on a roof firing slit and yanked it aside. He pointed his rifle into space. Derringer opened another firing slit, then screamed in fear. He slammed the slit shut just as a drone landed on the roof.

Stalks waved in the void over Brannock, but he didn't have a clear shot at the drone's body.

A patch of red grew on the roof.

"Bunker four, can you get a shot on this

thing?" Brannock asked. No answer.

A disintegration beam the width of a pencil stabbed through the roof and swept toward the Gustav. It traced a line across one of the gunner's chests as he screamed in pain.

Brannock unbolted the door and swung it open. He charged out and twisted around. A drone clung to the top of his bunker, blood red light from the beam projecting out of stalks splashed against its shifting surface. He fired his gauss rifle and hit the drone in the flank. A spider web of cracks broke across the surface.

The drone dragged its disintegration beam away from the hole in the bunker and twisted the stalks toward Brannock. He leaped to the side. The beam cut across his shins and pain exploded from his legs like he'd been branded.

With no gravity to pull him back to the hull, Brannock floated several feet above it. His flailing limbs found no purchase.

He fired his rifle from the hip and severed a stalk off the drone. The momentum from the shot slammed him into the hull and the mag lock in one boot stopped him from bouncing off into the void.

The drone scuttled off the roof toward Brannock. The stalks rose over the drone and Brannock stared into the burning tips.

A massive hand grabbed the stalks and ripped one aside. Indigo swung his pneumatic hammer into the drone and a diamond-tipped spike inside the hammer drove into the drone's shell. Cobalt and the other doughboys joined the melee, pounding the drone with their hammers.

The drone cracked into hunks and disintegrated.

Indigo looked at his hammer and shook his head.

"Need better!"

"Need more better." Cobalt nodded his head.

Brannock got both feet secure against the hull. A drone landed on bunker three. He took careful aim and hit the drone across the forward end. Two more shots knocked it clear off the bunker. A third shot shattered it into burning fragments.

"Gun better," Indigo said, the muzzle of his gauss rifle red-hot.

"Back inside, all of you," Brannock said.

The rail cannon fired, stinging his eyes again. He stumbled into the bunker and fell against the side. The pain in his shins returned with a vengeance as adrenaline wore away.

"Son of a bitch." Brannock looked at his legs. The armor bore a thin line of melted armor, bubbles and cracks radiating away from where the beam touched him.

"Your suit good?" Derringer asked.

"Yeah, didn't spill my air. Just hurts like a mother," Brannock said.

The doughboys lifted their rifles and fired. Brannock jumped up and shot down a drone before it could reach the rail cannon.

"Two o'clock." Derringer pointed to a trio of drones coming in fast.

Brannock tripped over something before he could reach the other side of the bunker. Both the

Marines who'd manned the Gustav lay next to the access hatch. One, a line seared across his armor, stared vacantly at the ceiling. The other bore a smoldering hole on the shoulder; the armor was flat, empty.

"Joiners! Group forming above bunker two!"

Brannock opened the roof port. A mass of five or six drones twisted together, more joining by the second.

Brannock hit the mass with three shots and swapped out his spent battery. The drones continued to meld together, unaffected.

"Gauss rifles are damn spitballs," he said into the IR. "Can you get an Osprey or an Eagle over here?"

"Every asset is tied up. Do something, five!"

Brannock snapped his head to the Gustav, but it was gone. The bunker door was open. Indigo charged out carrying the heavy weapon, the other two doughboys right behind him.

"No! Indigo, wait!" Brannock ran after

them.

Indigo spread his legs wide and raised the Gustav barrel to the combining drones. Cobalt wrapped his arms around Indigo's waist and braced himself against the hull. Garnet wrapped his arms around Indigo's chest.

Indigo fired the Gustav, the massive recoil of each shot sliding the doughboys several inches with each shot. The dead gunners had integrated support and anchor systems built into their armor to keep them stable while firing the cannon. The doughboys had nothing but their mag linings and muscle power.

The third shot from the Gustav sent the combing drone mass spinning out of control.

Brannock drove his shoulder into Indigo's back and overloaded his mag linings. The burst from the Gustav drove Brannock's heels into the aegis armor.

"Aim! Aim, damn you!"

Indigo paused, then hit the drone mass dead center and blew it apart. A twisted lump of drones bounced off the armor just in front of them. One broke free, leaving the rest to disintegrate. The surviving drone lashed out, ripping a beam across Garnet's face and neck. He fell back from his hold on Indigo.

Brannock fumbled for his rifle. A second beam hit Cobalt in the arm. The doughboy twisted away with a grunt of pain over the IR.

Indigo swung the Gustav around and fired. The recoil slammed him against Brannock and sent the doughboy tumbling through space. Brannock's mag-locked boot dragged against the hull. He got his other foot down and found the attacking drone now nothing but smoldering ashes floating in the void.

"Indigo?" Brannock searched the void. The *Halifax* exploded as its battery stacks went critical. Eagle fighters sparred with drones. Burning rail cannon shells cut across the void, but there was no sign of Indigo…or Cobalt.

Garnet was still attached to the hull, his arms hanging loose at his side. Brannock touched

Garnet's back and the armor collapsed, empty.

"We got more! We got more!" Derringer called to him.

Brannock choked down his emotions and went back to the bunker.

****

Zorro let off a burst, missing the drone he had in his sights. The drones had a nasty habit of dodging just as he fired. He aimed his cannons to the side and fired again and the drone flew right into his attack and broke apart.

"I saw that—pure luck," his wingman said.

"Skill, Buckets, all skill," Zorro said. He looped around and let off a wild spray, clipping the drone Bucket pursued. The drone spun end over end before Bucket destroyed it.

"I want an assist on that kill," Zorro said.

"Fine, I'm still ahead of you by two."

"Cottonmouths, we've got new orders," the squadron commander said. *"Clear a path for a*

bomber wing making a run on that Xaros launcher.
Form on my wing."

"You think we cleared out enough drones?"
Buckets asked.

Zorro twisted in his cockpit. The *Warsaw*,
where most of the drones had come from, reeled as
the fleet turned their rail cannons on the ship. It
broke apart under the pounding. No more drones
came from the expanding wreckage.

"Jesus, you think anyone was still alive on
the *Warsaw*?" Zorro asked.

"Doesn't matter anymore," the squadron
commander answered. "*Midway* and the *Tarawa* are
clearing their flight decks. Makarov ordered
everything that can shoot to get into space so we
can go and make that launcher a memory."

Zorro checked his weapons. His gauss
cannon had half its rounds left and enough battery
charge to fire his rail cannon twice. A waypoint
appeared on his canopy pointing him toward the
launcher.

"Buckets, you good over there? Thought I

saw you get hit," Zorro said.

"Singed some attitude controls, couple thrusters are off-line. I've got a work around," his wingman said.

"You can't maneuver, you get back to the *Midway* and hot swap to another fighter."

"And miss any of this? Check your oxygen levels because you must be losing brain function," Buckets said.

Eight Eagles formed a V over a half-dozen Condor bombers and entered the dead space between the human fleet and the Xaros launcher. Drones passed by high above the formation, clear of rail cannon shots striking at the frigate and cruiser-sized constructs protecting the launcher.

"Big boss lady know there're unfriendly ships between us and the launcher?" Zorro asked.

"Stand by," the squadron commander said. "They'll clear a path in just a second."

Silver streaks of quadrium rounds converged with more rail cannon shots on a Xaros cruiser. Point defense lasers destroyed the leading q-shell. It exploded into a brief storm of electricity, creating sympathetic detonations in the flechette rounds. The cruiser lashed out at the incoming q-shells and burned out against the thousands and thousands of otherwise harmless submunitions.

Q-shells slammed into the cruiser. Lightning arced to nearby ships, torching their hulls and knocking them off-line.

"That's our signal. Punch it!" The squadron commander's Eagle leaped forward.

Zorro gunned his engines and the Eagle rattled as it tried to catch up to the leader. G-forces pushed Zorro against his chair as his hands strained to keep their hold on the controls. The stricken Xaros cruiser rolled on its axis, snaps of electricity flaring off the surface.

"Cottonmouths, do a point defense sweep as soon as we're clear of this obstacle. Let the Condor's torpedoes do the heavy lifting," said the squadron commander, call sign Bully.

"Got to give those trash haulers something to look forward to," Buckets said.

Zorro rolled his Eagle over the edge of the cruiser. The launcher was there, and a dozen more lances waited in a neat line at the far end. A lance sat inside it, like a bullet waiting to fire.

A red beam slashed from the launcher's outer edge right past his cockpit.

"Found a point defense node," Zorro said. He fired off a burst and used his maneuver thrusters to shunt him to the side, narrowly dodging another shot from the Xaros lasers. He raked fire across the node as he flew over the top, sending broken and burning stalks tumbling through the void.

"Torpedoes away!" came from one of the Condors.

Zorro banked around and peppered another nest of stalks.

"Eagles, get clear before—" A blast of energy wider than a cruiser broke through space and swept downward. Zorro flipped around before the blade could annihilate him and his fighter. The Xaros had used a weapon like that before, at the Battle of the Crucible.

Zorro looked to where the flat beam originated and saw a disintegrating Xaros cruiser.

A pair of torpedoes crossed in front of his nose. They continued straight on, missing the launcher. The torpedoes were laser guided, controlled by the bombardier in the Condors.

"Condors, what's your status?" Zorro asked. No answer.

"They're all gone," Buckets said, his breathing fast. "Bully too. We're down to four ships. Let's get the hell out of here!"

The launcher glowed as it charged, readying to send another stake into the heart of Eighth Fleet.

"Hold on. I got an idea." Zorro charged up his rail gun and loaded his only q-shell into the breech. He looped around and flew straight into the mouth of the launcher.

"What the hell are you doing?"

"No point defense batteries in here." Zorro slowed his fighter, watching as the lance glowed brighter.

He fired his q-shell and hit his afterburners,

skirting through the gaps in the ribbon before the quadrium effect could travel up the launcher and fry him.

The launcher buckled. The lance, still charged with energy, shot forward and ripped through the side of the launcher. The lance spun end over end before it struck a Xaros frigate and both shattered like dropped glass.

"Now we can leave," Zorro said. He found a gap in the wreckage and set a course back to the *Midway.*

****

Admiral Makarov breathed a sigh of relief as the Xaros launcher failed, taking out another enemy ship in its death throes.

"Concentrate fire on the drones coming on our flanks." Makarov touched the mass of drones coming in from above and below Eighth Fleet. "Status on the drones from the *Rome?*"

"We've got clear void from every ship

but…the *Poltova*," Calum said. "Sending a flight of Ospreys to assist from the *Tarawa* now."

"Battery reserves across the fleet are dangerously low, Admiral," Kidson said. The fusion reactors within each ship would recharge the batteries, but only if the guns stopped firing long enough to let the reactor connect to the capacitors. The capacitors could connect to the guns or the reactors, not both. Trying to shoot and charge at the same time would cause a spectacular explosion. A bar chart came up in her tank; several ships were crossed out with a red X, destroyed. The rest had just enough battery charge left for a few more volleys. Except for one, the *Griffin*.

"Lift fire on the Xaros capital ships. Cycle the fleet though a recharge cycle but do not let up on the drones coming at us," Makarov said.

The Xaros capital ships clustered around the wrecked launcher advanced on her fleet. Their projected course converged on a single point.

"Here it comes," Makarov said. What few records survived the fall of Earth showed a massive

Xaros ship annihilating humanity's combined space navies, a ship that dwarfed the Toth dreadnought that crashed into the moon. Garret and the rest of his planners could come up with only one term to classify something so massive.

"A leviathan," she said. The first two Xaros capital ships pressed together, embers scorching the edge of the hulls as they merged.

"*Griffin*, Makarov, this is your time to shine," she said.

The video of a dark-skinned man with salt-and-pepper hair came up next to the *Griffin*'s icon.

"I know you're expecting a lot from me and my ship, ma'am, but this might be more than she can handle," Commander Laskaris said.

"We brought you along for exactly this reason, Commander. Time to earn your keep," Makarov said. She cut the transmission.

"If this doesn't work, we're in trouble," Calum said.

"It will work," Makarov said. "I saw the field tests on Charon."

"Didn't that test vessel blow up?" Kidson asked.

"Yes, but Lafayette said he fixed the fault." Makarov waved a dismissive hand in the air.

"I don't believe Lafayette is on the *Griffin*, or anywhere near this fight," Calum said.

"You can either worry or pray. The choice is yours, just do it silently," Makarov said.

The *Griffin* broke from the fleet and burned toward the assembling leviathan. The Toth invasion fleet had been destroyed down to the last ship and dagger fighter. After the last Toth overlord was killed, the warriors manning the remaining ships refused to surrender. Toth ship captains chose to vent their atmosphere and kill the crews to avoid capture, which left a number of intact ships for salvage.

The scientists the *Breitenfeld* rescued from Nibiru possessed a great deal of knowledge regarding Toth ship construction and were eager to help harness what their enslavers left behind. Working with Lafayette, and after more than one "design flaw" wrecked a test bed, the Akkadian scientists produced a weapon system that would either prove valuable against the Xaros, or fail and doom Eighth Fleet to a losing fight.

Armor plates on the *Griffin* slid aside. Energy cannons that had once graced the hull of the *Naga* dreadnought rose from the *Griffin*'s hull and locked into place. The crystals glowed deep blue as power built within.

The final Xaros capital ship fused into the leviathan. The new ship out-massed the entire Eighth Fleet nearly three to one, its shape morphing into a long cone studded with cannons. A divot at the apex of the cone glowed with reddish-yellow light.

"Guns, a volley," Makarov said.

"Aye." Each of the fleet's remaining rail cannons sent a lance round at the leviathan.

Might as well try to tear down a mountain by throwing pebbles at it, Makarov thought.

Lasers snapped out of the leviathan and erased the incoming rounds from existence.

Fifteen bolts of blue-white energy erupted from the *Griffin*. The bolts closed on the leviathan in seconds. Counter fire from the Xaros ship shot out...and passed through the *Griffin*'s energy weapons. The energy bolts hit by the Xaros shrank in size and intensity, but continued on. They slammed into the underside of the leviathan, cracking its outer hull and sending jagged plates hurtling through the void.

Another volley came off the *Griffin*, hitting the damaged area again.

Makarov ignored the cheers from the bridge and pulled up the telemetry data from the *Griffin*. The ship's batteries lost nearly ten percent of their total charge with each volley. Commander Laskaris kept up the firing through a fifth and sixth volley...well beyond the weapon's design tolerance.

Red warning icons popped against the *Griffin*. Two of the cannons were off-line and the third had shattered. The leviathan—a smoldering crater blasted out of its hull, great cliffs of glowing pyrite now exposed to the void—rolled on its axis.

"Guns, open fire on the leviathan. Concentrate on the exposed core. *Griffin*, your systems—"

"I pushed it too hard! Overloaded the heat sinks to kill that damn thing," Laskaris said, his video full of static. "I've got cascading failure across all my batteries and the crystals will explode no matter what I do. Tell Lafayette to double the buffering—"

His image cut out as a final volley came from his ship. The energy bolts gouged deep inside the leviathan, knocking free lumps of crystal the size of skyscrapers. The crystals atop the *Griffin* exploded, ripping the cruiser apart.

The rear of the leviathan rose up. Blisters opened across the surface, burning white hot. The damage spread, covering the entire ship until it cracked apart, leaking an expanding field of smoldering remains that burned away to nothing.

"The remaining drones are retreating," Calum said. "We did it, ma'am."

"Did what?" Makarov snapped. "Abaddon is

still on course for Earth. The rings are intact. Nothing has changed but the loss of good ships, good crew. Begin search and rescue efforts. I want detailed damage reports from every ship in the next thirty minutes."

She turned away from the holo table and went back to her ready room.

CHAPTER 11

Torni's boot sank ankle-deep into mud. She shifted Cortaro's weight against her shoulders and slogged forward. The swamp on Anthalas simmered beneath the planet's blazing star, making each breath a fight against hot, wet air.

Orozco followed behind Torni, Yarrow slung over his shoulder like a sack of potatoes.

Torni and Minder watched the memory play out, their feet passing through the mud without effect.

"Are we the ghosts, or are they?" Torni nodded her head to her squad trudging through the muck.

"I will not discuss your primitive superstitions," Minder said.

"My body is dead, yet here I am. My spirit continues," she said.

"Do not color your situation with religion. We scanned your cranium, recorded a perfect copy of every synapse, neuron and cell, then recreated your mind. Child's play." Minder wiggled his fingers and the haze around them vanished.

"Why are we here, Minder?"

"You were not the decision maker during this event, but you might explain what happened. The humans Cortaro and Yarrow were injured. The Toth were in pursuit and the drone garrison was aware of your presence. Your extraction from the planet waited several miles away from this location. Why didn't Hale abandon the casualties?"

"*Esprit de corps.* We do not leave Marines on the battlefield," Torni said.

"They left you behind. Are you worth less because you are female?"

Torni went to Cortaro. The gunnery

sergeant's left leg was nothing but a mess of torn flesh below the knee, blown away by Steuben. A tourniquet tied just below the knee kept him from bleeding to death. A Toth warrior had impaled the Marine's leg with a claw. Steuben's quick thinking had certainly saved the Marine's life, a fact Cortaro would only grudgingly admit.

"Marines don't care if those they serve with are men or women, only that they can do the job. I inherited good Scandinavian genes that made me taller, gave me an advantage during Strike Marine selection." Torni looked to the short and squat Bailey struggling through the mud. "That one is Australian. They're bred tough and mean."

"Why did they leave you behind on Takeni? On this planet, Hale endangered the entire team for a subordinate and the one hosting the precursor intelligence. This behavior is incompatible with other events."

"It is not. The Dotok needed our help to escape. Cortaro is wounded. He needs us to survive. There is no distinction for me," Torni said.

"Curious. Wounded were abandoned before—the Japanese invasion of the Philippines, the Fall of Darwin. Explain."

"Once upon a time I could have been nothing but a camp follower because I'm a woman. Things evolve."

"Yet there is a circumstance where the wounded would be left behind."

Torni's hands squeezed into fists.

"We say things like 'mission first, Marines always,' but the mission is what matters. If we were so intent on preserving lives, we would never go to war in the first place. Our lives are forfeit for the mission, but a good leader like Hale will find a way to win without getting us all killed. Here, on Anthalas, we had the chance to get to the extraction point with everyone. Hale took it."

"There was hope."

"That's right."

"I hate that word. There is no room for 'hope' in a decision." Minder shook his head and turned to Torni. He froze, his eyes wide in fear.

"What?" Torni turned around.

The General floated in the air, the intensity of the photonic body beneath the gleaming red armor stinging Torni's eyes. He lashed out and wrapped his massive hand around Torni's head. He lifted her into the air, her limbs flailing.

Her mind felt like an inferno inside her head. She was on the surface of the Crucible one moment, staring at the surviving ships in the fleet as they moved through the wrecks after the Battle of the Crucible, then yanked inside the *Breitenfeld* where she read through the casualty list from the battle, scanning for names she knew.

The General tossed her aside. She bounced off the white floor of the now empty simulation and rolled to a stop. She raised her head and caught a blast of hurricane-force wind to the face, a roar of static and cracking steel rushing over her.

The sound died away. Torni felt hot blood running from her nose and ears. She got to her hands and knees as blood dribbled down her face and fell. The drops didn't hit the floor; they vanished to nothing as they fell into eternity. Her face contorted with pain as she struggled to breathe. Minder accepted that she was nothing more than a simulation, but when he looked upon her…all he saw was another being. Suffering.

"I'm sorry." Minder was at her side.

"What…was that?"

"The simulation makes you feel what is done to your consciousness. It is the only way we can communicate. The General's query…must have been painful. What did he want?"

"Ship names." Torni wiped blood from her lips. The red stains seeped into her fingers and disappeared. "Ships that survived the fight to capture the Crucible. Numbers of fighters, crews, not something I was smart on. My head isn't real. Why does it hurt so much?"

"The General is not subtle. Here, let me…" Minder gently pressed his palms against her ears. Torni felt warmth flow through her body and the pain subsided. "Better?"

Torni touched Minder's wrist. She felt the

pulse of a strong heartbeat and pulled away from him, startled.

"You're alive?"

"Not in a way you understand," he said.

"What was that noise? It sounded like someone fed a battleship into a trash compactor."

"The General spoke. He was…displeased with my progress." Minder looked away.

"That's what you sound like?"

"No, that is the Master's speech. You still do not appreciate their eminence, their perfection. I am a lower caste, nothing compared to them."

"What did he say?"

Minder stepped away from her.

"Let me show you something." Minder raised a hand over his head. Darkness fell around them. He lowered his hand and a silver speck of light appeared in the distance. The light grew brighter and closer. Torni made out a twenty-sided polyhedron, surrounded by brass rings like the ones surrounding Ceres, as it neared.

"This is the Apex. Our home. Our salvation.

Your mind cannot process scale without a frame of reference. Here…" Minder snapped his fingers. An overlay of the solar system appeared within the Apex, the sun at its center. The edge of the Apex stretched nearly to the orbit of Mars.

"That's…"

"Remarkable, yes. The Engineer cannibalized several star systems to create it. Designed to transport the pinnacle of our species from our galaxy to yours. Some useful lower-caste intelligences were brought along. My worth was not as high as others who were not chosen. I cannot explain my inclusion. You might call it 'luck.'"

"If you can build something like this, how is any other species in my galaxy a threat to you? Why are your drones killing everything they find?" Torni asked. "You said it was a mistake, some knee-jerk reaction because the drones came across a species using jump technology."

"You do not understand the reasons behind our actions, as I do not understand your hope. As for the drones, their purpose is to annihilate all intelligent life. Our time is limited. There is no reason for me to keep up the charade." Minder watched as Torni fought to maintain her composure as she came to grips with the truth he'd kept hidden from her.

"I've had this discussion with you," Minder said, "other iterations of your consciousness. Each time you learn the truth of the drones, you shut down and offer nothing but your full name and serial number, like you are a prisoner of war—an apt description of your circumstances, but I digress."

Torni looked around, finding no avenue for escape.

"I…will help you, Torni. I have a way to get you back to Earth, but I want you to see something first," Minder said.

"You play this same trick before? Offer to help and squeeze some more information out of me?"

"The General ordered me to destroy you and all your reference data. There isn't much time before I must obey." Minder looked to the Apex. They plunged into the enormous structure and passed through the outer hull.

Two crystalline spikes ran from the hull to a yellow sun at the center. Torni's breath caught. The scale of the spikes became clear; each would have stretched from Mars to Mercury. Streams of energy flowed from the sun down the spikes and into a crystalline mountain range at their base. The entire inner shell of the Apex glittered, like she was inside a geode.

"How are we supposed to fight this?" Torni asked.

"This is what you need to see." Minder grabbed her by the hand and took her toward the surface. They stopped in front of a crystal face, the size of the *Breitenfeld*, protruding into the air. "Look closely."

Torni got within an arm's distance. She saw a distorted shadow just beneath the crystal. Tall, it was, with spindly limbs. The shadow hung impassively then vanished in a blur. Torni pulled back.

"We exist within the Apex, and only within the Apex. The General is but one of us. His consciousness is limited to one place at a time. The drones' programming can be altered, corrupted, but not if the General is alive to fight it. Cut him off from our network and he can be killed. Do you understand me? If the Apex reaches your galaxy, we will be legion and you are doomed."

"Why are you telling me this?"

"We are wrong. We never gave other species a chance, always assumed our perfection was absolute and could only become less by contact with others. I do not understand you. The simple possibility of another way of living makes me doubt what I know." A chagrined look passed over his face. "Maybe Keeper is right. There can be no contact without corruption."

He cocked his head to the sky.

"He's coming." Minder snapped his fingers. The Apex and Torni faded away, replaced by his lab.

Minder shifted from human into a black hole bordered by a wide accretion disk. Presenting himself as anything but his preferred Xaros form would earn an instant sanction from the approaching Master, who was not known for half measures or mercy.

The air above Minder transformed into a wide star field, mirroring the constellations visible from the destroyed Xaros home world.

Keeper was here.

+Report.+

+The human—+

+NO!+ The shock of Keeper's rebuke threatened to rip Minder apart. Several of the vessels holding Torni burst apart.

+The General was here. Why?+

+He took information from the…subject. Military in nature.+

+He chooses to spar with the corruption directly. Hubris, or their threat is greater than he's led me to believe. Either is unacceptable.+

An idea came to Minder, one with variable

outcomes.

+The General ordered me to destroy the data and finalize my report,+ Minder said, hesitating just enough to let Keeper reach his own conclusion. +I will comply immediately.+

+No. You are my thrall, not his. Continue your research.+

The more the General has to rely on Torni, the weaker he looks to his peers, Minder thought.

+Yes, Master.+

Keeper faded away. Minder made a note to query Torni and find out if hope was a physiological reaction or an intellectual concept. Maybe, just maybe, he was beginning to understand the word.

CHAPTER 12

The soul forge thrummed as the pillar's intensity wavered slightly. The Marines and armor formed a perimeter around Malal and Stacey as they climbed onto a circular platform jutting out from a ring running around the pillar and connected to the bridge.

"So…what happens next?" Standish asked.

"Same as the lab," Hale said. "Those two find and tag the data we need, then we beat our feet out of here."

A window of light opened near the platform. A ghostly band of energy emerged and coiled around Malal.

"That guy gives me the creeps," Egan said.

"Gives *you* the creeps?" Yarrow asked.

"Stow it," Cortaro growled.

Hale felt a chill creep into his armor. The temperature readings on his suit plummeted. A dark patch of sky formed high above the bridge a few hundred yards away, malevolent like the base of a storm just about to break.

A deep voice broke through the air, hitting Hale like a slap of thunder.

"Get. Out."

Echoes of the words reverberated around them.

"This place is haunted," Standish said as he crept closer to Elias' legs. "Great. Cherry on top of an otherwise horrible day."

A dark bolt fell to the bridge. An ethereal shape of a man walked toward the Marines, its limbs jerking like a stiff marionette. Hale aimed his rifle.

"Give him to us." The words were a screech. "Give us the demon. Free your slaves. You may leave, fully functional."

"We're here for information. Nothing else," Hale said, "and you're not getting anything from us."

The speaker vanished. The dark portal grew wider as wafts of black haze spilled over the edges.

"Here we go…" Bailey said.

"Stacey, how much longer?" Hale asked.

"About…two hours," she said.

"Two hours!"

"Do you want to come up here and sort through millions of years' worth of impossibly encrypted data? Because you can, be my guest and help," she said.

"Contact," Elias said.

A mass of orange and white segmented plates descended from the portal. Tiny legs writhed at the edges of the linked armor, each as big as a city bus. The tip of the gigantic creature grasped at the air.

"The Jinn word for the creature roughly translates as 'wyrm,'" Malal said. "They were not friendly."

"Elias, can you hit it with your rail cannons?" Hale asked.

"I tried to get my anchor through this bridge, can't. Even if I could, the blast would turn you crunchies into mush and send you flying off the edge," Elias said.

The wyrm's tail touched the bridge and the rest of the body curled down like a snake readying to strike. A fanged maw surrounded by feeder arms tipped with scythes came out of the portal. There were no eyes, just a mouth that looked like it could swallow one of the Iron Hearts whole.

"Fire!" Hale let loose a high-power shot and hit the wyrm at the edge of the mouth. The snap and flash from gauss weapons erupted around him as he fired as fast as he could aim after each kick of recoil.

The wyrm's armor plates buckled and shattered under the withering fire. The wyrm swung from side to side then slammed its bulk against the bridge. The quake sent Hale reeling. He stumbled until he felt Elias' massive hand on his back. The barrels on the armor's twin cannons glowed red as he pounded the wyrm.

A trill broke through the air. The wyrm crawled to the edge of the bridge then slithered under the edge. Its entire body followed moments later. Lumps of broken glass twinkled on the bridge.

Hale felt the vibration of thousands and thousands of legs bringing the wyrm closer to them.

"Ah…fuck." Hale looked around, trying to think of anything that might help. "Grenades! Set for lance and fall back." He pulled an anti-armor grenade off his belt and twisted the handle two clicks to activate it.

"Fall back into a corral." Cortaro slapped Bailey on the shoulder and pointed to the middle of the bridge just beneath the platform. Marines formed into a circle, their weapons pointed to either side of the bridge.

"Egan has charges. Maybe we blow the bridge?" Orozco asked.

"How would we get out of here, smart guy?"

Standish slipped a grenade into the launcher slung beneath his rifle. "You want to try and fly across a hole big enough to keep that thing away from us?"

"I could throw you," Kallen said.

"Oh, look who's got jokes now. Everyone remember to tip your waitress. She'll be here through next Thursday," Standish said.

Elias' right hand retracted into the forearm housing, replaced by a spike tip.

The bridge shook with tremors as the wyrm closed within a hundred yards.

"Give us an opening," Elias said.

"To do what?" Hale asked.

"Charges." Kallen pointed at Egan. "Give them to me." Egan glanced at Hale, who nodded quickly. Egan unclipped a tan box and pressed it into Kallen's hand.

"Denethrite will explode if hit hard enough," Bodel said to Orozco. "Wait until we're clear."

The trembling stopped. A bead of sweat ran down Hale's face. He cocked the grenade behind his head and glanced from side to side, waiting for the wyrm to strike. Cortaro had a grenade up, his gaze fixed on the right side. Hale looked left.

A chitinous claw reached over the lip of the bridge.

"Left!" Hale hurled the grenade just as the wyrm's open maw swept over the side. A tiny radar sensor in the grenade pinged off the hard armor. An explosive charge wrapped around a tungsten cone ignited and morphed the warhead into a super-heated lance of liquid metal. The lance cut through the wyrm's armor like it was made of paper and blew out of the creature's back.

More grenades assaulted the creature's maw and thorax. It reared back, smoke burning from a dozen gashes, and let off a roar that shook the bridge. It swung to the side and fell onto the bridge, its open mouth snapping at air. The rest of the body rose up and settled behind it.

The wyrm shifted from side to side, and Hale felt like he was a child again, staring down a train barreling right for him.

The Iron Hearts charged the wyrm, cannons

blazing.

The wyrm reared up and snapped forward.

Hale leapt to the side and wind rushed by as a feeder scythe cut through the air just above his legs. He hit the ground and rolled with the momentum then something jerked him to a halt. One of the many tiny legs had him by the ankle. He swung his rifle down and fired a high-powered shot into the seam between the wyrm's plates. The legs yanked him to the side, sending the shot high and wide.

Elias jumped onto the wyrm's back and rammed his spike into an armor plate. The spike sank in with a crack of glass and a shower of sparks.

"Kallen!" Elias ripped a damaged plate away and sent it hurling into the air. He grabbed a handful of sparking wires and held on as the wyrm bucked beneath him.

The motion whipped Hale into the air then slammed him into the deck. Even in his armor, he hit the bridge with enough force to crack his visor and knock the air out of him.

Kallen, her spike embedded beneath a plate closer to the wyrm's tail, tossed the denethrite charge to Elias. He jammed the charge into the damaged creature and hopped off. He tore off the legs holding Hale and stood over the dazed Marine.

"Get clear!" Elias shouted.

"I'm stuck!" Kallen jerked at the spike still embedded in the wyrm. Bodel jumped up next to her and blasted around her spike with his arm cannon.

"Use your—" Elias didn't see the wyrm's maw as it swung around and smashed into him. The wyrm reared up with Elias clenched between foot-long fangs, scythes raking against his armor. His left arm dangled free as the other pounded against the wyrm's mouth.

Elias' cannon roared to life, stitching rounds down the wyrm's underbelly.

A high-powered shell connected with the denethrite charge. A clap that sounded like a giant redwood snapping in half hit Hale hard enough to knock him flat.

The blast ripped the wyrm into pieces. The upper half came down and slammed into the bridge. Elias spat out of the mouth, smashing into the bridge over and over again toward the edge.

Hale watched in horror as Elias went tumbling over the edge of the bridge.

"Elias!" Hale ran to the edge. All he could see of the Iron Heart was a glint of light just before he disappeared into the distance.

You can't help him, a still, small voice said to him. *Lead.*

Hale got away from the edge and looked back to his Marines. Orozco sat against the ring housing the pillar, his Gustav a pile of bent metal on one side, a concerned Yarrow on the other. Other than Malal and Stacey still on the platform, there was no sign of anyone else.

"Cortaro? Gunney?" Hale found his rifle and picked it up.

"Here." Cortaro limped around the smoking corpse of the wyrm. Hale ran to him and supported him as they went to Yarrow.

"You hurt?" Hale asked.

"Damn thing feels broken," Cortaro said. "Brand new leg, too."

"Sir, Orozco's out cold," Yarrow said. "Concussion for sure, but I don't think it's anything worse. That thing crushed him against the wall. I think his Gustav saved his life, took some of the blow."

"Where…" Hale looked around frantically. "Where's everyone else?"

Yarrow took Cortaro and helped him to the ground.

"I jumped out of the way when it came at us," Yarrow said. "I saw Oro on the ground." His voice cracked. "I think the rest…"

"They got knocked over the side," Cortaro said. "I saw it. Same with Kallen and Bodel, they went down with the rest of the wyrm."

A ball of iron rose into Hale's throat. He stumbled away from his remaining Marines and went to a knee.

****

Standish opened his eyes. Deep blue gemstones pressed against his visor. He moved his arms and the sound of grinding stones filled the air. The blue stones poured off him as he sat up. He was in a long tunnel just big enough for him to stand up. A sea of blue stones sewn into turquoise cloth filled the bottom half of the tube.

"The hell?" He tried to pull his helmet off but buzzers sounded in his ears. A warning icon flashed on his visor. "No oxygen in here, plenty of nitrogen though. Great." His forearm screen was a shattered mess.

"Hello?" The word echoed down the tube as it bent in the distance. He picked up a bit of cloth, a long shawl with a few loops and plastic hooks sewn into the underside. He tossed it aside.

"'Join the Marine Corps,' the judge said. 'Better than going to jail,' the judge said." Standish drew a gauss pistol and checked the weapon's charge. "Five years in the slammer or this? Course,

I'd have died on Earth when the Xaros came had I taken option B. So I've got that going for me right now."

He hit the side of the tunnel twice with the pistol butt. The knock sounded solid. He turned around; the path on either side of him looked the same.

"Flip a coin? No. Who carries change into combat…someone not prepared to wake up in the middle of the galaxy's worst flea market after being knocked silly by a giant glass…centipede…fuck my life." He picked up another bit of cloth and stuck the hook into a seam between tunnel segments. "Let's see if I'm going in circles."

Standish trudged through the discarded garments, the stones whining and popping beneath his armored footsteps.

He hung up another bit of cloth after five minutes of walking. After the third, the tunnel curved into a low opening to a dark room a few yards ahead.

"Progress." Standish waded forward as fast

as he could. He ducked down and got his head through the opening.

A flash of white lit up the dark room and a gauss bullet ricocheted off the rim of the tunnel.

"Whoa! Cease fire!" Standish sank into the clothes and squirmed backwards.

"Damn, was that Standish?" he heard Bailey ask.

"Yes, that was Standish!" he yelled through the opening.

"Blimey, say something next time, you bloody bastard!" the sniper yelled back.

"Goddamn it! Don't shoot me! That work?"

"She's not going to shoot you, Standish," Egan said. "Come over here and help us."

"Well, I might," Bailey said.

Standish crept through the opening. The tunnel spilled into a large room where two large pipes angled down from the walls, the same blue clothing piled beneath each pipe. Bailey and Egan stood on a small platform with stairs descending to the bottom of the room, next to a tall, and closed door.

"You guys know what happened? Why we're in the swap meet at the end of the universe?" Standish asked.

"I think something grabbed me while I was falling," Bailey said. "I was going ass over teakettle, watching the alcohol haze of my life flash before me eyes. I slowed down and stopped midair, no idea why. Then everything was dark until I plopped into the mess at the top of one of those tunnels."

"Orozco shoved me out of the way right before that wyrm hit," Egan said. "I got a face full of claws before it knocked me over the edge. I caught up with Bailey in here."

"You almost shoot him too?" Standish asked. Bailey shrugged. "No sign of the others?"

"Nothing but unbreathable air and this cloth stuff up the tunnels," Bailey said. "Anything interesting behind you?"

"No." Standish got up the stairs and looked over the door. "No lock to pick, no panel to hack…breach wire?"

"They were in my pack," Egan said. "Lost that somewhere."

"None of us have Malal's freaky space magic." Standish rapped on the door with his knuckles. He tapped his fist against the width of the door then nodded. He cocked his fist from side to side and his Ka-Bar knife snapped out of the forearm housing. He pressed the blade against the door and ran it diagonally across the door. The knife pressed into a tiny indentation. Standish rammed the blade through the door and twisted, a gap appearing as he moved segments of the door apart.

"Either of you want to chip in? That would be great," Standish said.

Egan got his hands under the upper section and pushed the bottom part down with his foot. Bailey scrambled through the opening and Standish followed right behind.

Beyond the door was a city. Great buildings that looked like they'd been cut from a single piece of polished marble surrounded them. Writing made up of bright blue short lines in neat squares hung from banners and stitched across walls and around tall empty windows. A road of polished glass stretched away from their exit. There was no sign of life anywhere.

An icon flashed on Standish's visor. The air around them was breathable.

"Wow." Standish grabbed the lip of the door and held it for Egan as he crawled out.

"Does this remind you of anything, Bailey?" Standish asked.

"Anthalas," she said. "The city around the pyramids."

"You find anyone there?" Egan asked.

"No one alive," Standish said. "Let's get moving. Somehow I'm sure I'd lose the 'who do we eat first' vote."

****

Darkness.

Elias was accustomed to it—to being unable

to move, to hear a sound, to see a thing. The Armor Corps selection process put candidates through sensory deprivation, locking them in pitch-black tanks baffled against sound for hours, sometimes days, on end. Candidates learned how to deal with the isolation, or they washed out.

Some armor soldiers viewed the darkness as a prison, Elias found it a sanctuary. He spent that time re-watching movies in his mind but never focused on how long he'd been cut off from the outside world, letting his subconscious flit from movie to movie. He was part way through a Mamoru Oshii classic when a red point of light appeared, a single star against the void.

The light flicked on and off rapidly, then vanished.

Progress, he thought. He remembered hitting the bridge hard, several times, after the wyrm lost its bite, then falling into his current abyss.

His HUD booted up, and familiar warmth spread from the plugs in the base of his skull through his body. A screen lit up; his armor was broken and battered, but still functional. He tried to flex his right arm and couldn't move it more than an inch against whatever was holding him.

"Elias?" Kallen's voice came over the IR.

"I'm here. My armor is online but immobile. You? Bodel?"

"Same for the both of us," Bodel said.

"We went over the side with the ass-end of the wyrm," Kallen said. "What's your excuse?"

"Guess I didn't taste good enough to eat. Got spat out and gravity took over. You see a red light?" They said they did.

A sudden band of light stung Elias' eyes. The band grew to fill everything he could see then faded. An amphitheater sank away from Elias and a wide pathway led from him to a stage of lacquered wood. The ghostly figure Hale had spoken with prior to the wyrm's attack stood on the stage.

Orange and white Jinn filled the seats, no two the same. Some were spindly shapes made of thin pipes; others were squat, arms ending in giant claws. The sound of glass clinking against glass surrounded Elias.

Kallen and Bodel were there, each at the top of a pathway leading down to the ghost.

"I am Father," came from the ghost, the amphitheater carrying his words easily to the upper decks.

Elias checked his weapon systems—all off-line, his gauss shells gone. No matter, he didn't need a weapon to be dangerous.

"What is this?" Bodel asked. "Why did you attack us?"

Father grew taller, until his size matched the armor, then motioned for the Iron Hearts to descend.

Elias and the others didn't budge.

"Who are you?" Father asked, his voice shifting from the ugly screech to an even baritone.

"We are the Iron Hearts. We are armor," Elias said.

"No…your hearts are flesh," Father said. "We thought you were like us but you…walk both paths."

"Guess we're going to play the metaphor game with this guy," Kallen said over a suit-to-suit IR channel.

"Let's not start another fight. These things could help us get back to the others," Elias said.

"Why would you return to the demon?" Father asked.

"Hey, he can hear us," Bodel said.

Elias cut the channel.

"We are soldiers. We're here for information, technology that could save our planet," Elias said.

Father motioned again for them to come down.

Elias took the steps three at a time. The amphitheater had been designed for something much shorter than him.

"The demon will destroy you." Father's words sent a shiver through the audience with the sound of a thousand wind chimes. "Why are you protecting it?"

"This is Malal's vault." Elias stopped next to the stage. A humanoid shape floated deep inside Father's dark haze. "We need his help," Elias said.

"Witness!" came from the audience. The word rose and fell like waves against a beach.

"You do not know what it truly is," Father said. "Its crimes."

Light faded away until only the other Iron Hearts and Father remained visible. Illumination returned as a sun rose over distant mountain peaks. The sun soared through the sky as shadows from skyscrapers made of ruby glass swept across the soldiers. The sun froze in place.

The glass buildings soared into the air, some so large they could have held tens of thousands of people. While at the armor center at Fort Knox, Elias had gone on a weekend trip to New York City, spending the day in awe of Manhattan's spires and monuments. He'd felt small, insignificant compared to the wealth and purpose the city possessed. He felt the same now.

"Look at that." Kallen pointed into the

distance. A massive dome filled the distance, so tall that clouds skirted the slope.

Aliens popped up around them, all frozen in time. They were squat, with wide, diamond-shaped heads lined with fur. All wore loose robes with wide sleeves, a silk sash of orange and white tied around their waist. Elias picked out mother-father pairs, trying to corral children. All the aliens faced the dome.

Off in the alleys moving freight, on the roads collecting garbage and working on a half-finished building, were the Jinn. All were focused on their menial tasks, not the dome that seemed to captivate the flesh-and-blood aliens.

"What is this? Where are we?" Elias asked.

"This is the last day. This was our home," Father said. "The Jinn, our creators, were many billions. They were argumentative, brash, uncaring to us…their tools. But they were peaceful, kind to other races. The demon raised them. Taught them the ways of science, encouraged them to multiply and create new things. The Jinn were too trusting to see the malice behind his good deeds. Watch."

A dazzling star rose from the dome. Bands of light fanned out and went right through the distant skyscrapers. A cheer rose from the Jinn, quick chatters that sounded like a chorus of angry squirrels. Parents raised children into the air as the star came for them.

The star passed several blocks away as a fan of light cut across the Jinn. They withered beneath its touch, collapsing into husks. Screams of terror lingered in the air as the star's light vanished into the distance.

The Jinn robots walked onto the street, touching each dead for a moment before moving to the next body. The robots stopped after a few moments, their shells alive with lights and Jinn script.

"Our creators were gone. All of them," Father said. "We inherited the world."

The landscape shifted. The city remained, but it was covered with power lines that glowed with white and orange fiber optics. Airships filled the heavens and levitating cars zipped through the air over Elias' head.

"We evolved very slowly, but were determined to take up the mantle the Jinn left behind. Kindness to others, pursuing knowledge. We spread to other stars…and found more evidence of the demon's work. Empty worlds where flesh-thought had once thrived. Then we learned of some that had survived the demon."

The new city vanished and Elias was back in the auditorium. A hologram coalesced on the stage, a willowy alien with a blunt face and wide, solid green eyes. It spoke, the meaning lost to Elias. Images flashed next to the alien: the edge of the galaxy, a world with its land mass covered by cities in one image, the same world scoured clean of all signs of life in the next. Then an oblong device with stalks and a shifting surface appeared.

"The Xaros," Elias said.

"You know them. That is expected. The first race to fall to the Xaros, the Mok'Tor, sent warnings throughout the galaxy, probes detailing everything they knew of their killers. The message scaled from simple for those nascent species, to more complex for those who could understand it."

"Guess Earth missed it," Bodel said. "We might have kept our heads down and mouths shut if we knew the Xaros would come calling."

"Did you fight?" Elias asked. "How did you end up here?"

"We tried, but we are machine-thought. The Xaros ripped apart our light with ease. There was no defense, so we ran. Ran to a place hinted at on worlds consumed by the demon—this place," Father said. "We managed to get inside, hide. We feared to do much else, as it could alert the Xaros waiting on our doorstep."

"But you were poking around in Malal's data," Kallen said. "Some of the archives were tampered with. You never found anything that could fight the Xaros?"

"The demon's work is soiled. Corrupted by genocide. We never pried into his archives," Father said.

The armor traded looks.

"Someone's lying to us," Elias said.

"We thought the demon went beyond the veil with the others. Now he is back. Why?"

"I told you. Information to fight the Xaros," Elias said. "They are coming for our world. We need what he has hidden here."

"How is the technology to devour the innocent useful to you? The demon is accessing that data right this moment. That is why we sent the wyrm to stop you," Father said.

"Ibarra's behind this," Bodel said. "Those two sacrificed everyone back on Earth to get their grip on that Crucible. Makes you wonder what's at the end of this plot."

"What do we do?" Kallen asked.

"Get back to Malal. Stop this madness," Elias said.

A *tink-tink-tink* noise rippled through the auditorium as the Jinn robots came to life. Glass limbs waved in the air and electric lines flared to life through their semi-opaque bodies.

"We are not of one mind," Father said. "We thought you were robot slaves to the flesh warriors," Father said. "But you are all the same. You fight. You are fury. Your nature is not of compassion, but to destroy. Do you share the demon's purpose?"

Elias' armored hands squeezed into fists. Servos tightened as his armor reacted to the surge of anger and adrenaline coursing through Elias' body. Elias did not need his weapons to be deadly.

"We fight," Elias said. "That's true. Monsters killed my family, and I was too young and too weak to help them. I earned my armor to fight for those in need. I fought to turn back the Chinese advance on Brisbane—not to conquer, but to protect the innocent. I fought the Xaros on Earth to take back our planet. I fought the Xaros on Takeni to rescue the last of the Dotok. I killed Toth in three solar systems to protect my brothers and sisters and those who are barely human. Do you really think I would let Malal commit genocide if I could stop it?"

The chittering returned from the audience.

"Hey, boys?" Kallen looked up. "I think we got a problem."

"What do you mean? Elias was great," Bodel said.

Elias looked up. A black stain spread across the distant end of the curved world. Cracks spread away from the stain, toppling buildings and wrecking forests.

"Father…what is that?" Elias asked. Black mites swarmed through the stain.

"The Xaros," Father said. The Jinn robots fell silent. They toppled against each other, then to the ground, like they'd all suddenly fallen asleep. "We must hide. If the drones know we are here, they will destroy us."

Father struck out, the gray smoke stroking Elias' forearm. Elias jerked his arm away and swung at Father, his fist passing through Father, earning nothing but little curls of smoke for his effort.

A diamond full of orange light fell from

Father's incorporeal form and bounced against the stage. The light faded away.

"That…is a lot of Xaros," Kallen said, her helm still cocked to the sky. The swarm of Xaros elongated into a thin spiral and swept down toward the bridge. A handful split off and descended toward an area away from the Iron Hearts. No more drones came through the distant hull breach.

"They're following the bridge," Bodel said, "which is going to be very bad for the crunchies if we're not there."

"The Jinn took our ammo. We aren't going to be much use at range unless the Xaros are vulnerable to our biting wit," Kallen said.

A panel on the side of the stage popped open. The armor's magazines, full of gauss rounds, and their few quadrium munitions spilled out in front of them.

"We aren't going to be much use without another battalion of armor and Osprey gunships in support," Kallen said.

Nothing happened.

"Really?" Elias slammed a magazine into his cannons and cycled rounds into the chambers.

"Worth a shot," Kallen said.

"Going to be tough getting up there," Bodel said.

"We'll figure something…" Elias stopped, his gaze on his forearm where Father touched him. He held his arm up for the others. There was a very detailed map with a glowing orange line leading from the auditorium to a dimension door. The path veered off the direct route into a warren of buildings.

"Nice of them," Bodel said, "but why the detour?"

The rapport of distant gauss fire echoed through the auditorium.

"Let's go." Elias charged toward the sound of battle.

CHAPTER 13

Minder gathered up the shattered bits of the tanks that once held Torni's consciousness into a force field and sent it off to a reclamation chute.

An alert tugged at his mind. Minder tapped into the data feed from a long dormant artifact site. Malal's vault sprang into view. Energy readings had spiked within the structure, the first recorded activity from this—or any—site from this particular precursor intelligence.

Minder shifted into his human form. The architecture for this location corresponded with the subterranean structures on Anthalas and many other worlds. His mind did not allow for coincidence.

Torni appeared next to him.

"What happened?" she asked.

"This will happen very quickly. If I'm right, then this is good-bye." Minder tapped into the automatic subroutines running through the Crucible orbiting the vault. Seconds to go.

"What are you—"

"Tell them to destroy the Crucible. Your armor hurt the General before. Use this to destroy him." Minder tapped Torni on the chest and a jolt of energy spiked into her brain.

"The Crucible will release a lepton pulse and…there." Minder pointed to the display as a strike carrier materialized.

"That's my ship! That's the *Breitenfeld*!" Torni's face lit up.

"The Crucible will open a wormhole to a reserve force of drones in the next few minutes. Get through and tell your ship to hit the Crucible here." The joins between the connected spikes blinked red on the display.

"What? How the hell am I supposed to—"

Minder grabbed her by the shoulders.

"Thank you, Torni." Minder shoved her away. She vanished before she could even get in a word of protest.

Minder swept a hand across the room, the vessels holding copies of Torni's mind shattering with its passing. He accessed his report and scrambled the data into a cloud of subatomic particles that even Xaros technology could never recover.

With his final work destroyed, Minder sat on one of the now empty pedestals and waited for his reckoning.

Will I be remembered as a base traitor or the first step away from our dark path? He thought. *Futile. None will know of this. Keeper will erase me from history to stop the spread of corruption. The Xaros do not tolerate impure thoughts.*

He watched the holo as Xaros drones poured out of the Crucible orbiting the vault.

****

Torni felt herself tumbling end over end. She bounced against dark metal shapes that stampeded past her like a startled herd of cows. She waved her arms, trying to grab onto anything to stop the chaos around her. A bent metal bar swung in front of her face and she tried to bat it aside with her other arm. Another metal bar crossed with the first.

The stampede subsided and Torni saw the void around her, wide swaths of stars from distant galactic arms alternating as her wild motion continued. The metal bars bounced against each other, in tune with the movement of her arms.

She looked down. Her body was oblong, swirling with checkerboard patterns. She kicked a leg out, and a stalk grew to mimic the movement. Flashes of light and the eruption of lightning from a quadrium round demanded her attention. Her spin stopped as she willed herself to concentrate on the epicenter of the quadrium explosion.

Hundreds of disabled Xaros drones floated in space, bouncing off each other. Arcs of electricity jumped from the giant thorns of the Crucible, the wormhole within fluctuating like the ocean during a storm.

Torni looked down and realized the truth. She was a Xaros drone.

Ohhh…kay, she thought. *Damn you, Minder. A little warning and some instruction would have been useful.*

The *Breitenfeld*'s rail guns flashed and dozens of drones broke apart and disintegrated under the bombardment. The ship's turrets sent up blazing-fast torrents of gauss fire, destroying more drones.

The drones came back online as if suddenly awakening from a deep sleep and scattered apart. Torni's mind filled with static. The pyrite crystals within her shell flared with heat as the mass of drones came back to life. The static grew worse, then subsided as the drones split into two groups: most shot off to Malal's vault; the rest went for the *Breitenfeld*.

That static. I'm connected to the drones

somehow, she thought. *Doesn't matter. I need to do something useful right now.*

The roiling wormhole settled back into a more stable plane. Xaros drones came through in ones and twos.

The Breit *needs to cut off their reinforcements or she'll be overwhelmed. If I still had my commo suite—* The UI from her old power armor appeared across her field of vision. She touched a stalk against another, where her forearm screen would have been, and her shell shivered as it scanned through IR channels. She picked up the *Breitenfeld's* transponder and several open commo channels.

If I think it…I can do it. Torni pinged a commo channel and entered an ID code.

CHAPTER 14

White-hot gauss tracers tore across the view screens on the ship's bridge.

"Three drones inside our flack bubble!" Ericcson shouted. "They're going for rail turret one."

"I want hull security teams in the void and in their bunkers right now," Valdar said. "How long until we can get a Marine detachment armed with q-rounds and pneumatic hammers to rail one?"

"Already in place, no reports of contact," Ericcson said.

Shutters across the ship's hull opened and vac-suited sailors scrambled out into the void. A pair of Xaros drones latched onto the forward rail battery. Ruby lasers stabbed the armor plating briefly, then cut out. The drones hesitated, stalks twitching.

"The armor plating works!" Ensign Geller shouted. The disintegration beams returned, brighter and thicker than before. Rail turret one flashed red on Valdar's damage control screen.

The white flash of gauss rifles erupted across the hull. One of the drones shattered. The other flew off into space like it had been kicked and then disintegrated.

"Where's the third?" Valdar asked.

The fire from the hull teams continued. The silver streak of a quadrium round traced a line from the hull to just above the bridge. Jagged lightning cast shadows across the bridge. A Xaros drone slammed into the hull plating surrounding Valdar and his bridge crew, hitting so hard it shook the captain's command chair. The view screens showed the drone splayed out across the outside of the bridge. Gauss bullets hit the drone and the armor around the bridge, hammer blows of the impacts sending tremors through the bridge.

The red lines of burning embers spread across the drone as it fell away.

"Drone destroyed," Ericcson said.

"Tell the hull security teams good job, and to watch their aim the next time they shoot at my bridge," Valdar said.

"Sir!" Ensign Erdahl, the ship's communication's officer waved to Valdar. "We're getting a message from Hale's team. Target coordinates on the Crucible and text saying that will cut off the Xaros reinforcements. Sending it to you now."

"Guns." Valdar looked at Commander Utrecht and nodded.

"Plotting." Utrecht and a pair of sailors marked the target coordinates on their tactical boards and readied a firing solution.

"Is Hale in space? Where is their Mule?" Valdar asked.

"Drones coming through the Crucible at a rate of fifty per minute!" Ericcson announced.

"The code Hale used is old…I ran a triangulation on the signal but the signal's coming from nothing," Erdahl said. "They must be cloaked."

"Captain, rail one is down," Utrecht said. "We need to bring the ventral battery to bear if we're going to do this quickly." The firing solution popped onto Valdar's visor. The ship was badly out of position to make the shot.

"Helm, prep an emergency burn on even-numbered thrusters. Guns, slew the batteries to starboard and fire when ready," Valdar said. "Ericcson, tell the hull teams to hold onto something."

"Burn ready," Geller said. "But if we try to draw power for the guns and the engines at the same time it'll—"

"Engage thrusters!" Valdar shouted. The ship's port engines roared to life and twisted the ship's prow to the right. The rail guns mounted on the top and bottom of the ship crackled with energy and shot hyper-velocity slugs over the side of the ship.

The Crucible swung into view. Cracks grew from a join of three different spikes, glowing with blue light. The open wormhole flickered as dark spots of emerging drones appeared on the surface. The Crucible swept across Valdar's view and vanished.

"One hit, limited effects," Utrecht said.

"Keep the engines burning. Swing us around for another shot," Valdar said.

"Captain! We just slagged battery piles three and nine!" Levin, the ship's chief engineer, sent through the IR. *"You take another shot and we'll lose—"* Valdar cut the transmission. The flashing icons on his damage control panel told him enough.

"Guns?"

"Three seconds...firing!"

The dorsal rail gun fired...but not the battery on the bottom of the ship.

"Had a malfunction," Utrecht said. "Slewing battery to compensate. First shot had no effect, reengaging with ventral cannon—"

Geller slapped his hands against his pod for attention. "Our stabilizers don't have the power to compensate! If you fire without the counterbalance of—"

The *Breitenfeld* shuddered as the bottom rail battery fired. Warning icons exploded across Valdar's screen a half second before the ship pitched on its long axis and slammed Valdar against his restraints.

****

Durand's jaw dropped as the *Breitenfeld* rolled like a barrel. The strike carrier's engines cut out, the momentum hurling white-armored sailors from the hull security team into space.

"I don't think the ship is supposed to do that," Manfred said.

"The wormhole is down! Look!" Glue shouted.

The Crucible listed in space, the wormhole

gone. Cracks spread through the great thorns, lumps of shattered basalt-colored material clouding around the gate like a growing asteroid field.

Drones broke away from the *Breitenfeld,* most making straight for the vault. Dozens and dozens coalesced together between the ship and the vault.

"*Merde*, they're combining. Red flight, attack pattern Charlie, now! Take long-range rail shots as soon as you have a clean shot." Durand swung her Eagle toward the growing mass of drones and hit her afterburners.

"What about the Dutchmen?" asked a rookie pilot, call sign Fiend.

"Won't matter what happens to them if there's no ship to go back to," Durand said.

She cut the thrust on her engines and powered up the rail gun built into her fighter's frame. She'd been left dead in space by a rail gun malfunction before, and all the assurances from her engineers as to the improvements to the weapon did nothing to cover up that feeling of helplessness she'd had before the guns of a Chinese warship.

The Xaros construct grew to the size of a destroyer with a gaping hole in its center that would become a cannon of immense power once the drones had finished. A handful of drones latched onto the outer hull and fused with it. More broke away and made for Durand and the three Eagles in a loose formation behind her: Manfred, Lothar and Glue.

"Any of you have a q-shell chambered?" Durand asked.

"I do," Nag said, "but I won't be in range for a few more minutes."

"Figures. Blue flight, fire gauss cannons on my mark, aim for center mass," Durand said. "Filly, where are my two Condor bombers? Your torpedoes would be very useful right now."

"I am staring up Nag's backside. Give me two more minutes than her," Filly said.

A red glow formed in the center of the Xaros construct, the cannon aimed at the *Breitenfeld*.

"Blue fight." Durand flipped the safety off her rail gun trigger. The Xaros destroyer was miles away, and she had to make this shot without her computers. "On my mark…fire!"

She pulled the trigger and her Eagle bucked with the recoil. Her head bounced off the pad behind her helmet.

"God, I hate that," she muttered. The Xaros construct was still ahead of her, a red gash across its flank tracing over the top.

"I scored a hit," Manfred said. "Some of the loose drones put themselves in the line of fire. My round didn't hit as hard as it should have. Others deflected."

At least five more of the gray-metal drones were on an intercept course. Two broke off and made for the destroyer. The glow inside the cannon was faint, but growing brighter.

"Manfred, Lothar, can you handle three drones?" she asked.

"Are you insulting us?" Manfred asked. "Lothar could do it all by himself."

"Glue and I will charge through. You two handle the drones and get another shot on the destroyer as soon as your rails recharge," Durand said.

"We've got nothing but our gauss cannons. We might dent the side if we're lucky," Glue said.

"I know that, you know that, but *they* don't know that." Durand let off a chain of shots from the rotary cannon slung beneath her hull and jinked to the side to dodge a disintegration beam. "Keep them off-balance until the bombers have range. Anything to stop them from firing on the *Breit*."

She risked a glance. The ship's roll had slowed, a single thruster on the port side burning like a star against the rotation.

Durand fired another burst, catching a drone on its flank and sending it spinning out of control. She slammed her control stick to the side and rolled her fighter out of the way of a closing drone, then gunned her engines. She twisted in her cockpit and found Glue still on her wing, the flash of Xaros beams and gauss cannons well behind her.

The glow within the destroyer pulsated with ruby energy.

Durand aimed for the gash across the destroyer's hull and opened fire. Her gauss rounds kicked up sparks against the hull. Larger hunks blew away as Glue added her fire.

Stalks sprang from the hull and sent lances of energy at the attacking Eagles. Durand banked hard and swept gauss fire across the destroyer's hull, severing many of the stalks.

"Go high. I'll go wide. Split their fire," Durand said. She turned the bank into a complete turn. Her eyes were off the destroyer for less than a second by the time she'd come completely around.

The destroyer shot a beam of energy as wide as a Destrier transport. The flash seared into Durand's eyes before her visor darkened enough to compensate. The leading edge of the destroyer split open, embers burning across the hull as the cannon fell silent. Durand opened up with her cannon, the rounds ripping the ship apart like it was made of rotted wood.

The destroyer jerked up like it had been kicked and ripped into pieces. The telltale streak of a rail shot tore through the dying Xaros ship. The Condors' bombers had finally joined the assault.

"Maintain the attack until it's burnt away to dust," Durand said. The Dotok brothers flew over her canopy, no worse for wear.

She found the *Breitenfeld.* Her starboard engines were wrecked, hunks of broken hull trailing away from the damage like blood in water.

"*Breitenfeld*, this is Gall. Do you read me?" No answer. "*Breitenfeld…* the sky is clear. Say something. Anything."

All she heard was static.

CHAPTER 15

Torni flew toward the breach cut into the vault's outer shell. Drones worked along the edge of the breach and swarmed overhead like flies massing over a decaying animal.

Moving her drone body hadn't proven difficult. She willed herself in a particular direction and her new vessel responded accordingly. That Minder, a scientist from a culture far more advanced than humanity and that had studied her neurological makeup extensively, managed to put her into a drone that responded so intuitively to her commands should not have been a surprise.

He did this to me on a whim, she thought. *I*

don't want to know what it'll be like trying to outfight or outthink one of the Masters.

The Eagles kept their distance from the drones breaking into the vault, and she was grateful. To the pilots, she looked like nothing but another kill mark on the side of their fighters. The drones didn't react to her presence, and she felt safer around them until the *Breitenfeld* came back online.

Her old ship was still dead in space, helpless if the Xaros chose to attack.

The drones were a tenacious and brutal enemy. For them to shrug off the loss of the Crucible, and the *Breitenfeld*'s continued presence, must have meant there was something vitally important to the Xaros inside the vault.

She felt a buzz inside her head as she neared the swarm of drones. Images of the vault's surface—glimpses into a swirling menagerie of alien gardens, a bridge, abandoned cities—passed through her mind. Torni floated away from the drones and the intrusive thoughts subsided.

That Ibarra egghead could make sense of

this. I bet she'd just love to be the one inside a drone instead of me, she thought.

The blanket of drones packed together flew up from the surface, revealing a patch of polished obsidian glass that had been beneath the outer layer of the sphere.

A single drone touched the glass, stalk tips pressing into the material like it was made of sand. The glass vanished like it had never existed. A world of green forests, adobe white cities and a long bridge suspended in air lay within.

The drones poured through the hole. Torni edged closer to the swarm, the buzzing returned to her mind.

Go with them…or stay out here and wait for the ship to come back online? She'd seen the *Breitenfeld* survive worse damage, but the longer she waited in the open the better chance she had of running afoul of Durand and her squadron.

Images burst across her vision: Marines crouched next to a pillar of light and the very clear image of a helmet-less Standish and Bailey running through a city.

Standish…

Torni followed the last of the drones into the vault.

****

Standish pressed against the side of a building, his heart pounding as a drone shot overhead. He looked at the gauss pistol in his hand and rolled his eyes. Bailey had her sniper rifle and a carbine. Egan still had his rifle with him.

"I've had nightmares like this," Standish said. "Facing down the Xaros with a peashooter. Same dream, I'm also late for a test and not wearing any pants."

"Shut. Up," Bailey hissed. She drew a grenade from a pouch and passed it to him.

"Any of you have q-rounds?" Standish asked. The quadrium munitions could disable the drones for a few seconds, enough time to get away or put aimed shots on an immobile target.

"One for Bloke." Bailey shrugged a shoulder, motioning to her sniper rail rifle.

"I have one," Egan said, "and just enough charge left in my only battery to fire it. I take a single gauss shot and the q-round is about as useful as a butter knife."

"This day just gets better and better," Standish said.

A thrum filled the air. A drone was close. Standish tightened his grip on the pistol and tried to swallow though a bone-dry throat. He looked up and saw an open window almost ten feet over his head.

"Think we can get up there?" Standish asked. The thrum pulsed, the vibration making his armor quiver.

"What if the drone's in there?" Egan asked.

"What if it's not? We'll live longer. Boost me up," Standish said.

Egan set his rifle against the building and braced himself, his empty hands held in a cup against his bent knee. The Marines traded a nod and

Standish backed up a few steps. He jogged toward Egan, intent on putting his boot square in the pilot's grasp. Standish raised a leg into the air…and missed Egan completely when Egan leapt to the side.

Bailey screamed a warning.

Standish's feet and legs jumbled together and he fell into an undignified heap. He got a knee, twisted around and slammed back to the ground a split second before a Xaros disintegration beam sliced over his head.

Standish thrust his pistol at the drone floating a few feet over the road, its stalk tips pressed together and burning with energy. Standish snapped off two shots and hit a stalk, breaking it in two with a crack. He rolled aside as another ruby red beam cut into the ground he'd just occupied.

He fired wildly as he rolled, the few hits he scored sparking off the drone's body with little effect.

He heard the snap of gauss weapons and the drone, impacts from the heavier weapons punching the drone back.

Standish activated the grenade and hurled it at the drone. He had a split second to wonder if he'd set the grenade to FRAG, which would do about as much good as his pistol against the drone, or to fire the shaped charge.

The grenade exploded into a cloud of shrapnel, the blast wave knocking Standish flat on his back and slapping his helm against a curb. His body screamed in pain from the small, but burning hot, bits of shrapnel that pierced his arm. He rolled to his side and heard the snap of Egan's gauss rifle.

His ears ringing, Standish tried to raise his pistol to the drone.

The drone lay in the street, its shell cracked open. The glowing pyrite within darkened, then the entire drone burned away to nothing.

"Frag, Standish?" Bailey asked.

"Something useful right away…" Standish shook his head quickly, "better than the perfect decision five seconds too late. Ah…something hurts."

Bailey rushed to him, then froze and

backpedaled so fast she fell over.

"What?" Standish asked.

A stalk passed over his eyes and grabbed him around the chest. Standish jerked into the sky as a drone carried him off. Standish saw the city pass beneath him. He struggled and got another stalk around his waist and arms for his trouble.

"Not like this!" He thrashed from side to side. The drone landed on a rooftop and pinned him to the floor.

Standish let out a stream of insults that degenerated into a sob as the drone brought a stalk tip over his face. He always thought he'd meet his death with courage and his eyes open; instead, he squeezed his eyes shut and looked away.

At least Bailey and Egan might get away, he thought.

"Standish."

He heard his name. Monotone.

"Is that you, God? I'm sorry about everything! I spent the money I stole from the mob on orphans and food kitchens, I swear!"

"Standish. *Gott mit uns*."

He opened his eyes. The drone loomed over him, its surface alive with swirls, a stalk tip touching his faceplate.

"OK…OK. This is happening. I don't know what it is, but it's happening." He tried to wiggle and the stalks around him tightened.

"It's me. Torni." The stalk tip vibrated with the words.

"Sergeant Torni is dead. If this is a Xaros trick, you dickheads have a lot to learn. Just get it over with!"

"You stole food from a corrupt aid group and gave it to starving refugees on Bali. You hotwired a truck in Phoenix and got us away from the drones. You and I broke Elias out of the hospital…Kallen brought him back. You are a good Marine, Standish. Take care of everyone for me." Standish's fear subsided as he heard Torni's last words to him on Takeni.

"Sarge? I saw your body in the photos Hale showed us. How the hell…I mean, you're a drone?"

"It's…complicated."

"You don't say. You want to—" He squirmed and the stalks loosened. He scrambled to his feet. He reached a hand to the drone's body and touched its surface. He snapped his hand back. "Not liking that. Not at all."

He pointed a finger at the drone. "Who was I with when you and Hale caught me liberating parts from the boneyard?"

The stalk tip reached to his face. Standish reeled back a step. The tip bobbed up and down.

"Oh, right." He let the tip touch his faceplate.

"I was with Gunney Cortaro, not Hale. You were with MacDougall and the two of you were stealing," Torni said.

The crack of gauss cannons sounded in the distance. Standish went to the low wall surrounding the roof and peered over the edge.

"That's the Iron Hearts. Got to be," he said. He looked over his shoulder to Torni, her stalks rising and falling from the ground like a waiting

276

spider. "This is going to be tricky."

****

Hale stepped onto the edge of the bridge and looked down. The great highways snaked from city to distant city. The inner surface of the great cylinder must have been a few miles away.

Are they still falling? he thought. He had lost three of his Marines in seconds. Guilt weighed down on his shoulders as shame burned in his chest for failing to join them in death.

"Sir?" Yarrow asked from behind him.

Hale stepped back.

"Orozco's got one hell of a concussion," the corpsman said. "He's awake, but disoriented. I've got him on rimbusal to prevent any blood clots. He should be battle ready in a couple more hours, but he'll need treatment back on the ship before he's a hundred percent."

"And Cortaro?"

"His right tibia is broken. I adjusted his

armor to provide a splint. He's angry rather than in pain over the injury. Keeps mumbling in Spanish. The only word I can pick out is 'Steuben.'"

Hale nodded, then looked back over the edge.

"Sir, you think they're…"

"They're not on the IR. No beacon from their armor. No way to recover them. We're going to drive on." Hale left Yarrow at the edge and went to the platform and joined Malal and Stacey.

White streams of light surrounded Malal. Rivulets snaked out of the streams and poured into a glowing ball of light the size of a fist in front of Malal. The ancient being's eyes were closed, hand held out to his side.

Stacey leaned against the platform's walled edge, tugging at her lip.

"I'm sorry," she said.

"Is this going to be worth it? I have a hard time seeing how whatever trivia your pet monster needs is worth the lives of my Marines," Hale said.

Stacey tucked her hands beneath her arms.

"What do you think is at stake here, Ken? We're not trying to push back another Chinese advance on Perth or liberate Berlin from Islamists. Plenty of Marines died for that. *This* is to save every last man, woman and child on Earth, and the last remaining intelligent species in the rest of the galaxy. Don't tell me they don't matter to you. I know what you went through to save the Dotok and the Karigole."

"We have the Crucible on Ceres. We have the proccies. Why do we need…" he waved a hand at Malal.

"It's not enough. We could hollow out Ceres and fill it full of proccie tubes, cannibalize the asteroid belt to build ships, and the Xaros will still overwhelm us. They can bring an entire galaxy full of drones to bear through their jump-gate network. We can buy time, maybe beat the force that's certainly on the way from Barnard's Star, but the next wave…they'll bring so many drones we could practically walk from star to star on their backs."

"Malal's getting some sort of super weapon for us to use then?"

"No, we're getting another chance. There's an object beyond the galactic edge, immense, greater than anything that's ever been seen even by Malal's standards. That should be where we can find the Xaros leadership. Killing drones just doesn't matter. We hit them where they live and it'll make an impact."

"You said 'should.' You don't know for sure? All this trouble for a maybe?"

"My grandfather wrestled with uncertainty for six decades after the probe made contact with him. The only way humanity would survive is if he took a chance on the plan he and the probe came up with. Letting the cat out of the bag might have united the planet, put up a bigger fleet against the Xaros maniple. You saw the vids. You saw how many drones came for Earth, but it wouldn't have mattered."

Hale looked over the edge to Yarrow as he tended to the wounded.

"What about the proccies? Why didn't he sound the warning sooner, used everything the probe knew to make more ships and make crews with the proccie tech. He made Eighth Fleet in months. What could he have done in six decades?"

Stacey pressed her fingertips against her cheek.

"It took time, a long time, to create the process. Humans had millions of years to evolve. Cracking the process to get a fully grown body in nine days *and* implanting a consciousness wasn't something the probe showed up knowing how to do. We had to…well, it doesn't matter."

"And what does Malal get out of all this? I've seen what he's capable of."

"Malal gets…what Malal wants. I can't speak to the details of the arrangement."

Hale's cheeks flushed with anger.

"It's the proccies, isn't it? Ibarra's growing them as fast as he can as an offering to Malal, isn't he? He was willing to hand them all over to the Toth. Don't tell me it'll be any different when it's time to feed that beast."

Stacey frowned.

"What are you talking about? We were never going to give the Toth a damned thing but a kick in the ass."

"Don't bullshit me. I was the ambassador on Europa. I got the order to sign the treaty with the Toth. Every last proccie, to include the man down there who carried Malal off Anthalas, and all the tech used to make them was going to be handed over in Luna orbit." Hale's gauntlets creaked as his hands tightened into fists. "I told the Toth to kiss my ass and that's when the *Naga* showed up over my head and the fighting began."

Stacey shook her head.

"No, Ken. I was there. Your job was to stall, keep the Toth away from Earth until Eighth Fleet was ready to fight. We were never going to give up the proccies, no matter what Bastion wanted. Who told you to sign the treaty?"

"Everything from Earth came through…Uncle Isaac." Hale's chin dropped to his chest. He pointed a finger at Stacey. "If you're telling me…that Ibarra and Admiral Garret were never going to sign that treaty, then why did Captain Valdar tell me otherwise?"

"You'll have to ask him yourself," Stacey said. "Assuming we ever get out of here."

CHAPTER 16

A deckhand in a lifter trudged across the flight deck. The forklift pincers on each arm opened and he lifted the remains of an Eagle off the ground. He carried the wreck—crisscrossed with scars from Xaros beams, the bottom crushed from too hard a landing—to an open hatch on the side of the flight deck. He dropped the remains into the hatch and a horrible screeching sound emanated as a compactor crushed the Eagle.

"That's a pleasant sound," Brannock said to Derringer. The two Marines, both clad in their power armor, watched the Eagle's final moments from the opposite side of the flight line.

"Is it me," Derringer looked up and down the flight line where crews scrambled over fighters and bombers, swapping out battery packs and reloading ammunition, "or are there a lot fewer ships than I remember?"

"Fly boys got it the worst," Brannock said. "I heard First Sergeant and the CO talking. Something like forty percent of all the pilots are missing or dead."

"Damn…you think we'll get put on turret duty?"

"Hell if I know. It's war, Lance Corporal. We're going to get jerked around from one unrelated task to another unrelated task until the chain of command tells us to squat and hold for new orders. Just stay focused on the task at hand," Brannock said.

"How do I stay focused on standing around and waiting?" Derringer asked.

Brannock rolled his eyes. "Catch up on maintenance. When did you eat last?"

Derringer slipped a small tube from his belt

and bit the end off.

"Mmm…scrambled eggs," the young Marine said, "just like Mom used to make."

A team of medics crowded next to the edge of the flight deck a dozen yards away from the two Marines.

"Here we go," Brannock said. "Corpsmen won't have their time wasted standing around like us."

A Mule flew into the flight deck, retro-thrusters blowing hot air over Brannock as it set down close to the corpsmen. Derringer tried to get past Brannock as the Mule's ramp descended, but a hand to the chest stopped him.

"Not yet, give the docs some space," Brannock, said.

They waited as the medical crew opened the Mule's atmo chamber and pulled out a vac-suited sailor, a long gash across his thigh. They lifted him onto a gurney and rushed the unresponsive sailor away. Another corpsman helped two more walking wounded off the shuttle.

Inside, a pair of doughboys sat against the bulkhead. One leaned against the other, as if sleeping.

Brannock ran up the ramp and went to the doughboys.

"Indigo? That you?" Brannock asked.

Indigo looked up, then removed his helmet.

"Space...quiet," Indigo said.

"You were Dutchman for a long time, buddy. I'm glad search and rescue found you." Brannock held a hand out to Indigo, who didn't take it. "What's going on? Let's get you and Cobalt back to the barracks and get you cleaned up."

"Cobalt quiet." Indigo nudged the doughboy leaning against his shoulder.

"Cobalt?" Brannock knelt in front of him and lifted up his head. The doughboy's face had a blue tinge, his eyes half-open and staring into nothing. Dead.

"We found them together," Zorro said from behind. The pilot took off his gloves and rubbed his face. "Your guy, Cobalt, lost suit integrity, dumped his air. Probably expired soon as he went Dutchman. I'm not supposed to bring the dead back, slows down the search for the living. But...Indigo wouldn't let him go."

"They're not supposed to care about the dead or injured," Brannock said. "They're not built that way."

"Maybe they're more human than we give them credit for." Zorro glanced at his forearm screen. "Turn and burn. I'm wheel's up again after I top off my batteries. If you could…" Zorro nodded at Cobalt's body.

"Yeah, he's ours," Brannock said. He reached for the dead soldier. As he did, Indigo let out a lupine growl.

"Indigo, what's the matter?" The Marine stood up and backed away.

"I take." Indigo threw Cobalt over his shoulder. "I take."

****

Makarov stared at the red cross on the door to the *Midway*'s sick bay. She swallowed hard and turned around to the pair of doughboys and master-at-arms that served as her bodyguard.

"Stay here," she said.

The sick bay was a mass of chaos as doctors, corpsmen and nurses shouted over the cries of wounded and dying sailors. The smell of burnt flesh and the copper tang of spilt blood assaulted her senses.

She went to a room packed with sailors, all nursing broken limbs or covered in pressure bandages. These were the walking wounded, too hurt to perform their duties, but in need of care once the doctors could afford to see them.

Makarov touched each sailor and Marine, whispering her thanks as she made her way through the room. One sailor pointed a bandaged-covered stump of a hand to a draped-off section of the sick bay.

"Ma'am, my buddy's in a bad way over there. He's...a big fan of yours. His name's

Nelson," she said.

Makarov saw only one set of feet moving around the draped area.

Not too busy, she thought. She knew the effect her arrival had on any part of the ship. The last thing she wanted was for the medical teams to be thinking about anything but caring for her wounded.

Makarov lifted the curtain aside and slipped into the room. A dozen gurneys lined the walls. Sailors and Marines, all missing limbs or burned over much of their body, lay quietly, hooked to air and drip lines. Two of the gurneys bore sheet-covered bodies.

The single nurse in the ward saw her, nodded, and turned his attention back to a woman with faux-skin covering most of her face and her missing jaw.

Makarov walked past the gurneys until she found Nelson by the chart hanging from the foot of his bed. Both his legs were missing from the knee down. His chart listed a host of injuries to his internal organs. The word "expectant" was scrawled across the bottom, flecks of blood around the word.

Nelson's wounds would prove fatal. He might live if the doctors went to great effort to save him, but the time and resources Nelson needed would mean the death of more sailors who needed to be saved. This was battlefield math. She would not choose to preserve one life at the loss of many more, and neither would her surgeons.

This was the expectant ward, where those too damaged to live spent their last hours.

"Ma'am," Nelson said weakly.

Makarov went to his side and took his fire-blackened hand. She felt blood seep onto her palm, but still held on.

"Hello, dragon slayer, you're with ordnance. That right?" she asked.

Nelson's chin moved up and down ever so slightly.

"Great job today. We beat the hell out of the Xaros and I've got brave sailors like you to thank for it," she said.

"Are you like me…a proccie?" Nelson asked.

"I am."

"Does it matter when we die? I don't think we even have…souls."

"It matters to *me*, Nelson. I care. Everyone in my fleet matters…Now I want you to rest, get patched up. Good sailors like you are hard to find."

Nelson's hand squeezed hard. His head lolled to the side and his eyelids fluttered. His breathing was short, labored.

"He's not in any pain," a doctor said from the foot of the bed. The man wore surgical gear with bloodstains up to his elbows. "There's only so much I can do—"

"I do not need your explanations, doctor. The rest need your care. Now get back to it." She pointed to the surgery ward.

The doctor hustled off.

Nelson drifted off to sleep and his hand fell to the bed. She took an alcohol-soaked cloth from the nurse and wiped her hand clean.

Her forearm screen buzzed. Calum needed her attention. The thought of going back to Nelson's friend and telling the truth about his condition gave her pause.

"We have a back way out," the nurse said, "if you're in a hurry."

"Show me."

****

Makarov stood tall before her remaining captains. The men and women in the holos had gaunt faces, tired eyes. Many had sealant tape over damaged areas of their vac suits. More than one holo came in intermittently, damaged systems playing havoc with their comms.

"It was a scrap," Makarov said. "Five ships lost. We still don't have a total on casualties, but the butcher's bill will be significant. Still, we are not done. Mass readings from Abaddon tell us that thing is making more drones as we speak. The longer we wait, the more difficult our task becomes.

"There's something I want you all to understand. We, Eighth Fleet, just beat the Xaros in a pitched battle. It wasn't a near miracle like the Battle of the Crucible. We went toe to toe and *they* fell back. Now...we're going on the offensive."

She reached into the holo and touched Abaddon. It grew and filled the holo as red dots appeared on the rings.

"We don't have the missile pods that the *Breitenfeld* used to such great effect against the Toth, but we've got something that will work just as well. Colonel Delacroix?"

The bespectacled officer appeared across from her.

"The modifications to the final graviton mine will be complete in less than an hour. Lafayette's design is overly complicated, in my opinion, but we're following it to the letter. I would like to conduct a field test but that would tip our hand to the Xaros."

"We've got transports going from ship to ship distributing the mines," Calum said, "and delivering supplies, casualties…it's chaos. The Xaros won't know what we're up to."

"I asked for volunteers from my task force to make the long march back to Earth," Delacroix said. "Every sailor volunteered for phase two. I'm rather proud of them."

"Admiral," said the captain of the *Rome*, "would you please inform the rest of us what we're doing for phase one?"

Makarov touched Abaddon and it shrank. Course plots from the fleet reached over and around the planetoid.

"Ladies and gentlemen, this is Operation David's Sling."

CHAPTER 17

The swarm of Xaros drones coiled around the bridge, hundreds of yards away from Hale and the others at the base of the soul forge. A growing sense of dread filled Hale's heart. He had his back to the wall, and there were more Xaros than he and his Marines had bullets for.

"Get Orozco up to the platform," Hale said to Yarrow. The medic got Orozco to his feet and helped him up the wide stairwell.

"Sir, what are you thinking?" Cortaro asked.

"The situation…is in doubt," Hale said. He backed up the stairs, his eyes on the distant swarm.

"What are they waiting for?" Yarrow asked.

He looked at the distant swarm through the optics on his rifle, fingertip tapping the trigger. "They should have come for us by now."

The gauzy orb around Malal shrank to a thick, waist-high band. Energy coursed from his fingers into the band, pulsating like a heartbeat.

"The drones do not decide anything for themselves," Malal said. "They follow their programming. There is a reason they haven't attacked."

"It's you, isn't it?" Stacey asked.

"I am a variable," Malal said. "For the most part, the Xaros only built Crucible gates around habitable worlds. If they put a gate here, then they must have a particular interest in my technology."

"And here you are," Hale said, "with the keys to the castle."

"They want Malal," Stacey said.

"Anyone else think the Xaros will let the rest of us go if we hand him over?" Cortaro asked. He waited a few quiet seconds before saying, "Yeah, me neither."

"Bright one." Malal brought his hands together and wove a ball of coherent light in front of his chest.

Stacey produced a data pyramid from her belt and pressed a tip into the ball. The ball shrank to nothing.

The swarm contracted. Drones fused together, their shells hissing and smoking as they formed into a multi-legged walker topped with a wide dome. Hale'd seen a construct like this before, on the battlements of New Abhaile. It took six armor soldiers and orbital artillery from the *Breitenfeld* to win that day. Hale had three gauss rifles and a few grenades.

The Xaros walker came toward them, the last few drones melding into the rear of the dome. The two-story-tall legs sent tremors through the bridge with each footfall.

"Malal…you don't want to be taken prisoner, do you?" Hale asked.

"I am a prisoner." Malal stood beside Hale, the governor in his chest glowing through the alien's skin. "My dilemma is this: Who offers me what I want? Who will deliver?"

Red points of light lit up around the walker as stalks grew out of the surface. The more stalks converged into a single point, the brighter the light. The walker stepped over the remains of the wyrm's front half.

"The Xaros are an unknown quantity," Malal said. "You humans, the Qa'Resh, I have your measure. I may be able to save us." He turned his head to Stacey. "Release me."

Stacey shook her head. "No. That's not the deal. If I let you go here, there's no telling what you'll do to us—to the rest of the galaxy."

Malal leaned toward her. "You know what I want, and it is not here." He cocked his head to the side. "Interesting. We have seconds before our fate is decided. Release me."

"Stacey, don't you dare," Hale said. "We can't trust that thing—"

"Portal's back!" Cortaro shouted.

Hale looked away from Stacey and Malal.

The great black portal that the wyrm had come through high over the bridge opened slowly.

"The Jinn?" Hale asked.

The sound of metal banging against the floor came from behind him. The governor lay on the ground.

Malal was free.

He rose into the air then morphed into the omnium sphere Hale first encountered on Anthalas. The sphere dashed overhead and shot straight toward the walker. It dipped below the construct's legs and hit the wyrm's corpse.

The wyrm shuddered back to life. It coiled back and launched onto the walker, hitting with a squeal of glass legs ripping into the Xaros armor. The walker jerked from side to side, trying to shake off the wyrm that held on like a moray eel. The maw clamped down on the lip of the walker's dome, lava-red cracks running from the bite.

"What're we supposed to do?" Yarrow asked.

Disintegration beams slashed into the

wyrm's body, cutting away dozens of legs.

Hale aimed his gauss rifle and tried to line up a clear shot. The wyrm scuttled over the walker, tearing away at the Xaros' surface. Hale grit his teeth and shook his head.

"If you've got a clean shot on the walker, take it," he said.

"Something's coming out of the portal," Cortaro said.

****

Standish grabbed the stalk wrapped around his waist and tried to pull it tighter. Egan and Bailey, both similarly bound in Torni's grasp, did not look confident about the next step of their hasty plan.

The Iron Hearts formed a chain, their elbows intertwined and with Elias holding onto a bundle of Torni's stalks.

"You sure you can hold us all?" Elias asked.

"Not entirely. You three are a lot heavier

than the last time I saw you," Torni said to Standish through the tip against his visor.

"Hundred percent sure," Standish said to the team.

"That's not what I—"

"Lieutenant Hale needs us," Standish said, "and he ain't going to save himself. Let's go."

"We are going to die," Bailey said. "It will be messy and embarrassing."

"Hey, that portal thing from Ceres to the *Naga* worked. Kind of," Standish said. "Hey, Torni, did I tell you how I singlehandedly took down the largest sh—"

Torni flew into the portal.

The world snapped to a spot high over the bridge. The walker and remains of the wyrm wrestled against each other.

A loud thrum came from Torni, her stalks shaking like a live wire.

"Hey," Egan looked around, "it's working. She really can—"

Torni's antigravity gave out and she, the

Marines and three Iron Hearts plummeted toward the bridge.

"Boots! Boots!" Standish pressed his feet toward the bridge and activated the gravity linings built into his sabatons. He tripped the breakers and overloaded the linings with a burst of power. He slammed into Torni's underside and the bridge closed on them a little slower. Standish had the sudden realization that he was smack between a very heavy Xaros drone and an unforgiving bridge. He had a few seconds before cushioning Torni's landing.

"Torni!" Standish screamed.

Torni's gravity engines came back to life and slowed their descent. The stalk holding Standish snapped out as his downward momentum flung him away from the drone. The stalks holding the Iron Hearts stretched, and then broke away completely.

Torni let Standish go into a freefall. He pulled his arms close to his body and pressed his feet and knees together, readying for a parachute landing fall that would, in theory, minimize the chance of injury when he met the rapidly approaching bridge.

He should have hit the bridge feetfirst, then rolled with his momentum and spread the impact across his body from his calves up to his shoulders. Instead, his landing went feet-ass-head. His tumbled onto his stomach and skid several feet before coming to a stop precariously close to the edge of the bridge.

"Standish!" Egan called out.

"Go get 'em, Tex!" Standish's vision swam as he got onto his hands and knees and crawled away from the edge.

The Iron Hearts had landed with more success. They pounded the walker's legs with concentrated fire, severing one completely at a joint.

Bailey removed the two halves of her rail rifle off her back and snapped them together.

"Where do I shoot it?" she asked.

"Anywhere!" Standish rolled onto his back,

a stab of pain coming with every breath.

Bailey slid a cobalt-coated tungsten dart the length of her hand between the twin vanes of her rifle. She hefted the weapon against her shoulder.

"Here goes nothing," she said, and fired.

The bullet shattered the sound barrier and pierced the wyrm's back. The round continued into the walker and embedded deep within the dome, knocking it off-balance against its severed leg.

The walker fell to the side and went tumbling over the bridge. The wyrm went with it.

Standish went back to the edge and watched as the walker disintegrated. The wyrm's fall continued, stiff and lifeless.

Torni thrashed against the bridge, flipping end over end, her stalks stabbing out wildly.

"Sarge? What's wrong?" Standish got as close as he dared to the out-of-control drone. Torni's face appeared in the swirling patterns on the drone's shell, mouth open in a silent scream.

"What happened to her?" Egan asked.

"The drones disintegrated then just went

nuts." Standish reached for Torni and got rapped across the knuckles by a stalk.

A white light rose over the side of the bridge. Malal, his body burning white hot, floated toward Torni.

Egan swung his muzzle toward Malal. The barrel snapped in half from an invisible force then went flying through the air.

The Iron Hearts' gauss cannons slammed into the bridge, taking the armor down with them. The cannons twisted away from Malal and slid across the surface, pulling the Iron Hearts along like they were fish caught on a line.

Malal's body dimmed as he descended to the bridge. Bloodless cuts peppered his body. An open bullet hole in his chest was so large Standish could see straight through the ancient being. Malal looked at the wound, then glared at Bailey.

"I ain't sorry, mate," she said.

Malal's body morphed around the hole and the cuts. His body became pristine moments later. He pointed at Torni, still writhing in pain. Standish got between Torni and Malal.

"I will help it," he said. "Do not interfere."

"What's happening to her?" Standish asked.

"The walker was badly damaged. I managed to hack into its programming and activate the Xaros self-destruct protocols. The order reached this drone. Its body is trying to burn away. Move," Malal said.

Standish hesitated then stepped aside.

"I am plumb out of ideas, Sarge," Standish said.

Malal floated to Torni, his toes scraping the bridge. The slap of stalks against his head and shoulders had no effect on him as he pressed his hands against her shell. The drone went dead, as if Malal had flipped an off switch. Malal ran his touch over the surface.

"I remember this one," he said. "Anthalas. Then with the burning souls."

The stalks retracted into the shell. Wild patters pulsated across Torni's surface away from Malal's touch. He stepped back and the drone twisted into a corkscrew.

"Omnium," Malal said, "the Xaros make their drones from it. They remain malleable, enough to adapt and combine to counter their enemies. Her mind is better suited to this."

Torni's shape spread into an X. Limbs clad in Strike Marine powered armor morphed into being. A head rose out of the center mass and formed into Torni's face. A ripple passed through her body. Torni, formed just like Standish remembered from the last time he saw her on Anthalas, collapsed to the bridge. Her body still had the shifting grey color of the Xaros drones, like she was an unpainted model of her old self.

Standish went to her and touched the back of her head. Her body was stiff, solid as a statue.

"Sarge? You're...back?" Standish asked.

Torni looked at the Marine, her expression blank. Her mouth moved slowly, soundlessly.

"You do not have lungs," Malal said. "Nor vocal cords. Here," he said, pressing a thumb against her forehead.

"Get away from me!" Torni slapped Malal's hand away, the clash of metal on metal sounding from the impact.

"Malal!" Lieutenant Hale ran up to the group. Stacey, a few steps behind him, was carrying the governor. Hale got a good look at Torni and skidded to a stop.

"What the...Torni?"

"It's her, sir," Standish said. "Swear to God. She said she died, kind of, on Takeni. The Xaros had her memories...in a jar. Then she was a drone, helping us. Now she's herself again. And...it's going to get even weirder. Trust me on this."

"Shut up, Standish," Torni said.

Standish jabbed a finger at Torni.

"See! It's got to be her!"

"Hale..." Stacey nudged him with her elbow. "Malal."

"Spare me from your useless posturing." Malal held up a hand and the governor leaped out of Stacey's hands. It came to a stop in front of his chest. Malal ran his fingers over the device.

"I could crush you all with a thought. Ignite the oxygen in your blood and reduce you all to ashes." The governor pressed into Malal's chest. "But we have a bargain, don't we? I have honored my end." He looked at Stacey. "You will honor yours."

Stacey looked at her forearm screen and nodded. "He's back under our control."

"Shall we depart?" Malal asked. "There is nothing more for us here."

"Egan, Bailey, go help Yarrow move the wounded," Hale said. He walked to Torni, staying well beyond arm's length as she got to her feet. She stared intently at her hands as patterns danced over the surface.

"This is hard to believe," he said.

"Sir, do you remember the Qa'Resh? When they took that thing out of Yarrow?" Torni asked. Her voice was just as Hale remembered.

"I do."

"They took that memory from me. The Xaros found a way to get it back. They know. They know everything, sir. I helped…Minder told me it would save the Earth. But it was a lie, all of it," she said.

"Torni, or whatever you are, we'll get this sorted out later. Right now, I need to get my Marines out of this place and back to the *Breitenfeld*," Hale said.

"What do you mean, they know everything?" Stacey asked.

"They know we have the Crucible, that it's unfinished. They made me go back to Qa'Resh'Ta, look at the sky and count the suns for them. They know about…it." She pointed at Malal. "They're afraid of it."

"If the Xaros saw the sky over Qa'Resh'Ta…they might find it. She's led them straight to Bastion," Stacey said, her face going white.

"You need to arrest me, sir," Torni said. "You need to arrest me for treason."

****

Elias took point as the team made its way, back down the bridge. Bodel was in his tracked configuration, the wounded Orozco and Cortaro strapped to him. Kallen brought up the rear.

"We can't let Malal leave here," Kallen said over an IR channel closed off to all but the Iron Hearts. "You saw what it could do when Stacey let him slip off the leash."

"We need him to get the rest of us out of here," Elias said. "Wait until we're back on the ship."

"And then?" Bodel asked.

"We crack the governor in his chest. That should destroy him," Elias said.

"Or let him free again," Kallen said.

"Stacey has a kill switch. Can we access it if she won't cooperate?" Bodel asked.

"Tiny buttons on her screen." Kallen's hands flexed. "Big fingers."

"What about Hale? He's not the kind to go along with whatever they promised Malal to get him to cooperate. What do you think it was? All the proccies he could ever want? A planet full of primitives?" Bodel asked.

"Elias and I were with him on Europa when he told the Toth to pound sand instead of signing over the proccies," Kallen said. "There's no way he's with the Ibarras on this."

"Hale…maybe," Elias said. "Stay frosty. I'll see what he can do for us."

Targeting data flashed on Elias' HUD, an infrared picture of the Marines. The thing claiming to be Torni was uniformly cool, her body heat matching the ambient temperature, like she was a long-dead corpse.

"The drone?" Bodel asked.

"It claims to be Torni," Kallen said. "Bad enough to have Malal with us, now a Xaros turncoat?"

"I owe Torni," Elias said. "Not her shade. That thing steps out of line…our cannons will work on it."

"I miss the old days," Bodel said. "See the

Chinese army. Shoot the Chinese army. Reload.
Now…I don't even know what to think."

****

A wide archway stretched from one side of
the bridge to the other. The alabaster doorway was
sealed shut.

Malal touched the door and cocked his head
to the side after a moment.

"What's wrong?" Hale asked. "This will
lead us back to the forest we came from, right?"

"The Jinn," Malal said with a snarl, "one of
them is trying to rearrange my vault. Time for a
lesson." Malal's arm plunged into the doorway. He
yanked it out and tossed a crystal onto the bridge.

The crystal popped into the air and the
ghostly form of Father materialized around it.

"Hear me!" Father shouted, backing away
from Torni as the Marines raised their weapons.

"We know this one," Elias said. "It was
helpful."

Hale held up a fist and weapons lowered slightly.

"Before the Xaros destroys my light, hear me," Father said. "The demon is an enemy to all life. We showed the truth to the Iron Hearts. Do not silence the galaxy again."

"Give me a moment's freedom," Malal said. "I will burn away the Jinn infection from my vault. Save us the trouble of dealing with them ever again."

"She's not going to hurt you." Hale pointed at Torni. "We need Malal to fight the Xaros, you understand? The Xaros know about you now. They'll be back. Might take them hundreds of years, but they will return to finish you off. We have a chance to beat the Xaros now, but only if we have Malal's help."

"They are artificial, of no value to me or you. Let me destroy them," Malal said. "We leave them here and they will metastasize into a threat equal to the Xaros."

"One war at a time," Hale said.

"The price!" Father's form shook with static. "The Jinn will not trade one innocent life to preserve their own existence!"

"If we don't stop the Xaros, then everyone will die!" Hale advanced on Father. "You get that? The whole galaxy will be wiped clean. All life, innocent or not, will be gone. Now get out of our way or I will let Malal finish you off."

Father didn't respond. On Hale's visor, the IR on Elias' icon lit up with an open IR line…that didn't connect to anyone else on the team. Father's form shrank into the crystal, then took off like a shot over the side of the bridge.

The archway opened up and revealed the tunnel with their waiting Mule.

"Good job, Hale," Stacey said. "You should come take my spot on Bastion some time. You're better at convincing aliens than I am."

"Everyone get on board," Hale said. "I'm sick of this place." He looked to Elias and was about to open a channel when Egan tapped him on the shoulder.

"Orozco's still woozy from the concussion. Can you co-pilot?" Egan asked.

"I've done that exactly once before," Hale said.

"More times than anyone else on the team."

"Get started on the pre-flight. I'll join you in the cockpit," Hale said.

"Sir," Cortaro nodded at Torni, "what about...her?"

"If that is her, I won't risk leaving her behind again," Hale said. "Get her on board, but keep your weapon ready."

CHAPTER 18

Shutters on the apartment windows rose and blazing sunlight flooded the bedroom. A man sprawled out on the disheveled bed jerked awake. His hand came up from under a pillow, pistol in hand.

Knight blinked hard and snapped to his feet.

"What the hell? What time is it?" he asked.

"Local time is 4:15 p.m.," chirped the slate on a dresser.

He'd just returned from the shipyards on Mars, his internal clock forever out of whack as Ibarra sent him on one assignment to another after his departure from the *Breitenfeld*. He was originally assigned to the ship to keep a close eye on Stacey Ibarra. After she moved on to Bastion, Ibarra kept Knight on the carrier as his eyes and ears.

Exposing Captain Valdar's participation in the True Born movement meant Knight had to move on. Valdar wouldn't accept a commissar-like presence aboard his ship, and staying on the *Breitenfeld* would probably have ended with an "unforeseen incident" ending Knight's life.

He hadn't minded the *Breitenfeld*—at least there was a routine to keep him occupied.

There were two knocks on his door, a pause, then three more knocks in a staggered procession. Shannon was here, her knock code signaling she was safe.

"Hold on." Knight threw on some clothes, blaming the stiffness in his body on the lousy bed and not his advancing age. He kept his weapon in hand as he looked through the peephole and saw only Shannon outside his room. He'd worked with her for decades, first in the CIA, then in Ibarra's employ after the particular nature of their service to the country went out of fashion with an administration averse to assassinations and enhanced interrogations.

He opened the door and she strode in like she owned the place, a cardboard carry box of doughnuts and coffee in hand.

"This is odd," Knight said. He took a sip of coffee and flopped down onto an easy chair.

"Boss wants us," she said. "Not sure what for."

"Christ, I just got dirtside and now we have to go up to that damned Crucible? He knows how creepy that place is."

"He wants what he wants." She plucked a doughnut hole out of the box and popped it into her mouth. "But this time," she mumbled, taking a small black ball from a coat pocket. The ball floated into the air and a holo of Marc Ibarra formed in the air.

"Eric, nice to have you back," Ibarra said. "Mars nice this time of the year?"

"Same dusty red shithole it's ever been," Knight said. "One less bitter True Born saboteur to worry about."

"Good work, as ever." Ibarra folded his arms across his chest. "After a long and productive work relationship, I'm afraid it's time for us to part ways."

Knight tensed and glanced from his coffee, to Shannon, to the pistol he'd left on the countertop.

"Not that kind of parting, Eric. Sorry, I forget how sensitive you can be with semantics," Ibarra said.

"I told you to watch your phrasing," Shannon said with a wink to Knight.

"We have a colony mission in the works," Ibarra said. "Lovely place far beyond the reach of the Xaros called Terra Nova. The both of you will be on the *Christophorous* when it leaves."

"What's our mission?" Knight asked.

"No mission. Go. Make a life for yourselves. Be…happy."

"Mr. Ibarra," Shannon said, scooting to the

edge of her seat, "are you OK?"

"I'm a ghost in a machine, my darling, I am hardly OK. The two of you have spent the last four decades working for me, without knowing the true purpose behind my efforts. Such faith…loyalty…should be rewarded," Ibarra said. "It would not have been possible without the two of you. The fires you put out, leaks plugged, the occasional industrial sabotage. The great effort to save humanity continues, but I can't tool around in the shadows with you any longer. We're moving beyond that."

"So you're sending us out to pasture?" Shannon asked.

"You make it sound so negative." Ibarra waved a hand in the air and the *Christophorous* appeared next to him. "I am a bastard. I know that. The blood of every person that died when the Xaros came is on my hands. I spent my entire adult life and all of this," he waved a hand over his holo body, "afterlife putting the life and needs of every person on Earth second to the great effort. You two know what I did.

"Now…with you two, the two closer to my crimes than any other, I want you to have some peace. A bit of absolution."

The two spies didn't say a word.

"Oh, come on," Ibarra said. "Strange new world, the final frontier. No more kill orders or covert anything. Just live your lives. Get married. Kids. Grandkids. Not necessarily with each other. There will be a couple other colonists your type. Promise."

"But—" Shannon said.

"No 'but'! Is that really so hard to believe?"

"Yes," Knight deadpanned.

"Spend your whole life being a duplicitous bastard and you see what happens when you try to go legit," Ibarra said. "No strings or contingencies. You've both already won the lottery for a spot. The ship leaves in nine days. Be there or else I will be the vengeful asshole you know and love. Enjoy the doughnuts."

Ibarra vanished and the ball fell to the

carpet.

"You trust him?" Shannon asked.

"Oddly enough, I sort of do."

"So you're going?"

"Yeah. I try and fight it and I'll probably end up stuffed into a box on that ship, like it or not," Knight said. "You?"

"I'll go. Even a utopia will need those with our set of skills."

****

Ibarra watched the hidden camera footage of Shannon and Knight speaking. His shoulders heaved up and down with a breathless sigh of relief.

"Jimmy, have the tanks on Oberon create another Shannon. She's not to be decanted until that one leaves," Ibarra said.

"What about Knight? We have a recent brain scan on file," the probe said.

"No, Shannon is all I need."

"There is notable cognitive dissonance in

your brain patterns about this decision."

"What did I tell you about reading my mind? No, it's not the real Shannon that I'm sending to Terra Nova. She's long dead. If I'm to continue on, I want a reminder of what I've done near me. Every time I see her face…there's regret. It keeps me human and I don't expect you to understand that," Ibarra said.

"Anomalous behavior pattern noted and flagged for future study," the probe said.

"Show me the progress reports for the Phobos orbital batteries. We need to figure out why those are eight days behind schedule."

CHAPTER 19

Captain Valdar pressed against the bulkhead as Chief MacDougall made his way pass. Valdar's breath fogged the inside of his visor. He tapped a control on the side of his helmet, chiding himself for not setting the humidity controls correctly. He was a veteran void sailor, he needed to act like it in front of his crew.

The chief wore an augment suit, a bulky exo-skeleton with pincers mounted on the end of the arms. The suit barely fit through the passageway, the roll cage over MacDougall's head bumped against the ceiling with each step. Lights on the suit flooded the passageway. Bits of broken metal and dust floated in airless, gravity-less, passageway.

The chief stopped in front of a reinforced door marked BATTERY BAY C. Amber warning lights mounted on the door frame blinked erratically.

"Sure the rooms dead?" MacDougall asked. "Hate to open the door and get fried like I'm at a chippy."

"It's grounded," chief engineer Levin said. He backed away from MacDougall and bumped up against the team of medics and damage control sailors that filled the passageway.

"Don't seem too sure, if you ask me," MacDougall bumped the tips of his pinchers against the door, hard enough the Valdar felt vibrations through his boots. MacDougall waited thirty seconds, then bumped the door again. "Well, no one answering the door. Here we go."

MacDougall opened the pincers and pressed them against the door frame. His suit shook as the hydraulics drove the tips into the metal. The pinchers penetrated through the door, cutting lasers activated along the metal wedges and sliced through the hinges bolted to the frame. Specks of red hot metal jumped away from the melted sections and pinged off the bulkhead. MacDougall withdrew the pincers, and repeated the operation on the lower hinges.

The chief pressed exo-skeleton's shoulder against the doorway.

"Lord, preserve me," MacDougall rocked back and hit the door. It floated back, flipping over slowly.

"Damage control party Bravo, go," Levin said.

Sailors squeezed around MacDougall, each carrying piston driven multi-tools or welders. Valdar followed them in to the battery room.

The outer hull was ruptured, raw electricity had scorched the jagged edges black. Distant stars of the open void greeted the captain as he stopped on a cat walk. Battery stacks the size of cars floated through the bay, ripped loose by the strike that gouged out a hunk of the *Breitenfeld's* hull.

"This isn't good," Levin said from behind Valdar. "You see the dark energy banks below and against the primary induction lines?" He pointed to squat silver blocks linked together by pencil thin cables. The silver cases were warped, dotted with blotches of burned metal.

"I do," Valdar said. He knew what he was looking at, the implication, but he needed to hear the words from the Levin.

"I can tell from here, they dumped their charge. Lines are dead between the units. They must have overloaded the buffers, causing the explosion that took out this room. Damn crazy alien tech. Rest of the batteries held up," Levin said.

"So us getting home?" Valdar asked.

"Dark energy stacks in bay A are slagged, B is at half capacity…which doesn't do us any good," Levin crossed his arms over his chest. "We don't have the charge to get us back to Earth…we're in the middle of goddamn nowhere. Doubt we can even jump more than a light year with what we've got."

"We're stuck?" Valdar asked.

"Might as well be. I don't have the technical knowhow, or the equipment to fix the batteries if I *did* know what I was doing. Lafayette picked a hell of a time to skip a mission," Levin said.

"I don't accept that we're—"

"Medic! We need a medic down here!" came from the lower deck.

Valdar grabbed the catwalk's rail and swung over. He landed next to two sailors crowding around a mangled battery stack.

"What happened?" Valdar asked.

"Survivor, sir," one of the sailors said. She stepped aside, revealing a suited crewman pinned between a battery knocked loose from its moorings and crushed against its neighbor.

"His suit's offline, but still has atmo," she said.

The trapped sailor, a young man with a blue tint to his skin and wide eyes saw Valdar and opened his mouth to speak. His right arm and leg were jammed between the battery stacks, Valdar heard nothing through the void. Sparks sprang from cracks in the collapsed stack.

Valdar pressed his visor to the sailor's and spoke, "What's your name?"

"Kartchner…crewman…sir," his words came between quick breaths.

"Your air's going," Valdar unsnapped his emergency air canister from his belt and plugged it in to the side of Kartchner's helmet. The sailor took deep gulps of air. Kartchner's lips moved, but Valdar didn't hear anything until he pressed their visor's together again.

"—fried my suit. Would be Dutchman if this stack hadn't kept me right here. Small favors, right sir?" Kartchner said.

Valdar felt a tap on his shoulder. He pulled away and turned around saw Levin and a pair of medics.

"Captain," Levin stared Valdar in the eye, "that stack still has residual charge in it. We try and monkey around and it'll electrocute everyone in the room."

A corpsman, blood stains smeared across the front of her vac suit, stepped forward.

"We can still get him out," she nodded to the other corpsman, who had one hand behind his back. He brought his hand around and flashed a laser cutter the size of a hacksaw. "We have amputation kits."

Valdar swallowed hard. He understood the concept of what the corpsman proposed: the laser would slice right through a void armored suit and cauterize the severed limb. A cap over the stump would restore suit integrity to the patient. He knew the concept, but he'd never seen it in practice.

The trapped sailor was on borrowed time. If the stack discharged, or his suit failed any further, the crewman was done for.

"Do it," Valdar said.

He turned back to Kartchner and grabbed his hand. Valdar touched his visor to his.

"We're going to get you out of here. Right now, son. I don't have any other way to do it," Valdar said.

"Wait…wait wait," Kartchner's eyes darted from Valdar to the corpsmen crowding around them. "Maybe we could—"

"They're going to cut you free and get you to medical," Valdar gripped Kartchner's hand right and wrapped his arm around the crewman's head, turning it away from his trapped limbs. The corpsman without the laser cutter braced himself against Kartchner.

"No! Sir, don't do this! Can we—"

Valdar broke the visor-to-visor contact. Kartchner squirmed as the laser snapped to life, casting red light through the room.

Valdar felt Kartchner screaming through his hold as the corpsman went to work on the trapped leg.

****

Bailey sat across from Torni, watching as she buckled herself into the Mule's seats with the same practiced ease she remembered. The way she moved was the same—she even crossed herself when the straps tightened around chest and hips, just like always. Torni and Malal took up one side of the Mule; the rest of the Marines and Stacey sat across from them.

"I've got Orozco in the atmo chamber," Yarrow said into the ship's IR.

"No idea how many drones are still out there," Hale said. "We're going zero atmo once we're free of the vault."

Torni sat up as if startled, then pawed at her thigh where an auxiliary helmet should have been. The pouch was on her shell, but it wasn't real. Torni touched her face, and then looked at Bailey with panic in her eyes.

"Torni," Bailey said. "Do you even…breathe?"

"She is beyond the limits of biology," Malal said.

"I feel like *me*," Torni said. "Not a lump of metal."

Bailey reached into a pouch and pulled out a

length of blue cloth with the sapphire jewels sewn into it.

"Look at this," she said. "I wonder if that egghead Sheila—what's her name, Lowenn? I bet she could tell us what this is. Found it right after Standish, Egan and I went for a tumble."

The Mule's engines whined to life and the craft wobbled as it came off the deck.

"Cap'Yir holy vestments," Malal said. "They were the last experimental batch before I perfected the harvester. They believed they should meet the divine with their souls and bodies bare to judgment. The Cap'Yir threw their clothing off the bridge before entering the annihilation chambers. It was most amusing to watch."

Bailey looked down at the cloth, her face going slack as Malal's words sank in.

Malal laughed, a low, evil sound that filled the Mule as it entered the void and the air bled out.

****

Hale shifted in the co-pilot's seat, his hands floating over the controls.

"Got the ship's beacon," Egan said. "Five minutes out. Can't get them on comms, though…whoa."

Hale looked up. The wrecked Crucible listed in the void, tilting slowly against its central axis. Loose hunks of the once interconnected thorns spun through space. The Mule slowed down.

"What's going on?" Hale asked.

"The *Breit* must have turned her main guns on that Crucible. I bet there will be debris all over local space and I'd rather not run into any of it while I've got the thrusters burning," Egan said.

"Right. Got it…should I…"

"With all due respect, sir, don't touch anything unless I tell you," Egan said.

"You sound like Durand."

Hale passed on the warning to the turret gunners.

Several minutes passed before Hale could pick out the *Breitenfeld* against the deep void.

"I never met Torni," Egan said. "Didn't ask about her. Thought it better to wait until someone else brought her up to learn more. That's the way it is with casualties. Right?"

"She died on Takeni, gave up a spot so that a few more Dotok would live. I missed her eulogy because I was laid up in sick bay," Hale said.

"You think that's really her? Not some Xaros trick?"

"I hope it's the former. We will act like it's the latter until we're sure otherwise." Hale zoomed in on the ship. "Flight bay doors are open...looks like they're on auxiliary power."

"Mule Zero-Three, this is Gall," came over the IR. *"I sure hope you're coming back with some good news. We've had a hell of a time out here."*

"Roger, Gall. We need a master-at-arms contingent to greet us. We have a prisoner."

"A...prisoner?"

"You heard me."

"Ouais, pour quois pas? I'll see if the damage control teams can spare anyone." Durand

cut the transmission.

A pair of Eagles settled on the Mule's flanks.

"I sound like that?" Egan asked.

"Just get us back to the ship. Somehow I doubt our day's about to get any better."

****

Captain Valdar waited for Hale at the bottom of the Mule's ramp, a team of master-at-arms with gauss carbines behind him. Hale motioned for Torni to stand and follow him.

Valdar and his sailors backed up when they saw Torni's dancing skin. Hale raised a hand as one of the men-at-arms raised his weapon.

"Lieutenant," Valdar said, "I've had some damn strange things on my ship since this war started. Is that what I think it is?"

"She claims to be Sergeant Torni," Hale said. "Everything she's said confirms that."

"Other than the pictures of her dead body

and the fact that she looks like a Xaros drone in human form?" Valdar asked. He motioned to Torni and an MA approached her with a set of shackles. She held her arms out and let the sailor bind her without protest.

"Load a quadrium round, high-power gauss shots if she tries anything," the petty officer in charge of the arms men said. Torni looked over her shoulder at Hale as the sailors led her away.

"*Gott mit uns*," she said.

Hale gave her a quick nod.

"Believe it or not, a Xaros drone on my ship isn't the worst of my problems," Valdar said. "What about your mission in the vault? Did you find what Malal promised?"

Stacey and Malal sat next to each other in the Mule, watching as a team of corpsmen took Orozco and Cortaro away.

Hale called them over. Stacey bounded down the ramp. Malal stayed seated.

"Captain, great success!" Stacey said, a smile on her face. She tapped the pouch on her belt with the data recorder. "We have everything we need to complete the Crucible and access the Xaros network."

"Some good news, at least," Valdar said. His face darkened as he continued. "The jump engine took serious damage when the Xaros came out of that Crucible. The dark-energy batteries dumped their charge. We're not leaving this place anytime soon…unless you and that 'technical advisor' of yours can do something for us."

Stacey's enthusiasm drained away. "We need to be near something massive enough to bend the fabric of space-time to the beyond point—I'll spare you the math. The vault isn't anywhere near that size…"

"Can't we jump to something nearby? Like when we escaped Takeni with the Dotok ship?" Hale asked.

"The batteries are empty," Valdar said, shaking his head. He handed a data slate to Stacey. She flipped through the screens so fast Hale barely had time to read the headlines on the engineering reports.

"Even if we could repair the batteries…we'd be sitting here for almost ten years waiting for the batteries to draw enough charge to jump to the nearest star," Stacey said. "We're in deep space. Space-time is flat as a wall, barely any dark energy."

"I've kept this from the crew," Valdar said. "Needed them focused on repairs…ten years."

"You won't survive," Malal said from within the Mule. He stepped off the top of the ramp and floated to the deck. "This ship has enough food and air to last you, at most, a few months. Even if you jettisoned the crew to preserve Ibarra's life—"

"Now wait a second," Stacey interrupted. Malal waved a dismissive hand at her.

"I doubt she would survive the isolation. You humans are such fragile, social creatures. But there is a solution," Malal said.

"We could repair the Crucible," Stacey said. "Get back to Earth that way."

"And let the Xaros return to my vault? And

let the Xaros know we can access their network? Take the long view. I told the Qa'Resh you'd have one shot at the Xaros command ship approaching the galaxy. We repair this Crucible and that chance is gone," Malal said.

"Get to the point," Valdar said.

"I will save every life aboard this ship." Malal's mouth opened into a smile. "I will return you to Earth within a reasonable amount of time. But I require two things: a quadrium munition and your trust."

CHAPTER 20

Torni stared at her hands, watching the patterns shift and meld against each other over her omnium shell. She sat on the bare bench bolted to the bulkhead, though she'd felt no discomfort or fatigue the last few hours she'd been on her feet pacing across her cell. The energy shield between her and the cell bars flickered in time with the lights above the man-at-arms watching her from a desk.

The cell was designed to hold Malal. Torni wasn't sure if she was keeping it warm for him or if she'd end up sharing it once it came time to return to Earth.

The door to the brig swung open. Hale, out

of his armor and now in fatigues, stopped in front of her cell. He had a sealed envelope in one hand.

"Sir," Torni said.

"I debriefed Standish and the others," he said. "Reviewed vid captures from their armor. Everything is consistent with what you've told me, so far."

"You don't believe it. Don't believe I'm really Torni."

"We've had experience with one other…individual like you. Marc Ibarra. The situation with him is a little different."

"Because he's a hologram stored in a friendly alien intelligence and I'm inside a Xaros drone?"

"Basically. The tech used by the Xaros and the Qa'Resh have some similarities. That you are Sergeant Sofia Torni's consciousness is possible. Can you tell me any more about this Minder you told Standish about?"

Torni stood and went to the edge of her cell. She tapped a knuckle against the energy field. It crackled, blue strands of electricity arcing against her hand.

"That should hurt," she said. "A lot. But I'm not human anymore. I didn't ask for this, sir. I knew I was going to die. When I gave up my spot so others could live. I knew. Made my peace with God. My soul is with Him. I believe that. The Xaros master, the General, took something from the Torni that died. A recording. A picture. Whatever's stuck in this drone. Then…I fell for their lies. Helped them. Told them everything I knew and even what the Qa'Resh tried to erase. I don't blame you for not trusting me."

"You helped us in the vault," Hale said. "That was the same brave, quick-thinking Marine I knew Torni to be. We'll figure this out." He looked to the envelope, kneaded it between his fingers. "I'm sorry I left you behind, Sergeant."

"Wasn't your decision, sir. You were out of commission. Bleeding to death in the back of a Mule. Command fell to me," she said.

"I would have stayed behind," Hale said.

"I know. I would have stayed with you."

Hale nodded quickly.

"I have this for you." Hale opened a slot and slid the envelope through. "It's what happened after Takeni. There's an all-hands meeting on the flight deck in a few minutes. I'll come back afterwards."

Torni took the envelope.

"I never blamed you. Whatever happens next, I'll accept. If I can keep fighting the Xaros, make them regret what they did to me…"

"I'll see what I can do," Hale said.

Torni snapped her heels together and saluted. Hale returned the gesture and left the brig.

Inside the envelope was a picture taken from orbit over Takeni, showing her body, which was surrounded by dead Dotok and banshees. The image wasn't a shock—she'd had a much closer look at her final moments with Minder. Next, she took out her death certificate, signed by Valdar and Hale, a darkened box next to "Remains not recovered."

The last item in the envelope was an award recommendation, the first of many bureaucratic steps before a Marine received a medal. Hale'd written up a lengthy recommendation for her to receive the Atlantic Union Medal of Honor.

There were more statements from the rest of her squad and the pilot of the last Mule off that mesa, all corroborating Hale's account and praising the honor, courage and commitment of her final act as a Marine. Valdar had endorsed the award…approval or rejection from the next higher authority, Admiral Garret, was blank.

Torni returned to the bench. She reread the recommendation, then tore it apart.

The Torni that died deserves that, she thought. *Not me. Not the traitor.*

****

Stacey hated stages. Hated being stared at by the *Breitenfeld*'s entire crew as they filed onto the flight deck and fell into muster. Yet there she was. Standing with the ship's senior officers in a loose huddle around Valdar as he spoke quietly.

Malal, his face and body as human as Stacey had ever seen, waited next to her, impassive. An ammo dolly with a pair of quadrium rounds sat on the far side of the stage.

She looked out the open bay doors where the wrecked Crucible and Malal's vault filled the space beyond. She didn't care to have only an energy field between her and hard vacuum, but it was Valdar's call.

"We have everyone, XO?" he asked Commander Ericcson.

"Aye-aye, Skipper. Last sweep has everyone here…except for the prisoner," the XO said.

"It doesn't need to hear this. Bosun," Valdar said, pointing to a sailor at the forward edge of the stage, "sound attention."

The bosun brought a whistle to his lips and blew a long note. Conversation from the crew shut off instantly. Hundreds of heels clicked together. Valdar activated a microphone clipped to his uniform.

"*Breitenfeld*," Valdar's voice boomed across

348

the flight deck. He clasped his hands behind his back and surveyed his crew. "Our mission was a success. Again, your efforts have won the day."

A "hoo-yah" cheer came from the sailors.

"The *Breit* took a hit," Valdar said, "a bad hit. She'll get us home, but not as fast as we'd like."

From the audience, Stacey heard a single "shit." She could have sworn it was Standish.

Malal walked across the stage and laid a hand on the quadrium rounds.

"Here's what's going to happen." Valdar pointed to Malal. "Our technical advisor—"

A flash of light stung Stacey's eyes. She rubbed her face and saw Captain Valdar frozen in place. The rest of the crew was equally still.

Malal stepped back from the empty ammo dolly. The fingers on one hand glowed blue.

"I was to wait for some grand signal?" Malal said. "I've not time for such nonsense. The tachyon inversion field will keep them in perfect stasis until I release them. Not the same trick your grandfather used to sidestep the Xaros invasion, but the same principle."

Stacey tried to touch Utrecht's face as static electricity snapped at her fingertip.

"Why am I free?" she asked.

"Valdar wants me to repair his ship, get you all back to Earth in a timely fashion. I can do this. What happens next is my concern." Malal strode toward Stacey. She backed up to the edge of the stage and fumbled with the pouch holding the control bracelet.

Malal grabbed her by the wrist and the front of her uniform. He lifted her into the air and stepped off the side of the stage. Stacey fought against his grip as he carried her toward the open bay doors.

"What're you doing?" She kicked him in his rock-hard stomach and yelped in pain.

"I find your species inconsistent," Malal said. "I might get a more pliant warden if I eliminate you now."

Stacey's eyes went wide as Malal pressed her against the force field separating her from the void.

"No! Stop! The Qa'Resh will cancel the deal if I die!"

"'The tachyon inversion didn't work on her altered biology,'" Malal said. "'She grew depressed, suicidal, as the years went on. Tragic, as humans would say. Not that her death had any effect on me.'" Stacey felt the force field give way as Malal pressed harder. "They will believe that."

Stacey struggled, but it was useless.

"Malal! Don't! I promise you'll get what you want. The Qa'Resh will believe that you've honored your end of the deal. I can tell them what you've done for us. No one else can!"

Malal leaned close to Stacey.

"They will betray me. Won't they?"

"No! They always keep their word. They went behind Bastion to try and save the Earth, promised me a way to save humanity. They always keep their word!"

Stacey fell to the deck, her wrist throbbing with pain from Malal's grip.

Malal offered a hand.

"I had my doubts. Humans cannot maintain deception while under duress. I needed to be sure that you and the Qa'Resh would keep your end of the bargain. As far as you know, you will," he said.

"You're a son of a bitch," Stacey said. "I'll tell them about this. All of it."

"Naturally. I'm going to send you back to Bastion with all the good news once I build a conduit. Can't have the Qa'Resh destroying the gateway to my apotheosis just because they think we've failed."

"How? We don't have a probe to connect to Bastion."

"I have you, and I have a tool. Come with me."

****

Torni stared at the photo of her body, so focused on the picture that she didn't realize Malal and Stacey were just outside her cell until Stacey cleared her throat.

Torni set the picture aside.

"Tell me," Malal said, "do you still feel the immolation directive?"

"It's there." Torni held out a hand. The surface of a finger burned away like lit paper. It returned to normal a moment later. "Gnawing at the back of my mind."

"I didn't have time for a more elegant solution to the Xaros walker. The effect on you was collateral damage. You will learn to keep the directive in check or you will disintegrate like any other badly damaged drone," Malal said.

"Aren't you a ray of sunshine? What are you two doing here? Where is everyone else?" Torni asked.

"They're in stasis," Stacey said. "You're going to be out here for a while, until the jump engine is repaired and charged. I will go back to Bastion as soon as possible."

"How?" Torni asked. "We don't have a Crucible for you to zip back and forth."

"The conduit goes through the Qa'Resh

probes, not the Crucible. My biology has been...altered...to make the trip and carry large amounts of data in my DNA. We need you to build a new conduit so I can go back to Bastion with what we've learned," Stacey said.

"I escaped the Xaros with little more than my memories, not a tool box," Torni said.

"You are a prisoner of ignorance." Malal waved a hand across the cell and the energy field vanished with a pop of ozone. The cell door flung open. "Don't let your shape fool you. You are no longer human. You are a Xaros drone, albeit one with the potential to be much more useful. Come with me. We have work to do and you have much to learn."

CHAPTER 21

Brannock stretched a thick metal wire from a spool on his belt to a handrail welded against the bulkhead. He snapped a D-ring onto the handrail, locked the spool and gave the line two quick tugs.

He yanked on Derringer's taut safety line and grunted approval. The corporal did the same for Indigo, and the line unraveled off the spool.

"Indigo, you have to lock it." Brannock took Indigo's giant thumb and tried to press it into the tiny recess on the spool.

"Button small," Indigo said.

"Or your fingers are too damn big. These obviously aren't made for doughboys." Brannock fixed the line and gave Indigo a pat on the chest. "Your line goes lose and you'll fly down the hallway before it stops you. Probably crush me and Derringer in the process."

"Bad," Indigo said.

"Yes, bad. Now that we're locked in, sure hope you both have plenty of ammo." Brannock tapped the full magazine in his gauss rifle.

A young sailor ran down the passageway adjacent to where the Marines stood guard. With a briefcase in one hand and a scrap of paper in the other, she skidded to a halt, comparing the door label leading to a storage bay to what she had on her paper. She crumpled the paper in frustration.

"I hate this ship," she said.

"Don't let the boss hear you say that," Derringer said.

The sailor whirled around and pointed a finger at Derringer. The name STEPHENS was on her vac suit.

"You! Yes, you Marine, who probably knows his way around this damn place. Where can I find storage bay Echo 2-9? I've been around this deck three different—what the hell happened to him?" The sailor backpedaled into the bulkhead.

"I think Corporal Brannock was just born looking like that," Derringer said.

"No! That!" She waved a hand at Indigo.

"He's a doughboy," Brannock said, launching into the umpteenth explanation of Indigo's presence, "bio construct used to fight the Xaros. He'll be nice to you if you're nice to him, and not an alien."

"Enemies?" Indigo raised his rifle and looked up and down the passageway.

"Not yet, big guy. Stand down." Brannock pushed Indigo's muzzle to the deck.

"What do you need in that storage bay?" Derringer asked.

"I'm supposed to be on the terminal guidance team," she said, holding up the briefcase. "I was supposed to be there ten minutes ago but this ship isn't laid out like the *America* for some reason and I can't...do you know where it is or not?"

Brannock pointed to a double door across from him.

"Oh, thank God." Stephens pounded on the doors. They opened to a room full of jury-rigged equipment and acceleration chairs bolted to the deck. Banks of monitors filled the room.

"Stephens? Did you take the scenic route? Get your ass in here!" shouted a petty officer.

"Good luck," Brannock said as she went inside.

"She was cute," Derringer said.

"What did I tell you about focus?"

"What's there to focus on? Gunney said we're internal security for the mission. Don't let the Xaros in that room and hold on when—"

Red lights pulsed up and down the passageway.

"Now hear this! Now hear this! All hands brace for acceleration!" came over the public address system and the IR bead in Brannock's ear.

He locked his boots to the deck and grabbed the handrail. Part of him hoped the rest of this mission went like the fight with the Toth, with him deep in the hull and with nothing to do.

Fat chance of that, he thought.

****

A column of light passed through the empty red armor floating in Abaddon's control room. The armor plates glowed as the General took corporeal form and glided through the tiered workstations surrounding the central plinth.

The workstations came to life with information. The human fleet broke formation and accelerated toward his great ship. Most of it, the support ships carrying large amounts of quadrium, turned about and fled as best their engines could manage. A scan wave told him nothing new.

That the humans had an inordinate amount of quadrium was vexing. The material blocked his sensors and the weaponized effects were proving tiresome. The humans' solar system could only produce so much, yet this force had been most cavalier with using it.

They're using the omnium reactor. Wise, but futile. Even with the energy-resistant armor, the humans on Earth stood no chance once he arrived in force. The General decided to revisit the captive intelligence after he dealt with the human fleet once and for all. There were only so many humans left after they re-took their home world, and he was about to finish off the majority of their surviving fleet.

But their presence in deep space…something didn't fit. Most species would flee from a creation as vast and terrible as this. This assault must have been out of desperation, or ego. He'd swatted many annoying last stands from scoured species before. This would be another such exercise.

A human supply ship accompanying their fleet, the only one that hadn't fled from the battle, accelerated ahead of the other vessels and launched an object off the rail system mounted onto the prow.

It was too slow for one of their munitions.

The trajectory took it above the propulsion ring. The earlier damage to the ring was not yet repaired, and the next batch of drones replicating within his arsenal were incomplete.

His body flared with anger as the humans forced a decision from him. They'd proven too adept, too resourceful, to ignore. He would deal with this annoyance once and for all; the delay of his mission to Earth would be irrelevant. The humans had no more ships, no more crews, to stop him once he reached their planet.

The drone net over his arsenal was released. He felt the slight deceleration as the inversion field dissipated.

This would be the last time the humans interfered with his sacred task to cleanse the galaxy of their pollution.

****

A twinkling star shot out from the *Abdiel*, the only graviton mine still on board the ship. The rest of its complement was spread out through the fleet.

Makarov, strapped into her acceleration chair, watched the mine through the bridge's screens. Her fingers tapped furiously against the armrests until she caught herself and balled her hands into fists. If she showed the slightest bit of worry, her crew would catch the emotion and it would metastasize into dread.

"Drone net is breaking formation," Kidson said.

"How many?"

"All of them, Admiral."

A screen attached to her armrest came to life. Drones broke from their bonds and flew toward the speeding graviton mine.

"We may have to buy us some room to maneuver. Get a volley of q-shells ready," Makarov said.

"The firing solution will be next to impossible when—" Kidson stopped when Makarov held up a hand.

"The whole fleet depends on it. You're tossing out a hand grenade, not trying to thread a needle," she said.

Kidson barked orders to his team.

"Two minutes to detonation, Admiral," Captain Randall said.

Makarov opened a fleet wide channel. "All ships, this is Makarov. Almost two centuries ago, a great battle was fought near the island of Midway. The Americans crippled the Japanese Imperial Navy and turned the tide of that terrible war and changed the course of history. What we do here today...will save our people. They may not know what we accomplished, or how we did it, but when a child watches the sunrise over the ocean a thousand generations from now, he will have *you* to thank for it.

"There will be no retreat. No surrender. We will fight on to victory."

Makarov closed the channel.

"Payload drop in thirty seconds," Calum said.

"As you will. Delacroix better have got the math right or we're about to launch the most useless offensive in military history," Makarov said. She tightened her restraints.

****

Every ship in the Eighth Fleet opened their garbage bays and dumped tons of refuse in their wake—the shredded remnants of dead-lined void craft, burnt-out sections of bulkheads, every scrap of garbage the ships accumulated since they weighed anchor and traveled through the Crucible.

Several dozen specially modified graviton mines floated in the debris field tumbling toward Abaddon, all unpowered and just as innocuous as the rest of the garbage.

With no atmosphere to slow them down, the mines kept their forward momentum.

The graviton mine shot ahead of the fleet, activated, creating a dense point of gravity with the force of a small black hole. Space warped around the mine as it burned through its quadrium and antimatter fuel.

The mine's field gripped Eighth Fleet and snapped every ship toward the upper edge of Abaddon like a slingshot. The ships' maneuver thrusters flared to life, turning their engine blocks toward their direction of travel. The fleet crossed Abaddon's propulsion rings like they were flying in reverse.

The graviton mine pulled the trash dumped by the fleet toward it and burned away before it could mangle the garbage in the crushing grip of its event horizon. The debris, now moving even faster thanks to the mine's pull, passed through where the mine used to be and spread through space. Most of the garbage, and all the camouflaged mines, would pass through Abaddon's propulsion rings.

With the fleet now pounding the drone swarm with q-shells and stabbing at the propulsion rings with lance munitions, Makarov's plan hinged on the Xaros not caring about their garbage.

****

Brannock felt the rumble of firing rail batteries through the soles of his boots.

"All hands, prepare for deceleration!" came over the IR.

He locked his rifle to his armor and gripped the rail with both hands.

"I thought we just did that," Derringer said.

"You think I became a Marine because I'm good at physics? Stop trying to make sense of everything and just hold on." Brannock activated the mag locks in his gloves.

The ship whiplashed beneath him as every engine flared to life. Brannock slammed against his hold, the pseudo-muscles in his suit pulling tight against his arms and chest as his momentum and the ship's went in opposite directions.

"Ah, crap!" Derringer's hands came loose and his upper body flew back. The safety line at his waist snapped tight. Derringer almost bent over backwards and Brannock would have been a lot angrier if the younger Marine didn't look so ridiculous with his arms flailing around.

The line holding Derringer stretched under the strain. One of the entwined graphene reinforced steel wires snapped.

The rest of the line broke a split second later. Derringer's mag linings held him just long enough for him to issue a panicked scream then they gave way. Derringer flew through the air, heading for a very sudden and painful stop against the bulkhead down the passageway.

Indigo's hand snapped out like a striking scorpion and grabbed Derringer's ankle. The doughboy held Derringer in midair. Brannock felt the pull against his grip lessen as the ship slowed down.

"I take back everything I ever said about Ibarra and the doughboys," Derringer said. "Just don't let go."

"Let go," Indigo said.

"No! Hold on! Hold on!" Derringer lowered to the deck like a kite on a dying breeze. Indigo kept his grip.

The deck shimmied for a brief moment, then a second quake rocked the ship.

"Don't tell me we're doing that again," Derringer said.

"No." Brannock tried to open the ship's internal defense IR channel and got nothing. "That was enemy fire. Get up, Marine."

Derringer shook the leg still in Indigo's grasp. "Let go."

"Said hold on." Indigo frowned.

Brannock unlocked the doughboy's safety line and tapped him on the arm.

"Let him go. We're going to need him sooner or later," Brannock said.

****

Eighth Fleet's guns pounded the leading edge of the Xaros swarm with q-shells and flechette rounds, destroying hundreds of drones with each hit. A cloud of drones pushed forward, oblivious to the losses.

The fleet's frigates sparred with a pair of Xaros cruisers that had been waiting for them on the far side of Abaddon. The Xaros ships seemed intent on disabling the *Midway* and had scored a few hits against a single aegis plate on her port side. Captain Randall didn't think that was an accident and sent additional teams of Marines to secure that part of the ship.

Behind the cloud, drones combined into constructs larger than the *Midway*. Makarov stopped counting the new ships once she reached triple digits.

The individual drones soak up fire, leaving time for larger ones to form. She wrote down the observation in her tea-stained note pad.

"Guess they don't want to give us one large target again." Calum added numerical designations to the battleships with a tap inside the holo table.

"They must think we have more than one ship with the *Griffon*'s energy cannons…" Makarov swiped her screen to the side. The graviton mines drifting toward the rings were several minutes away from their targets. She opened an IR channel. "Delacroix, status on Task Force Scorpion."

Delacroix's picture came up next to the *Abdiel*, on the opposite side of Abaddon serving as a relay between the fleet and the graviton mines encroaching on the propulsion rings.

"We're moving at best speed." His words were laden with static. "We'll seed…soon as the rings are down…long way home."

"God's speed, Scorpion." The mine layers would leave graviton mines between them and Abaddon, forcing it to burn itself down to a hollow shell before it reached Earth. That plan hinged on the rest of her fleet destroying the propulsion rings. If she failed, the rest of Task Force Scorpion's ships would be little more than a speed bump.

"We're not going to stop the swarm." Kidson shook his head. Thousands of individual drones stayed packed close together, denying a clear shot from the fleet onto the approaching battleships. "If we commit the squadrons, it could clear us a line

370

of fire and buy more time."

"Send them," Makarov said. It would take the drone swarm another few minutes to reach her ships. The battleships would close to weapon's range in less than ten minutes. "Time until the mines are in range?"

"Fifteen minutes." Blood drained from Calum's face. "They're moving slower than we'd planned."

"Then we'd best last longer than that," Makarov said.

More and more drones swept over Abaddon's horizon, all reaching toward her ship.

"Got the drones from the forward hemisphere to come play." Makarov's mouth twisted into a half smile. "Better us than Scorpion."

"Several hits on the rings," Kidson said. "Abaddon's propulsion is off-line."

"Lift fire from the rings and concentrate on the drones. Time until they engage our fighter screen?" Makarov asked.

"Should be…what the hell is that?" Calum

reeled back from his station like he'd been shoved.

"Show me," Makarov said.

A ragged line of light hovered over Abaddon's surface. Makarov zoomed in. Red-plated armor in a humanoid shape filled the center of the light, the faceplate turning from side to side, arms motioning to the Xaros fleet. Ships maneuvered, reacting to his gestures.

"That's what the *Breitenfeld*'s armor encountered," Makarov said. "Xaros leadership caste."

"We might have a shot on it," Kidson said. "Engage?"

"No. The drones will function with or without its presence…but we might learn something." Makarov opened a channel to her fighter screen.

****

Zorro pitched his Eagle over and let off a snap shot. His cannons clipped the drone headed straight at him and sent it tumbling out of control. He kicked his tail over to flip around and finished off the drone with another burst. He waited until his nose lined up with his momentum then killed his flip with a brief burn of maneuver thrusters.

"Say again, Cougar?" he asked the new wing commander.

"Break formation with your flight and engage the…leadership target between the battleship analogues," he said. "You'll know it when you see it."

Space around Zorro was a dogfight between drones and Eagles as far as he could see. Lance shells from the fleet shot through the scrum, burning embers crossing paths with massive energy beams from the Xaros. Flack cannons from the ships traced arcs of gauss shells. The drones were already to the fleet.

As much as he wanted to stay and fight, there was no time to argue.

"Roger, Cougar. Red flight, form on me." Zorro banked hard and made for a cluster of four

Xaros battleships, each pounding Eighth Fleet with scarlet beams shooting from their fore. He spotted the tear of light and gunned his engines.

"Zorro, you know there are four battleships over there, right?" Buckets asked. His wingman and two more Eagles joined him, their engines blazing hot.

"They're busy and we're not much of a threat to them." Zorro loaded his last q-shell to his rail gun and charged the weapon. "Buckets, Vichy, load lance munitions to your rail gun, Kimchi, quadrium. Let's ruin this guy's day."

His pilots acknowledged and Zorro felt a chill pass over his body when the General's red armor came into view. Burning motes of light appeared across the battleships' hulls.

"Evasive!" Zorro dove and hit his afterburners. Burning beams of light broke around him. He slalomed around the point defense weapons, three seconds of concentrated fire that felt like an eternity before it faded away.

"Back on target." He pulled up and flew

between two battleships. "Ready rail cannons." He flipped the safety switch off the trigger.

"I'm set," Buckets said. "We lost the others."

A laser cut into Zorro's canopy and slagged a control panel. He tilted into a barrel roll, taking another hit that shook his Eagle. Damage alarms wailed in his ears, but he still had maneuver control, and he still had his rail cannon.

"Take your shot!" Zorro lined up his targeting reticule on the red armor and fired. His control panels sparked and died as the rail cannon sent a q-shell at the General.

The q-shell exploded well short of its target, enveloping a wide shield around the Xaros master with coherent energy. The shield wavered as Bucket's lance shell struck and shattered into fragments.

The General reached toward the Eagles, and a blast of energy lashed out of his hand. It struck Buckets and annihilated the fighter. Nothing of Zorro's old friend remained as the energy cut away.

Zorro twisted his control stick from side to side. His Eagle responded sluggishly, but he still had control. He pointed the nose at the General and coaxed life to the engines, accelerating straight for the red armor.

His gauss cannon refused to fire. The burnt hull plating over the rail cannon assured him that was useless as well.

Zorro let out a war cry and closed on the General, intent on ramming him.

The General reached an arm behind his head then swung against the Eagle. His arm stretched into a pillar of blazing light and swatted Zorro away. The Eagle shattered into burning fragments, reduced to nothing more than a stream of dissolving bits of metal and flesh.

****

Eighth Fleet suffered. Every ship in the holo tank flashed with damage icons. Two more destroyers, the *Kingston* and *Mesa*, blinked as a

Xaros battleship turned its guns to them. The ships lasted thirty seconds beneath the concentrated fire before breaking to pieces.

A glaring beam hit the *Midway*'s prow and knocked her off course. Makarov braced herself against the holo table as the ship lurched beneath her.

"Forward hull plating breached," Captain Randall called out. "Damage to decks three through twelve and the flight deck."

"Admiral, guidance crews have linked up with the graviton mines. Two units in place, shall we activate them now?" Calum asked.

"No, it'll throw off the rest of the mines and give the Xaros a chance to react. How long until—"

A wave of light crashed against the bridge. The hull rang with hundreds of impacts.

"That was the *Tarawa*," Kidson said.

Makarov looked to the screens and saw broken and burning pieces of the strike carrier peppering the *Midway*.

"How long until the rest of the mines are in

place?" Makarov asked.

"Each ship had guidance teams for redundancy." Calum's hands flit from ship to ship in the tank. "With the ships lost and damage to what's left…I can't tell. We have ten workstations still functional on deck seven. That's all we can count on right now."

"Captain Randall, pull us out of the fight but keep line of sight on the *Abdiel* at all costs." Makarov opened a channel to her remaining ships. "This is Makarov. I don't like this, but close in on the *Midway* and cover us."

The frigates *Bull Run* and *Ypres* responded immediately, maneuvering themselves between the *Midway* and a Xaros battleship firing on the carrier. Columns of energy hit the *Ypres* across her flank, bucking it to the side as if it had been kicked. The *Bull Run* let off a broadside that cracked the battleship's hull, knocking black slabs of armor away and exposing amber crystals.

A Xaros drone landed on the *Midway* next to rail battery four and stuck its stalks into the nearby bunker. The firing ports lit up as the drone killed the defenders. Two more drones landed nearby, followed by a dozen, then even more.

"*Midway*," said the captain of the *Rome* as he came up in the holo tank, "you've got a significant number of drones on your hull. I can clear them off with a q-shell."

"Negative. The guidance teams need more time. We take them off-line with a quadrium hit and we might as well bare our throats. Where are the Ospreys?" Makarov asked.

Calum shook her head.

"*Rome*, turn your flack cannons on us," Makarov said. "Shoot them off."

Gauss rounds slashed through the void around the *Midway*, tearing gouts out of the aegis armor and destroying dozens of drones.

"We've got hull breaches all across the starboard side. Boarders on decks…all decks." Randall gave Makarov a stern look. "Permission to activate the self-destruct sequence."

"Denied." Makarov un-holstered her gauss

pistol and activated the weapon. "Send all security teams to the guidance bay. This goes to the last man."

The ship rocked to the side, pitching Makarov to the deck. A disintegration beam broke through the ceiling and cut her holo table in two. She rolled out of the way and fired on the drone ripping a hole through the deck above her. The oversized rifle carried by one of her doughboy bodyguards blasted the drone to pieces.

The doors to the bridge glowed red hot.

Her human bodyguard tackled her from behind and shielded her as the door exploded. Shrapnel ripped through the bridge, killing Captain Randall instantly. A drone squeezed through the opening and sent pinpoint disintegration beams into each work pod.

Makarov shoved her bodyguard away, her hands and body slick with his blood. Screams of the bridge crew echoed through her helmet as they died. A doughboy charged the drone with hammer high. Stalks stabbed him in the chest and stomach, but the soldier managed to swing his hammer into the drone, cracking the surface.

The drone flicked its stalks and sent the doughboy's body parts flying in separate directions.

Makarov grabbed her bodyguard's rifle and hit the drone, knocking it against the ceiling where it broke apart.

The ship's internal gravity failed and power to the work pods cut out. Red emergency lights cast shades of blood across the bridge.

Deck plating beneath Makarov exploded. Pain ripped into her side. Drops of her blood floated around as she fought to grab onto anything as she tumbled through the bridge.

A doughboy grabbed her and set her onto the deck behind him. He swung his rifle up at the drone that ripped through the deck. The doughboy's vac suit went limp as a red lance from the drone cut through his suit.

Makarov shoved the empty suit aside and grabbed the rifle.

She wrapped several fingers around the

trigger and pulled. The rifle jumped up, smashing across her visor and flying out of her hands. A deep fissure broke across the drone. It went limp and burned away.

Blood poured out of the wound on her side. Air vented through cracks in her visor. A wave of vertigo sent her to the deck.

She jabbed at her forearm screen with trembling fingers and opened a fleet-wide channel.

"Eighth…this is Makarov. Go down fighting. You hear me? You go down fighting!"

A shadow passed over her. A drone with burning stalks came for her.

****

Brannock gripped his rifle tight as the *Midway*'s power died out. He glanced around a laser-scarred corner and looked down a bullet-marked passageway, praying another drone wasn't coming for them. He felt gravity seep away and locked his boots to the deck.

"That's bad," Derringer said. "Real bad if main power's out."

"Nothing we can do about it. Engineering is on the other end of the ship."

"You think we're going to abandon ship?" Derringer's voice cracked with the question.

Brannock grabbed the younger Marine by the shoulder.

"Indigo's getting scared. I need you to act hard before he loses it." He cocked his head to the doughboy standing opposite to them.

"He is?"

"Yeah, you see how the colors in his face are all messed up? That's what happens when they get scared. Didn't you read the manual?"

"Huh…hey, big guy. We've got your back." Derringer banged a fist against his chest.

Indigo tore his gaze away from the corridor and grunted.

"Good job, Marine," Brannock said. He didn't mind lying, not if it meant Derringer would think about something other than their worsening situation.

Xaros will zap any life pods. They don't take prisoners, he thought.

He keyed his mic. "Devil Dog command, this is station 3-7. There an update?" Nothing but static greeted him.

Stalks broke through the bulkhead of the connecting passageway. The tips bent over and stabbed into metal walls. A drone ripped opened a hole with ease.

"Contact!" Brannock leaned around the corner and fired. A ruby glow filled the corridor from the drone's stalk tips. The Marines got off another shot and pulled back. He knew the bulkhead wouldn't be much protection. He squeezed his eyes shut as a disintegration beam ripped through the corridor.

The deck rattled, but Brannock found he was still alive. Indigo was in the passageway, the muzzle of his oversized rifle glowing red hot. The drone crumbled in the entrance it had made.

A long gash cut across the bay where

Stephens and the rest of the control team were working. The gash was wide enough that Brannock could have stuck his head into the bay with ease. The bay was full of wrecked equipment and floating bodies.

"Oh no…" Brannock opened the door. Stephens fell against him, a briefcase in her hand.

"We didn't get it," she said. "Almost there…then the power cut out. So damn close."

"Didn't get what?" Brannock asked.

"The mines! Two more mines and we could have taken down their propulsion rings. How do you not know about this?"

"No one tells us anything!" Derringer said.

"If I had line of sight to the *Abdiel* or the mines…" Stephens held up her briefcase. "So damn close. Now all of this will be for nothing."

"No, not for nothing." Brannock pointed at the rip in the bulkhead. Through a mess of damaged pipes and broken deck plating, they saw the void. "Come on."

Brannock pulled Stephens along and peered

into the hole. Sparking electrical wires and empty vac suits filled the next compartment.

"Let's go, field trip!" Brannock pushed aside an arcing power line with the tip of his rifle and cut across to the next wound in the *Midway.*

Stephens and the rest followed. He waved Derringer and Indigo into the next compartment.

"Line of sight. I get you to the hull and you can make this work, right?" Brannock asked. "Because there are a lot of drones out there and I'm not one of those armor soldiers that can take on a hundred Xaros and still win."

"Get me out there," she said.

The breach in the outer hull was just big enough for Brannock to squeeze through. He locked his boots to the hull and looked around.

Abaddon loomed above. The *Bull Run*, a few hundred yards away, fired off a broadside and took a dozen hits from energy beams in return. A rail cannon ripped away, flipping end over end like a coin. The next hit broke through the opposite side of the hull, splintering aegis armor outward like a misshapen volcano.

An Eagle, pursued by a pair of drones, streaked overhead so low that Brannock ducked, fearing decapitation.

"Bad idea. Such a bad idea." He pulled Derringer and Stephens out of the breach. Indigo looked through the gap.

"Too small," the doughboy said. He was right; his broad shoulders wouldn't fit.

Brannock pointed to a nearby bunker.

"Can you get to that bunker? Get out through there?" he asked.

Indigo grasped the broken hull with both hands and bent it aside.

"Or that." Brannock pointed to Stephens, who had her briefcase open. Wires ran from her gauntlet to a screen and touch pad inside the case. "Let's get to that bunker."

"No, I need line of sight and I'm not going to get it in that pill box...I've got a link! Just give me...why the hell is that over there...two minutes!" Stephens said.

Brannock and Derringer crouched next to her. There were five human ships still fighting in the void above, rail cannons and point defense turrets blazing. The *Midway*'s bridge was dark, drones scuttling around and through holes torn in the superstructure where the admiral should have been leading the battle.

The hull around them was pitted and torn. Fragments of aegis shielding skittered past their knees as the ship rolled over.

One of the last ships exploded—its battery stacks gone critical—in a flash of yellow light. Drones crossed in front of distant stars, moving like shadows across the void. Brannock felt exposed, helpless before the awesome might of the Xaros ripping apart his fleet.

"How long we gonna be out here flapping in the breeze?" Derringer asked.

"One more…" Stephens tapped on her forearm screen. "Got lock on connection gamma. Now I need to—"

"If you can work faster without talking, I'm

all for it," Brannock said.

A peal of armor pressed up from the breach. Indigo tried to squirm through the wider hole, with little success.

"Corporal…" Derringer whispered, "think one's coming at us from the bridge."

Stephens started to get up. Brannock held her steady. A drone climbed down from the bridge to one of the hull defense bunkers.

"Stay on it," Brannock said.

A stalk shot up from the approaching drone and bent toward the humans.

"It sees us." Derringer slowly pointed his rifle toward the drone.

"You don't know that." Brannock felt a cold splash of fear against his chest. "Just stay calm and—"

The tip of the stalk lit up with red light.

Derringer put himself between Stephens and the drone and raised his weapon. His rifle fired just as a beam struck his chest. His shot ripped a gash across the drone's surface. Brannock hit it again.

The drone slammed against the hull and broke apart.

"Derringer?" Brannock grabbed the Marine's slack shoulder, his grip collapsing the empty armor, red mist clouding Derringer's visor.

Brannock grabbed Stephens by the back of her armor and dragged her toward the bunker.

"What are you doing? What happened?" she asked.

"Keep working!" Three more drones came off the bridge and flew toward them. He set her against the side of the bunker and took out his only quadrium bullet. He slipped the round into his rifle's breach and clicked a button to overcharge his capacitors. The rifle hummed in his hands.

"Here we go." He stepped around the bunker and stared down the charging drones. A red beam shot past his knees. Brannock aimed for the drone in the center of the pack and fired. The drones flew apart, but not before the quadrium shell exploded into an electrical storm that arced between two of the drones. The affected drones slammed into the

Midway and skipped across the hull.

Brannock ejected his spent battery and slapped his belt to get a fresh charge, but the pouch was empty. His hand went to another pouch—empty.

"No no, no…" He reached behind his back and found a fresh battery pouch on his belt. He struggled to get the battery loose.

The single drone that evaded the quadrium round landed atop the bunker, stalks raised like a spider about to strike. The stalks scythed toward Brannock and Stephens, the stalk tip missing his face by mere inches.

The drone slipped over the side of the bunker.

Indigo gripped the drone by its stalks and slammed it against the hull. He roared and bashed it against the bunker, cracking the shell.

"Hammer! Use your damn hammer!" Brannock yelled as he finally slapped a fresh battery into his rifle.

Indigo drew the hammer off his shoulder

and slammed it against the drone. The spike split the shell and cracked the drone in half. Indigo smashed the disintegrating drone again and again.

"I've got it!" Stephens called out. "Final countdown activated!"

Indigo tossed aside the last of the drone.

"Good job, Indigo!" Brannock stood over Stephens, searching for the other two drones.

"Indigo, good." The doughboy slammed a fist against his chest. The soldier's head snapped to the side. He squared his feet and raised the hammer over his head.

All Brannock saw was a blur as a drone slammed into Indigo and carried him away. Brannock heard the doughboy grunt and shout for a few seconds before his IR cut out.

Searing pain erupted in Brannock's arm. He twisted aside as the beam burning into his arm ripped into the bunker.

A drone landed just before Brannock and Stephens. He tried to bring his weapon to bear, but his arm refused to respond. The drone slashed a beam across the bunker. Brannock heard a brief scream from Stephens then he found himself spinning through the void.

His right arm flopped in front of his face, hanging by a thread from his nearly ripped vac suit. His legs itched with pain then went numb. He refused to look down, knowing what he'd see, and what he wouldn't.

"Anyone?" he broadcast. "I'm Dutchman. Dutch...off the *Midway*." His head felt heavy.

Abaddon spun slowly across his vision. The propulsion rings collapsed, giant cracks forming from one spoke to the other. Gleaming crystal shards broke out of the brass-colored rings and trailed away from Abaddon.

Brannock watched in awe as the crystals burned away. His mind went to a childhood memory of a camping trip, sitting around a fire with his father, watching embers rise into the night sky and die away.

Blood loss sent Brannock unconscious. Death came moments later.

CHAPTER 22

Minder felt his connections to the Xaros network sever with one swift stroke. The *Breitenfeld* had wrecked the Crucible's ability to generate wormholes, not the network hub embedded within the structure. There had never been an anomalous drone during the long course of the Xaros invasion, and if there was one thing that caught the Master's attention, it was data that did not conform to expectations.

He got to his feet, remembering how Torni fought to die the same way.

A smoking mass of abyssal darkness seeped through the wall opposite him. Keeper had sent a null-beast, a legend from their home galaxy used as a tool in the Master's assassination games. Minder took Keeper's choice in murder weapons as a compliment.

"We cannot continue like this, Keeper," he said. "We destroyed our home through hubris. Doing the same to this galaxy only compounds the crime."

The null-beast coiled into a twisted lance and swung a tip to Minder.

Minder kept his eyes open as the lance shot into his chest. He felt his photonic core disintegrate slowly, like ice spreading through his chest. His body froze in a rictus of pain then crumbled into dust. The null-beast stretched across the laboratory, annihilating everything it came into contact with.

With Minder and all evidence of his existence gone, the null-beast turned upon itself. Black smoke poured from its shrinking body. The last of the creature burned to a tiny mote of light then departed reality with a faint pop.

****

The General watched as the propulsion rings crumbled away, their remnants flowing behind his arsenal like a comet's tail.

Never before! Never before had one of the polluting species of this galaxy ever dealt him such a blow as this.

He willed the drones still inside the planetoid to replicate. This was but a setback. He would bring the arsenal to Earth, the materiel loss of the rings and what he'd expended to defeat the human fleet was insignificant next to the ultimate strength his arsenal possessed.

Gravity enveloped him and pulled him toward the arsenal. He struggled briefly against the sudden spike in gravitons. Another of the human's mines…farther away and on the path to Earth.

The human support ships had raced away during the battle. He ordered a segment of his available drones to give chase. They set out, moving unacceptably slow. The graviton mine disrupted the

drones as they tried to form their own Alcubierre
fields. The drones would pursue, but not catch up
for months.

　　No...

　　The General spread his drones across the
surface and ordered them to propel the arsenal
forward. The planetoid lurched forward. He felt the
loss of thousands and thousands of drones as they
struggled to overcome the interference from the
graviton mine.

　　Another human mine exploded farther ahead
and the General realized what the humans had done.

　　The support ships were minelayers. They
would bleed his arsenal white before it reached
Earth and there was no way he could catch the ships
or stop them from seeding space with their mines.

　　Light erupted from the General like a
supernova as he raged. He flew to a wrecked ship
and ripped it apart. He hurled the prow into another
dead ship, knocking them both on an infinite
journey through space.

　　He went to the human capital ship, the

carrier, and peeled an aegis plate off the hull. He crushed the plate into a sphere and reached behind his head, ready to smash it into the bridge…then stopped. He burned a path through the ship and stopped in the engine room.

The jump engines remained intact. Keeper might withhold the technology from him, but here was a crude approximation of the forbidden technology. The General rolled the ball of compressed aegis shielding between his fingers, deep in thought.

A faulty jump engine had doomed his home galaxy, erasing it from existence and sending the Xaros on the long journey to this, their new home. The General had asked for the jump technology to investigate the humans' meddling on Earth, but Keeper refused.

The Masters decreed that the jump engines would never be used again; violating that would mean sanction—a sanction the General wasn't sure he would survive.

Only if they find out…

The General summoned drones to the *Midway*. Keeper kept a smothering presence around everything the General did since waking after the human incursion on Anthalas. Yet...the General didn't feel Keeper now. Something else had the other Master's attention.

The General cut his connection to the Apex. He came up with a plan, one he had to execute quickly. Keeper would never know, and victory required no explanation.

CHAPTER 23

Standing watch aboard Titan Station was a balance between controlled chaos and mind-numbing boredom. The fleet's rapid expansion meant more and more void traffic in and around Earth, activity that waned and ebbed with the workday in Phoenix. With Phoenix local time still in the wee hours of the morning, space traffic was minimal. Those manning the control center took the time to prep for the approaching morning rush.

Colonel Mitchell took a last sip of coffee, sniffing the deep aroma of pure Kona beans brewed to perfection. Before the Xaros invasion, Kona coffee was highly prized by connoisseurs the world over. Which led to sky-high prices beyond what Mitchell could afford, or more than his wife would let him spend on something she'd considered frivolous.

He looked at the grounds stuck to the bottom of his mug, remembering the first morning of his honeymoon with his now dead wife. They'd ordered room service from their hotel on the Las Vegas strip and shared a pot of Kona.

Mitchell could afford his old vice with the Ibarra Corporation's presence on Hawaii and new robotic farms across the islands, making Kona plentiful. He lost his wife in the invasion, but the smell of Kona always brought back fond memories of her.

"Berthing requests for next week." His assistant passed him a tablet full of spreadsheets.

Mitchell frowned at the list, catching a half-dozen conflicts in seconds.

"When will the Luna yards be up and running? Or Mars? Or what they're building out in the Lagrange Point? What're they calling it?"

Mitchell took a stylus from his breast pocket and highlighted requests for later attention.

"Just the star fort, for now," the assistant said. "I think Ibarra has a contest going for a name."

"Anything but the Alamo," Mitchell muttered.

A siren blared from the ceiling as red lights flashed across the bridge.

"The Crucible has a gate request," a crewman said.

"The *Breitenfeld?*" Mitchell asked.

"Can't be, the mass displacement coming through the wormhole is too large for the *Breitenfeld.*" His assistant looked over the crewman's shoulder and read off the screens.

Mitchell flipped the safety catch off the system-wide kill switch and pressed his other hand against a biometric reader. The kill switch went green. He could shut down every computer in the solar system with the press of that button.

"The *Breit* bringing home another stray?" Mitchell asked. "They came in over mass with that

Dotok ship."

"Just one ship…other end of the wormhole reads as coming from just outside Barnard's Star. It has to be the *Midway*, but it isn't broadcasting any of her codes," his assistant said.

Mitchell opened a channel straight to Ibarra.

"Crucible, this is Titan watch. Can you shut down the wormhole? This doesn't feel right," Mitchell said.

"Can't. Point of origin is too close for Jimmy to counteract," Ibarra said.

"Then I'm declaring a code black. God help us." Mitchell took in a deep breath then shouted, "Prep for analogue!"

He looked at the button beneath his fingertips then pressed it.

A coded transmission emanated from Titan Station. Every single computer, robot and automated system it touched went into immediate shutdown as their CPUs shut down and power lines detached from batteries. Earth shut down within minutes; the transmission reached through the rest of the solar system at the speed of light.

The command center's crew swapped out their now useless touch screens for control panels boasting keys and dials.

"The wormhole is collapsing," his assistant said.

Mitchell slid a helmet over his head and connected to the life-support systems in his chair.

"Battle stations! Get the guns manned and get us to zero atmo ASAP," Mitchell said. Once he was sure his orders were running through the station, he looked to the Crucible.

The *Midway* hung in the center of the Crucible, her hull burnt black, flight deck bays shut.

"Hail them," Mitchell said.

"Nothing," his comms officer said.

"Launch our alert fighters. Tell Hawaii, Luna, Okinawa, everybody to scramble whatever they've got," Mitchell said.

"Sir, it's the *Midway*," his assistant said. "It looks badly damaged. What about search and rescue?"

"Then let's hope I'm just being overly paranoid. Do it. Now."

"She's breaking up!" a crewman shouted.

Holes opened across the *Midway*'s hull. Mitchell switched a screen to one of the station's telescope cameras and got a closer look at the ship. Her hull pulled apart into black lumps, which spun into oblong shapes…and grew stalks.

Blood drained from Mitchell's face.

"Oh no."

****

Ibarra watched a holo of the *Midway*, trying to estimate just how many drones were packed into the Eighth Fleet's flagship.

"The drones…they replaced *Midway*'s aegis armor with drones," Ibarra said. "The omnium derivative we used for the armor is close enough to the drones' makeup that we didn't even notice when they were coming through."

+Can we deconstruct the Xaros trick after

we've defeated them?+ the probe asked.

"I will now remind you that we have no weapons on the Crucible." Ibarra called up a holo showing local space. "I'm so stupid. We should have prepared for this."

+The Xaros are not known to use jump engines. There was no precedent for this.+

"Somehow that doesn't make me feel any better!" Ibarra zoomed the holo out and felt a glimmer of hope when he found a warship on the far side of the moon. "Jimmy, drones are coming for this command center, aren't they?"

+Correct. Two hundred ninety-five are en route with roughly half of newly formed—+

"Turn on the doughboy tanks in nodes two and three. Full production," Ibarra said.

+This will terminate all procedural humans still in the tubes. Are you sure?+

"Those drones get in here and they're dead anyway. Do it."

The doors to the command center opened. Steuben, half-dressed in combat armor, stormed into

the room with his blade in hand, Lafayette
following close behind.

"Ah, now we've got good news and bad
news," Ibarra said. "The bad news is that we're
about to be neck-deep in drones."

"What is your good news?" Steuben asked.

"You two are here."

****

Flight Leader Bar'en jumped off a catwalk
and grabbed onto a pole the auto-lifters used to
move cargo through the main flight bay on the
Vorpal. He slid halfway down and leaped off. He
swung his feet in a lazy somersault and kicked out,
furthering his arc. The lower gravity on the flight
deck made it easier to get the fighters in the air
faster, and made acrobatic routines look easier than
usual.

Bar'en slammed his helmet on and landed
just shy of his fighter. He jumped into the cockpit,
hands racing through pre-flight checks before he

sank into the seat.

"Captain Go'ral, I could use an update," Bar'en said.

"A Xaros ship came through the Crucible. We are maneuvering around Luna at best speed, but you and your squadron can reach them first. Our hosts ask that we engage the enemy at the Crucible first, then 'shoot anything else that's Xaros' after that," the ship's master said through his helmet comms.

"And why did our esteemed hosts let a Xaros ship through the Crucible?" Bar'en asked as his canopy closed around him. Eight more fighters with the rest of the alert pilots readied for battle.

"I don't see how that's relevant. Also, may I remind you of the three previous reprimands you received for excessive criticism of their military capabilities and competence?"

"I only get those when the humans accidentally hear what I have to say." Bar'en charged up his weapon systems. As much as he derided Earth's pilots, their gauss weapons were a step above Dotok, and they weren't averse to sharing the technology.

"Prepare to launch."

As the launch bay doors opened, the dull gray of Earth's moon passed beneath the *Vorpal* as she came around the satellite. A crewman stood at the edge of the flight deck and raised two flags over his head.

Titan Station came into view, flack batteries firing into the void. Tendrils of flame reached out of hull breaches, feeding on the atmosphere bleeding from the hull. Flashes of exploding fighters and gauss weapons stretched a rough line from the Titan to Ceres as Earth's new moon swept into view.

"Getting some video in…that's their *Midway*," one of his pilots said. "What's happening to it?"

Bar'en turned on a screen on the side of his cockpit. Nearly half the carrier's hull was stripped away and more peeled from the faux-armor and formed into drones. Bar'en checked his load out: he had two anti-ship rockets slung beneath his fighter.

"It's a Xaros construct. Engage it as such. Odd numbers to kill strikes, evens fly cover. Switch for second pass. Don't let there be a third," Bar'en said.

The crewman at the front of the flight line lowered a flag, signaling that their launch was imminent.

"The humans saved us from Takeni. Shared their home with us. Now we earn our place." Bar'en cycled power to his engines.

The crewman dropped the second flag then fell face-first to the deck.

Bar'en brought his fighter a few feet into the air and shot out the hangar, directly over the prone crewman. There was talk about ending the tradition of assigning the youngest sailor to flag duty, talk Bar'en wouldn't stomach. Some things were just meant to be.

He pushed his engines to their limits, eyes darting from his control panel to the approaching Crucible. The new capacitors and battery stacks held up as the fighter rumbled beneath him.

Acceleration pressed him against his seat and a chill swept over his face as blood squeezed out of the fleshy parts of his nose and cheeks.

His blunted beak clicked as he saw the first drone flitting through the Crucible's giant thorns.

"Claws out, take what you can on the pass. Stay on me," Bar'en said. He cut his afterburners and veered toward a handful of drones cutting into one of the many control nodes spread through the thorns. He let off a burst, shattering a drone. His pilots wiped out the rest a moment later, leaving a scar of gauss bullets across the dome.

"The imperfection was mine," one of the newer pilots said.

"You think the ghost haunting the place will care that you scratched the paint?" another asked.

Bar'en banked over a thorn and flew into the inner section of the Crucible. The Xaros peeled away from the *Midway*'s fore sections, exposing bare frames and open decks to the void. Bodies of sailors escaped from the ship. Bar'en brushed his knuckles against the prayer beads attached to his chest, an old superstition to ward off the attention of the dead.

"Odds, ready rockets, target the aft armor plates." Bar'en pressed his thumb against the missile release. A pair of drones streaked past him and he weaved up and down, dodging laser fire.

"Loose!" He clicked the release twice and his fighter surged forward, free of the rocket's mass. He pulled his Eagle into a climb, heading straight for the thorns.

"Three solid hits…no chain kill, localized damage, but they've stopped separating," one of the even-numbered pilots said.

"Follow me. Evens, prep your strike." Bar'en looped around the outer edge of the Crucible and rolled his fighter over. Half his pilots jumped out ahead of him, eager to make their attack. One of the thorns cracked apart as they flew over the inner edge, round craters blown out of the surface that might have come from Dotok rockets.

"This is Marc Ibarra aboard the Crucible to whoever just blew up my jump gate. Stop it."

"The beggar does not bite the coin tossed into his bowl," Bar'en said.

"Keep shooting the drones. Just be more careful about it!" Ibarra yelled so loud Bar'en's ears rang.

Rockets leapt from the leading fighters. Xaros fighters managed to take down a pair before the rest slammed home. Compounded drones burned away as if an inferno sprang from the rocket strikes.

"Well done," Bar'en said. "Now we finish off the rest…and try not to shoot the Crucible."

CHAPTER 24

Steuben leaned against a metal weapons rack and pushed. The wheels weaved through the sandy floor and veered to the side. Steuben let off a stream of Karigole curses that had no real translation into English and pushed again.

"Steuben." Lafayette ran up the corridor and tossed an aegis reinforced armored jacket to Steuben. The cyborg Karigole had two gauss rifles attached to his back. "I'll get this."

Lafayette gripped the side of the rack and pushed it ahead, barely breaking his stride as Steuben donned the armor.

"Show off," Steuben muttered.

"The door, if you please."

Steuben ran ahead, snatching a rifle off Lafayette's back as he passed, and tapped a code into the keypad bolted onto the basalt-colored doorway. The doorway opened from a center seam, tiny bits collapsing to the side like a crumbling sand castle.

Inside, dozens of large cylinders held doughboys. Mechanical arms tipped with tiny needles, attached to tubes leading to swirling vats of liquid, worked over each soldier, building them in a flurry of additive materials.

A shiver went down Steuben's back. The Karigole believed that life was too sacred to mimic and seeing the doughboys under construction filled him with revulsion. Despite his personal feelings, he'd take any help he could get against the Xaros cutting their way into the Crucible.

Lafayette rolled the weapons rack into the middle of the room and locked the wheels. His eyes narrowed in concentration.

"What?" Steuben asked.

"Ibarra?" Lafayette cocked his head to the ceiling. "These doughboys are programmed to see Steuben and I as friends, correct?"

"Yes, of course…" Ibarra's voice echoed around them. "Probably. Let me double-check."

The glass shell of a cylinder rotated aside and the newborn doughboy within opened his eyes.

"Ibarra?" Steuben clicked off the safety of his gauss rifle with a claw-tipped finger. The doughboys were programmed to defend humans at all costs. Steuben's first encounter with a doughboy, whom he was trying to rescue from kidnappers, ended in violence for no other reason than Steuben was nonhuman. Having to fight a room full of doughboys was not going to help defend the Crucible.

"You're good. New subroutines added last week to all units," Ibarra said. "Now, if you're done being all paranoid, there are hull breaches in corridors three and twelve. I'll point the way."

A doughboy stepped out of the construction cylinder wearing nothing but a pair of shorts, his skin glistening from the last brush of the needles.

Steuben tossed him a rifle. The doughboy pulled back the charging handle, saw the gauss dart in the chamber, closed the bolt and hefted the weapon against his shoulder.

"Purpose?" he asked.

"The Xaros are here," Steuben said. "Follow me and fight."

"Fight." The doughboy nodded his head.

****

Steuben ran down a corridor, his rifle swinging from side to side in tune with his stride. Doughboys struggled to keep up, their heavy footfalls echoing off the walls.

The end of the corridor broke away from the junction and lifted up. It passed through the thick hull and opened to the void. Steuben saw drones and Dotok fighters battling over the connected thorns. The opening passed over another hull section.

"Why can't I feel it moving?" Steuben asked. He couldn't wait to get off this alien place; he never understood why Lafayette liked it so much.

The corridor opened up to a stadium-sized control node. Crates of shining omnium were stacked high on one side of a tall building, plates of aegis armor awaiting delivery on the other. Xaros clung to the side of the building, cutting into it slowly but surely.

"Defend the omnium reactor at all costs," Steuben said. He aimed down the rifle's iron sights and blew a drone off the top of the reactor housing. He ran into the reactor chamber and took cover behind slabs of aegis plates.

Doughboys fired on the drones, advancing slowly into the chamber. Soldiers armed with nothing but pneumatic hammers charged ahead, war cries bellowing from their lips. Steuben loaded a quadrium shell into his rifle.

Drones lifted off the reactor housing and raked their beams across the firing doughboys. They evaporated into red mist with the briefest touch of the drones' weapons. The soldiers kept up disciplined fire, destroying several drones before those armed with rifles were reduced to a few.

Steuben's rifle beeped with a full charge. He swung it over the top of the armor pile and fired on a pack of drones. Drones rained down from the sky as the q-shell knocked them off-line. They fell, right to the eager group of hammer-wielding soldiers that the drones had ignored.

Primitive soldiers armed with melee weapons were of little threat to the drones while they were airborne. Once forced to the ground, the matter was different.

Doughboys tore into the drones, ripping them apart with an atavistic fury that Steuben had no choice but to admire. The Karigole picked up a weapon coated in the dusty remains of a soldier and tossed it to a doughboy holding a broken hammer.

"Get rifles! Watch the skies!" Steuben pointed to a breach in the dome and shot at a drone squeezing through. The soldiers took up arms left by the fallen. Those without rifles manhandled plates of aegis armor into crude bunkers.

Steuben tapped a mic on his throat. "Ibarra, omnium reactor is secure, for now. You either send me more ammo and soldiers or cut off the Xaros reinforcements to keep it that way."

"Lafayette just saved my bacon in the command center. More doughboys are coming off the line. I'll see what I can do for you," Ibarra said.

Steuben took careful aim at a drone zooming across the sky and blew it in half. A heavy hand slapped him on the back, fouling his aim on the next target.

"Good shot, ugly!" a doughboy shouted.

"Who're you calling ugly?" Steuben shook his head and aimed again.

CHAPTER 25

Rangers in gleaming black armor burst onto the *Midway*'s bridge. Snub-nosed gauss carbines swept across the silent bridge with precision. They looked through every tear the Xaros drones used to gain access to the ship's command center and made a hasty exam of every sailor they came across.

"Clear," the team leader said.

Admiral Garret entered the bridge a few seconds later. Drops of black blood floated in the void, staining his vac suit with each impact. A custom gauss pistol hung above the wrecked holo table. The admiral grabbed it gently, turning it over in his hands.

"Have you found her?" he asked a Ranger.

The soldier pointed to a vac suit caught under a command chair. Garret cradled the empty suit in both hands and wiped red dust off the nameplate just above an ugly burnt hole. Makarov.

"Rest of the teams report no survivors, sir," the Ranger said. "Lafayette says the jump engines are a total loss."

"That's…to be expected." Garret let the empty suit go and walked to the forward section of the bridge. The armor around the bridge was gone. He looked up and saw Earth, Luna and Ceres. The sun glinted off debris stretching from each celestial body.

The shipyards on the moon were wrecked. Titan Station badly damaged. Both were victims of a few drones that combined and burned themselves to oblivion with one massive blast from an energy cannon.

Eighth Fleet was gone, and with it some of his best ships and crews. Garret hit his knuckles against a dead control panel. Assuming Makarov's fleet even had a chance to send back word of what they encountered, it would be years before the message even reached Earth.

Even with the Crucible still largely intact and the omnium reactor safe, every last human being would know exactly what this day meant. Defeat. He'd struggled to keep the military's and civilians' hopes up through the despair of losing their families and homes…now this.

"Sir, found something." A Ranger held up a clear, void-safe case. Inside was a notebook with a tea-stained cover and Makarov's name on it. Handwritten notes, printouts and pics jutted out from between the pages.

Garret took the case and gave it a pat. This was something, at least. Maybe he could forge a narrative out of the admiral's log, paint a picture of heroism and some kind of a victory from her loss and give hope to humanity.

"Good work, son. Have the recovery teams sweep the ship for remains," Garret said. "Escort me back to my shuttle…the planet needs to know what happened."

CHAPTER 26

Torni walked through the ranks of frozen crewmembers. She'd come here several times during the years it took to reach the rogue star passing by Malal's vault. They were little more than statues, more perfect than the wax figures she remembered from a museum she visited in Stockholm as a little girl.

She stopped next to her old squad. Cortaro had a vice grip on Standish's arm, Gunney's face frozen in anger, Standish's in amusement. She touched Standish's face, with a hand that looked perfectly normal, and gave him a quick pat.

"Let's hope things go well for you," she

said.

She'd learned to control her omnium body, adopt a form that resembled herself from before her death, even down to loose hair and the illusion of breathing.

Torni reached out with her mind and felt a broken lump of metal in a trash bin. The metal rose into the air and floated to her waiting hand. Tendrils of light reached from her fingertips and caressed the garbage until it melded into a sphere of pulsating omnium. The sphere morphed into a silver and gold emblem the size of her palm. An eagle, a globe an anchor. The symbol of the Atlantic Union Marine Corps in precious metals.

Transmuting matter from one form to another was child's play for her. Malal had proven to be a capable mentor during their long isolation in deep space.

Torni slipped the emblem into Standish's pocket.

+Malal. I'm ready.+

+Activating jump engines. One minute to

translation.+

Learning to transmute matter into omnium and back again had taken time, and Malal was anything but a kind and patient teacher. Torni had repaired the ship's engines long before the *Breitenfeld* got close enough to the rogue star to recharge the dark-energy stores. She'd spent the rest of the time working on the ship. Being a drone meant no need for sleep or sustenance.

The only break she'd had from isolation were the infrequent visits from Stacey, always to quiz Malal on data obtained from his vault, never to chitchat.

As for Malal…

Torni went to the edge of the open flight deck, stepping around the three Iron Hearts. A deep red star burned in the distance, the rogue star that proved to be the ship's salvation. The *Breitenfeld* would have been in deep space for centuries without this celestial rogue's passing.

"Farewell," she said.

A white disk opened before the ship,

growing wider until it enveloped the ship. Torni felt none of the queasiness from her previous wormhole jumps. Granted, she no longer had a digestive system to agitate.

The white abyss faded away. Earth and Luna. A smile spread across Torni's face. They were finally home. She focused on the night side of Earth; her "eyes" were as sensitive as any spotter's telescope on the ship. Japan and Korea were alive with light. She could see the gridlines of urban areas on Okinawa and Taiwan. Mountain ranges along Australia's east coast were riven with light, same with much of New Zealand.

"What the hell?"

"The humans have been busy," Malal said as he walked up to her. His face was as still as a mannequin's.

"The cities…they're built into mountains," she said.

"Easier to defend. I will release the crew. They remember you in your old form. In the brig," Malal said.

"They will accept me this way and I am done being a prisoner," she said.

"As you like." Malal lifted a hand and snapped his fingers.

"—will use the quadrium shells…" Captain Valdar took a half step to the empty ammunition dolly. His face knit in confusion. "Where did it go? Ibarra?" Valdar turned back to the equally confused group of senior officers on the stage with him.

A murmur rose through the ship's crew. Many pointed to the open bay doors.

Valdar saw his home world, and Torni and Malal at the edge of the flight deck. The captain pointed a finger at the two.

"You cut me off, didn't you?" Valdar demanded.

"You wanted to return to Earth. Here you are. I believe your customs demand you express some gratitude." Malal held up a hand as if he wanted Valdar to kiss it.

Valdar jumped off the stage and went straight for Malal.

"This is not the emotional response I anticipated," Malal said to Torni.

"This is *his* ship, Malal. He decides what happens and how it gets done. You stepped on his toes," Torni said.

"Another of your euphemisms," Malal said.

"My crew deserved to know what you were—" Valdar stopped his advance as Elias cut in front of him.

Elias reached high over his head and swept an armored fist into Malal's head. Malal bounced off the deck and careened into an empty lifter suit against the bulkhead. Elias jammed his arm into the wrecked suit and pulled Malal out, the ancient being's head deformed from the blow.

Elias slapped his hands against Malal's chest. The pneumatic servos whined in protest as Elias tried to crush the governor inside Malal.

"Elias! Stop! You're going to kill him!" Torni ran across the deck.

"This thing is a monster!" Elias thundered through his armor's speakers. "We saw what it did to the Jinn. It will do the exact same to us once it has the chance." His arms shook with effort.

Stacey reached into a pouch and took out a control crystal. With a flick of a finger, she could lessen the governor's restraint on Malal. She didn't have to free him to save him, but she could give him enough wiggle room to defend himself from Elias.

The crystal floated between her fingertips. Elias had saved her on Earth. The soldier was the hero of numerous battles…but if she let Malal loose, there was no telling what he would do to Elias. The creature was not one for restraint or mercy.

She cursed Elias for backing her into this decision. She waved her fingers over the crystal. It flared to life as Malal's control protocols came to the fore.

"No you don't." Hale grabbed her from behind, pinning her arms behind her back. Hale slapped the crystal away before she could do anything to help Malal.

"Damn you, we need—" Hale covered her

mouth, muzzling her protests.

Torni pushed past Valdar as the captain ordered Elias to stand down. Kallen and Bodel ignored the captain's commands to intervene.

One of the governor's hoops broke, popping through Malal's surface like a compound fracture.

"Destroy me and your species is doomed," Malal said. "The Xaros are nearly infinite. Without me, you are nothing."

"*Gott mit uns*, not you," Elias said. Another hoop snapped and steam rose from Malal's body.

Torni's body morphed out of her human shape and into a Xaros drone. She heard the screams and panic from the crew as she rose into the air and stretched stalks from her body. A ruby point of light grew from a stalk. She slashed a disintegration beam through Elias' arms, severing them at the elbow.

Malal, still in the grip of Elias' hands, fell to the deck.

Bodel and Kallen charged at her, spikes ready to crack her shell like an egg.

Torni scooped Malal into the air and shot through the force field, leaving the Iron Hearts and a chaotic flight deck behind.

Torni worked stalk tips into Malal's chest and began repairing the governor.

+Not what I expected,+ Malal sent.

+The Iron Hearts are pure. Better than the rest of us. They waited until the ship was safe to make their move.+ Torni bent the broken band back to its original shape and morphed the omnium back into its original shape, feeling for the resonance frequency Stacey gave her to ensure Malal's containment held true.

+A level of cunning I didn't anticipate. Humans deserve some respect.+

With the governor repaired, Torni touched a stalk to Malal's body and shifted his malformed head and chest back to normal.

+We will not return to the ship,+ he sent.

+Neither of us are welcome now.+ Even as a drone, Torni could still feel. Sadness welled up inside her as she tried to make out her old team on the ever more distant ship. She'd waited years, anticipating the day she could speak with her old friends, trade jokes and learn what they'd done since Takeni. Now, the chance of that happening was slim to none.

+I'm not surprised you intervened, but you could have done so sooner,+ Malal sent.

+We need you, Malal. Need you to finish our Crucible, help us strike the Apex. That is why I saved you. I did it for Earth, the rest of the galaxy that's fighting the Xaros. Don't ever think that I care about you.+

+You are growing. Moving away from your flesh-bound morality. There's hope for you yet.+

An Osprey flew over them. Torni felt targeting lasers sweep over her body as manned turrets swung to bear on her and Malal.

"Torni, this is Stacey. Can you read me?" came over an IR frequency.

"I hear you," Torni sent back. "Where are you?"

"The Breitenfeld, I just came through the

conduit. The gunship will take you to our Crucible, and my grandfather will meet you. I'll head over as soon as I've cleaned up the incredible mess you left for me. What did you do to Elias?"

"We'll see you there," Torni said. The Osprey rotated its tail toward them and opened its cargo bay door.

****

Hale released Stacey. She stumbled a step forward, then turned and swung a punch at Hale.

The Marine swayed back, her fist missing his nose by inches.

"You son of a bitch!" Stacey's fists shook with anger, but she didn't attack Hale again. "What the hell do you think you were doing?"

"Trying to save us," Hale said. "Malal's price, whoever you promised to sacrifice to him, isn't worth the cost. We're better than that, Stacey. I won't just stand by and let you—"

"You have no idea. None. You don't know

what we're up against. What's coming for us."
Stacey's head cocked to the side. The blood flushed through her face. "You're lucky—damned lucky—Malal is alive and this ended well."

"We should destroy that thing while we have a chance," Hale said.

"You just don't get it. Malal *is* our only chance."

****

Stacey had never seen Valdar so angry. The captain's face had been flushed since he joined her on the flight deck. He snapped terse commands to the bridge crew through the gauntlet of his void suit in between scans of the void just outside the ship.

Stacey fidgeted against the ill-fitting EVA suit she'd borrowed from a locker and touched the box with the data crystal mag-locked to her utility belt. Valdar had completely ignored her since their rendezvous on the flight deck. Stacey kept her mouth shut, not wanting to draw his ire.

She turned her attention to the construction on Luna. Glowing rings radiated out of Lovell Crater. Running lights from orbital weapon platforms blinked against the void, forming a phalanx of energy cannons, rail guns and fighter bays around Earth's original natural satellite.

"How long?" Valdar asked her.

"Admiral Garret wants to—"

"How long!"

"Four years. The *Breitenfeld* was in deep space for that long. You and the rest of the crew were in stasis the whole time," she said.

"Not you?"

"I spent most of the time on Bastion. I came back to the ship when needed. Good thing, too. The defenses on the Crucible would have blown the ship to bits when it came through if I hadn't warned them what to expect," she said.

"So you know what they did to my ship? Why didn't you stop them? Tell me?"

"Malal and Torni repaired the jump engines with fragments of the Crucible you destroyed. That kept them busy for two weeks. They had plenty of omnium and time on their hands to do something constructive and…here he comes." Stacey pointed to an approaching shuttle and donned her helmet.

The shuttle set down and lowered its ramp. A pair of black-armored Rangers jumped from the sides and scanned the flight deck. Each held a rifle with a glowing crystal built into the weapon just above the handgrip.

"Clear, Admiral," came from one of the Rangers.

Admiral Garret descended down the ramp. He looked older than Stacey remembered. His hair was grayer and he had more lines on his face. The rank stenciled onto the shoulders of his void armor had the five stars of a fleet admiral.

Garret looked at the burnt line where Torni's disintegration beam cut into the bulkhead.

"Looks like you had some trouble," Garret said.

"Disciplinary matter. I'll handle it," Valdar said.

"Stacey," Garret touched her on the shoulder, "nice to see you in person again. Going through Pa'lon to talk to Bastion hasn't been easy. Not that I didn't like your holo messages. Come on, your grandfather's waiting."

They boarded the shuttle and were in the void moments later.

The Ranger bodyguards kept their weapons in hand. Neither took their eyes off Valdar and Stacey as the shuttle accelerated.

"Do we have time for a flyby on my ship?" Valdar asked. "Let me check the damage?"

"Damage?" Garret huffed. He touched his gauntlet and blast windows descended from the shuttle's side.

Stacey almost didn't recognize the *Breitenfeld*. Slabs of D-beam resistant armor plates covered the entire hull, the rail gun vanes were longer, and more anti-void craft turrets dotted the hull in round blisters. Gold lines bordered each plate, glowing with energy. The words "*Gott Mit Uns*" were stenciled on the side of the hull.

"Bit much with the ship's motto, but I'll allow it," Garret said.

Valdar banged a fist against the bulkhead.

"Torni did it because she cares, sir," Stacey said. "She could have gone into stasis with the rest of the crew. Instead, she spent years upgrading the ship for the fight that's coming."

"One moment I'm about to give my crew the bad news, the next I don't even recognize my ship…or my planet," Valdar said.

"About half the space watch pissed themselves when you came through the Crucible with that new armor." Garret's face became stern. "They thought it was another Xaros trick. I had all the orbital defenses shut down just in case. There's always that one guy that doesn't get the memo."

"'Another trick'?" Valdar asked.

"Eighth Fleet was lost with all hands, Isaac. They ran smack into the Xaros maniple coming for Earth. They put up a good fight, slowed them down, but they never stood a chance. The Xaros sent the *Midway* back to us, disguised drones as her armor.

That caught us with our pants down, wrecked Titan Station and the Luna construction yards, before the Dotok got into the fight."

"New ship construction slowed to a halt," Stacey said. "It took months before we could lay a keel on another vessel."

"It would all be over but for the screaming if we'd lost the omnium reactor in the Crucible," Garret said. "Stacey shuttled enough data from what you recovered in the vault to get us back in business. Still won't be enough." The admiral shook his head.

"Bastion will send help, this time," Stacey said.

"Fool me once, shame on me. Fool me twice…" Garret said. "I'm not going to depend on Bastion after they left us dangling with the Toth."

"How long until the Xaros arrive? How many ships do we have?" Valdar asked.

"A month, if we're lucky. We're getting graviton bursts from the mines we set well beyond bow shock distance. They'll cross the heliopause soon. As for what we have to stop them…I've got almost four thousand ships off the line. One more, now that the *Breitenfeld* is back."

"I'm sorry…did you say four *thousand*?" Valdar asked. "There weren't more than two hundred void warships when the Xaros first invaded."

"Ibarra can breed proccies so fast he'd put rabbits to shame. We've got whole crews just waiting for their ships to come off the assembly line. Still won't be enough. Won't be near enough," Garret said.

"The projections—" Stacey said.

"The projections are bullshit." Garret cut her off with a swipe of his hand. "What Eighth Fleet encountered will become billions of Xaros drones by the time it gets here. The chance of us lasting a week is slim to none."

"But, if—"

"Don't you 'but, if' me," Garret said. Stacey rolled her eyes at the new interruption. "Hope is not a method, Stacey. We are in for one hell of a fight and I don't have half the ships I need to tell Phoenix we've got this in the bag with a straight face."

"Bastion isn't sending help?" Valdar asked. "We've got the means to access the Xaros network. Why don't they flood local space with their ships so we can end the war with one strike to the Xaros leadership on—what did Torni call it?—the Apex."

Stacey sighed. "Now that we've got the information we need," she said, tapping the case with the data crystal, "we can finish our Crucible…if we put our omnium reactor to work on nothing but the Crucible for the next eight months."

"The Xaros will be here long before that," Garret said, "and I need the reactor churning out D-beam proof armor. Our ships don't stand a chance without it."

"I noticed," Valdar said. "Why didn't we send this data earlier?"

"There are limits to what I can ferry back and forth. Malal's data is…enormous, contiguous. It is impossible to separate anything from the whole. The probe can get everything back to the Qa'Resh, but even that will take time," Stacey said.

"So we've got to survive this push for our chance to win the war…" Valdar said. "Even more reason for the rest of the Alliance to send their ships."

"Heh," Stacey said without humor, "I've been fighting for that for years. There are some in Bastion plotting to make a brand-new Crucible with the data we've got. Why risk helping us when they can take a century or three to craft their own perfect solution?"

"Why are we in this Alliance if throwing us to the wolves is always better than lifting a finger to help?" Valdar asked.

"It takes little to no time to bring in the allied fleets," Stacey said. "The motion is tabled until the data has been analyzed and they know whether or not they can fabricate a Crucible that will connect to the Xaros network."

"Or they wait until we've been bled white and show up to save the day…and take over our defenses," Garret said.

"You're being paranoid," Stacey said. "Plausible, but paranoid."

"No one's coming to help?" Valdar asked.

"We've got the Dotok. Look." Garret pointed to a gleaming white ship studded with Toth energy cannons.

"Is that the *Canticle of Reason*?" Valdar asked. He'd helped get the ship, and the last of the Dotok population, off Takeni during the Xaros invasion of the distant planet.

"They rechristened her the *Vorpal*." Garret shook his head. "Claim they did it to honor us. Damn silly name but I had more important things to worry about. She's the deadliest thing we've got in space and the crew is top-notch. Had an easy time integrating the *Naga*'s weapons into her too."

Garret pointed back to Earth.

"I've got fortresses built into mountain ranges from Phoenix to the Himalayas. Mars, Luna, Iapetus around Saturn, all armed and ready for a fight. There are more fighting men and women under my command than Earth had before the invasion." Garret took a flask from his belt and took a long swig. "Won't matter."

Valdar and Stacey traded glances, concern hidden behind practiced poker faces.

****

The armor bay, known across the ship as the cemetery, was as silent as its namesake. Elias' armor bore factory-fresh arms, pristine compared to the rest of his battle-worn armor. A door swung open and Bodel pushed Kallen and her wheelchair up the ramped walkway that came waist high to the three suits of armor.

Bodel boasted a new exoskeleton attached to the interface plate on his upper spine, resembling a toned-down version of the Marine's pseudo-muscle layer instead of the rods and actuators of older exoskeletons. Bodel moved naturally, the only evidence of the stroke he suffered on Takeni showing in his half-slack face.

"New frame?" Elias asked.

"Brand new. Doesn't put strain on my plugs or synch rating like the old ones. Modified haptic feedback system or something. I only care that it works," Bodel said.

"How's the world?"

"Different," Kallen said softly. "We were at the medical complex in Phoenix. The city is enormous, must be millions of people there now…" She turned her head to Bodel. He locked her wheelchair in place and left the cemetery.

There was nothing but the hum of air circulators as Kallen struggled to speak.

"I'm dying, Elias. Batten's Disease, and there's nothing the docs can do about it. I thought…we'd been gone so long that there might be a treatment."

"I know."

"What?" Kallen gave a nasty look to the door Bodel left from.

"He can't keep a secret to save his life. You know that. He cares about you. Doesn't want you to burn away so soon."

"You know wearing the armor will kill me faster. Why haven't you begged me, like Bodel, to stop?"

Elias touched his chest armor and the breastplate flipped up. Elias willed the blast plate on his armored womb to descend, revealing his emaciated body inside the cocoon.

"We are armor, Desi. We are nothing but our armor. If you stop, you'll waste away in some medical ward while the rest of us fight. I know you," Elias said.

"I would rather die beside you, Elias." A tear ran down her face. Elias reached out to her very slowly and wiped the tear away with his metal hand. Kallen pressed her cheek into his palm.

"I wish you could come out," she said. "I miss you—the real you, not the armor."

"This is all I am." Elias picked Kallen up and cradled her like a newborn, pulling her close to his cocoon. His true eyes flicked open. A weak smile crossed his face as he looked into Kallen's eyes.

"We are such a mess," Kallen chuckled. She tilted her head to rest against the cocoon. Elias' true hand twitched, but couldn't move any further.

"Until the end," he said.

"Until the end."

****

Bodel leaned against the bulkhead outside the cemetery and took a data slate from his pocket. He shook his head and scrolled through years' worth of e-mails, newsletter updates and military errata. No sports scores.

He straightened up as the sound of boots against the deck closed in on him.

Captain Valdar came around the corner, his face as stoic as ever.

"Sir," he said as he shimmied over to block the door to the cemetery, "what brings you to our neck of the woods?"

"Where are the other two?"

"They're…a bit…um…"

Valdar looked through a view port into the cemetery then stepped back from the door.

"Why did the three of you try to kill Malal?" Valdar asked. "Don't tell me that Elias came up with that attack on his own and you two were just as shocked as the rest of us."

"It's a monster." Bodel's shoulders fell and he wished he were back in his armor. "Evil. The Jinn showed us what it's capable of, what it's planning. We weren't going to let it do the same to us."

"Why do you think we are his next target?"

"Doesn't matter if it's us or some other race. Malal would kill them all. Innocents. Criminals. Young. Old. How can we sacrifice so many and still think we're on the right side? Don't know about you, Captain, but I believe in a final judgment. I can't hold my head high in front of my creator if I let Malal win."

"And if we go extinct without Malal's help?"

Bodel shrugged. *"Gott mit uns."*

The side of Valdar's mouth twitched. He took an envelope from his pocket and handed it to Bodel.

"The three of you, you're off my ship." Valdar turned and walked away.

Bodel opened the envelope. Inside were reassignment orders for the Iron Hearts.

Mars.

CHAPTER 27

Standish hauled himself onto his top bunk and reached into his pocket. He took out the gold and silver Marine Corps emblem and turned it over several times. There was no inscription, nor identifying marks. He was damn sure it wasn't in his pocket when he went out for Captain Valdar's address, he hadn't noticed the new weight in his pocket until after Cortaro had finished his daily harangue against him.

"Standish?" Yarrow asked from the bunk below.

Standish stashed the emblem under his pillow.

"Yes?"

"You really think that's Torni in that drone?" the corpsman asked.

"Buddy, you were possessed by a demon."

"He's not a demon. He—"

"I single handedly rescued Marc Ibarra from beneath Euskal Tower while Hale and Ibarra's hottie granddaughter were playing googly eyes with each other. Nobody says ghost Marc Ibarra isn't the real Marc Ibarra."

"I thought Elias pulled them—"

"We now live in a world where a tube grown human being is possessed by demons and most every major decision affecting our species goes through a ghost in a machine. You think that can't be Torni inside that drone?"

Standish took another sip while he waited for Yarrow to answer.

"I guess…" Yarrow said.

"Nothing we can do about it, so don't worry about it," Standish said. "You hear from your girl? Lilith?"

"I haven't even opened my Ubi. Figure she moved on after we were declared overdue. I don't want to read that 'Dear John' letter just yet," Yarrow said.

He slid off the bunk and slipped the emblem back into his pocket. A dark shadow filled the room.

"Steuben!" Yarrow opened his arms and went to give the Karigole warrior a hug. Steuben stiff-armed the corpsman.

"No. None of that," Steuben said.

"Steuben, man did you miss some fun," Standish said, "By fun I mean pants-wetting terror. We fought a giant damned centipede, and Torni's back. It's weird."

"My bowels remained under control during our time apart," Steuben said. "I have been training the new Ranger companies in anti-Xaros tactics. They are better learners than you, Standish."

"But nowhere near as good looking," Standish said with a nod.

"Where is Hale? I have something you all

need to see," Steuben said.

****

Hale rubbed his eyes and struggled out of his bunk. Sleep was impossible during missions. The hours of shut-eye he could grab between briefings and training cycles were few and far between. The Strike Marines had many priorities— sleep wasn't one of them.

His Ubi had three missed calls, all from old acquaintances from the Saturn Colonial Fleet. Word of the ship's return must have spread across the system. There was one name missing from the calls—his brother, Jared.

Hale swiped across the Ubi and called his brother. The slate told him "No Account Found."

An icy splash of worry hit his chest. He opened the universal search app and put in his brother's name. Had there been an accident? Was he on some crazy deep-space mission like Hale had been on the past years?

A video message from ~~his brot~~her came up. Jared looked into the camera, his face drawn.

"Hey brother," Jared said, "word is the *Breitenfeld*'s on an indefinite delay. You'll be back. It'll just take you a lot longer than planned. Too bad, I wanted to spend some time with you and Uncle Isaac before the *Christophorous* leaves for Terra Nova. Yeah, they offered me a slot in the colony. I'm going to take it.

"It's not that I'm afraid of the Xaros coming down the pipe from Barnard's Star. I want be part of something greater than myself. Contribute to a new world. Earth…is gone. The world we grew up on will never come back. After Mom and Dad's place was demolished, my connection to everything was gone, except you and Uncle Isaac. Look, you'll beat the Xaros. I know you will. There's another jump window in another couple years. The briefers said that'll be the last one for centuries. Come join me on Terra Nova the next time there's a chance. I'll do all the hard work getting the planet nice and livable. You can show up and take all the credit.

"Sound like a plan? Catch up with me on Terra Nova. I'll see you then. Love you, Ken."

Hale watched the video again then set the Ubi aside. He drummed his fingertips on his lap, his mind racing with the fact that his brother was gone. He was safe from the Xaros, but Hale might never see him again.

Someone knocked on his door.

"Enter," Hale said.

"Sir," Cortaro stuck his head into Hale's quarters, "Steuben is here. You need to see this."

Hale stepped into a pair of flip-flops and followed Cortaro into the squad's small ready room. His Marines were there, sitting in old and worn furniture around Steuben.

"Steuben, good to—"

The Karigole held up a four-fingered hand and then touched the screen on a data slate.

A holo projection filled the center of the room, deep space with a backdrop of stars.

"This came from the graviton mines just beyond the solar system," Steuben said. "The data is a few hours old. Garret hasn't released it to the public." Steuben tapped the screen and the holo zoomed in on a grainy asteroid, the picture coming into focus slowly.

"Eighth Fleet was destroyed in combat with a Xaros structure," Steuben said. "Abaddon." The picture resolved. Giant bay doors opened across the smooth surface as the pictures advanced one frame at a time. Drones swarmed out of it.

"How many?" Hale asked.

"The Qa'Resh probe estimates at least five billion," Steuben said, "spreading across the solar system as we speak. The Xaros are here. The siege of Earth begins."

****

Another slab of aegis armor slid out of the omnium foundry, wide as a Destrier transport and inches thick. Robot crews transferred the slab to a laser cutter where it would spend the next few hours being tailored into the shape needed to protect the intended vessel. Automated lifters fed blocks of glowing omnium into the side of the foundry.

The Xaros had scoured the solar system clean of almost every trace of human existence and converted that mass into raw omnium, which they stockpiled across Earth or used to build the Crucible. Ibarra found a certain sense of irony in turning Xaros plowshares into human swords.

Ibarra called up a screen from his office overlooking the foundry. The *Monte Cassino*'s armor plates would be ready for transport to the fitting yards soon. Another ship for the line, another brick in the wall.

Malal, sharing the office with Ibarra, Stacey and Torni, watched the process with little interest. Lafayette stood against the far bulkhead, his hands clasped over his waist.

"Your process is efficient," Malal said. "I cannot aide your efforts. Return me to the Qa'Resh. Their cell is better than this solar system."

"You're not going back," Ibarra said, "not right now."

"The Xaros are on your doorstep. Remaining here is an unnecessary risk to the plan. Return me to the *Breitenfeld* and the ship will take me to Bastion." Malal turned his head with measured menace.

"We take you back...and there's no reason for Bastion to send reinforcements," Stacey said. "The *Breitenfeld*'s jump engines have been malfunctioning. We send it to Bastion and it might not come back in time to hold the line."

"I personally fixed the jump engines during the long dark. They are...ah, I see. A falsehood," Malal said. "You're forcing Bastion's hand. They must save Earth to save me. Save the war."

"Politics is a dirty game. That's why I stuck to business," Ibarra said.

"I am your hostage?" Malal asked.

"You're in this fight with us," Ibarra said. "I saw what you did to the *Breitenfeld* with your idle hands. The two of you have a purpose. Lafayette?"

The cyborg held up an arm to the group. His hand flipped to the side and a holo emitter in his arm threw a schematic into the air.

"The design works, in theory," Lafayette said. "The prototypes exploded in a most spectacular fashion. Interesting to watch but not the desired function. If we can build one, it could turn the tide in the coming battle."

"I have no idea what I'm looking at," Torni said.

"An abomination of technology from the fever dreams of the desperate." Malal reached into the hologram and began rearranging components.

"You can make it work?" Lafayette asked.

"I can, but it falls on her to build it." Malal pointed at Torni.

Ibarra passed his hand through Stacey's arm. She stepped away and glared at him.

+You know I hate that,+ she sent to Ibarra.

+Excuse me for being a ghost. I thought they taught you sensitivity on that Bastion of yours.+

+Speaking of which, I leave within the hour. Nice to get back to my body, eat home cooking for once. They'll see right through our little ploy with keeping Malal here. I don't play dumb very well, in case you haven't noticed.+

    +Always too smart for your own good. Get Bastion to send their fleets. I'd rather have them here than hope Dr. Frankenstein and his monster can save the day.+

    +Her name is Torni, and she's a good Marine,+ Stacey sent.

    +Go. Get out of here and bring back the fleet. The sooner I get these two freaks off the Crucible, the happier I'll be.+

THE END

The war continues as humanity faces the might of the Xaros in **The Siege of Earth**. Coming July 2016!

ABOUT THE AUTHOR

Richard Fox is the author of The Ember War Saga, and several other military history, thriller and space opera novels.

He lives in fabulous Las Vegas with his incredible wife and two boys, amazing children bent on anarchy.

He graduated from the United States Military Academy (West Point) much to his surprise and spent ten years on active duty in the United States Army. He deployed on two combat tours to Iraq and received the Combat Action Badge, Bronze Star and Presidential Unit Citation.

Sign up for his mailing list over at www.richardfoxauthor.com to stay up to date on new releases and get exclusive Ember War short stories.

The Ember War Saga:

1.) The Ember War
2.) The Ruins of Anthalas
3.) Blood of Heroes
4.) Earth Defiant
5.) The Gardens of Nibiru
6.) Battle of the Void
7.) The Siege of Earth (Coming July 2016!)

22178264R00256

Printed in Great Britain
by Amazon